Fiction International 51

World in Pain

Fiction International is a journal of arts and culture published at San Diego State University. *Fiction International* was founded, published, and edited by Joe David Bellamy at St. Lawrence University from 1973 to 1982.

Business correspondence, including that related to shipping and advertising, should be directed to:

Harold Jaffe
Editor, Fiction International
Department of English
San Diego State University
5500 Campanile Drive
San Diego, CA 92182-6020

E-mail: hjaffe@sdsu.edu

Journal typeset by Left Fork (O'Brien, OR)

ISSN 0092-1912
ISBN 978-0-931362-15-6

Editorial Staff

Call for Submissions: Body

Fiction International is accepting submissions for an issue on Body. Submissions will be accepted online or through mail from October 1, 2018 to February 15, 2019. We consider submissions of fiction, non-fiction, visuals, and indeterminate texts which reflect the theme.

Online submissions must be submitted through **Submittable** at https://fictioninternational.submittable.com/submit. Hard copy submissions must be printed out, accompanied by an SASE, and mailed to:

Harold Jaffe
Editor, *Fiction International*
Department of English
San Diego State University
5500 Campanile Drive
San Diego, CA 92182-6020

We exercise all due care in handling manuscripts, but we cannot be responsible for loss. Please allow one to three months for reply. If submitting through Submittable or mail isn't possible, we may accept emailed submissions **providing you receive approval in advance**. Should you have any questions, please email the editor at: hjaffe@sdsu.edu.

Subscriptions

Fiction International is published once yearly.

Annual subscriptions:
Individuals:
$16 plus $2 postage for U.S.
$16 plus $4 postage for international addresses.

Institutions:
If subscription is issued through a subscription service, their terms and rates apply. Otherwise, the rates are:
$35 plus $2 postage for U.S.
$35 plus $4 postage for international addresses.

Some past issues are also for sale. Please see page 208 or our website (http://fictioninternational.sdsu.edu) for a complete list of available past issues and prices. Remember to add applicable postage when ordering.

Use of FI in the Classroom

Please consider assigning this issue (or one of the past issues) as part of your reading list. Ask your bookseller to contact Harold Jaffe (hjaffe@mail.sdsu.edu) for information on availability of multiple copies.

Donating to FI

Although we maintain an office at San Diego State University, *Fiction International* is 100% independent of financial aid from the university. Outside of sales and subscriptions, our continued existence relies on supporters who make cash donations. That is why we are asking people who support the artistic merit of the journal and the progressive political thinking it advances to support *Fiction International* by making a tax-deductible donation.

If you would like to donate to *Fiction International* using a credit card, please visit our website (http://fictioninternational.sdsu.edu) and use the "Donate" button to link to our PayPal account. You may also mail a check to:

Fiction International
Department of English
San Diego State University
5500 Campanile Drive
San Diego, CA 92182-6020

Support FI Online

Fiction International maintains an active online presence through its website, Twitter, and Facebook group pages. Please support us by visiting the following addresses and by recommending us to family and friends.

http://fictioninternational.sdsu.edu
http://www.twitter.com/FictIntl
http://www.facebook.com/FictIntl

Contents

Hisham Bustani

One Moment Before the End

Your head, hit by a brick hurled bitterly by a professional murderer, will not stop bleeding before my eyes.

The white matter of the brain will not stop seeping out of the cracks and winding around my neck.

Come sleep beside me, I will heal the fiery marks that iron rod left on your body. I will heal the gaping hole the Kalashnikov bullet made between your eyes, I will make my flesh a pillow for your weary, desecrated body.

Was I deaf, or did I not hear your screams? Maybe you swallowed them. Maybe you swallowed your tongue. Tell me that you suffocated yourself; tell me you did not hear the cracking of bones, snapping one by one and breaking apart; tell me you did not hear his voice saying "on his head…"

This earth is the legacy of a filthy species of servile gods. A god who is enslaved to an enslaved god, and so on, ad infinitum. Ad inifinitum, but the end is coming: when I clench my fist and press my teeth together, I expand, becoming a cold, blue colossus – crushing that filth underfoot. From the periphery of my all-knowing gaze, drops of acid fall. May all of you

dissolve

evaporate

I raise a glass to your death and sit, alone on an empty planet awaiting my death that will not arrive.

But life is not a graphic novel, and the novelist cannot invent another future for me, or for you. And this slaughtered body before me is not an event embalmed on paper – brought alive by the mind when it desires, and put back on a dusty shelf after reading.

This blood before me will not stop flowing, and the brick that was hurled at your head (brick breaking bone, bone breaking brick) will keep spinning around my head – a performance fast, slow, reversed – as I writhe, tossing and turning in my bed like a body being hit with an iron rod, and exploding like a head hit by a brick.

[Zoom in on the face of the killer]

Thirty-two years. I am married with three children: two girls and a boy. I take care of the garden in my house, in the village. I kiss my mother's hand when I visit her every evening, and she strokes my head. "God bless you son", she says. I have sex with my wife three times a week, and sometimes argue with her. But I don't let her stay angry for longer than two days, I buy her favorite sweets to make up with her.

I enrolled in the army, just like that. A steady salary, health insurance, benefits and prestige. I hadn't been in a battle in my life. By the time I was born, the front had been calm for years. The only war I've known is an internal war, a war to root out a cancerous tumor, to exterminate the parasite that does not stop eating away, a war that turned our people into "them" and "us". They are the disease, and we are the remedy.

They caught that young man in a big warehouse while sweeping the area. He was one of them, he was hiding weapons. One of my guys grabbed an iron rod and kept swinging and swinging as the boy writhed on the ground covering his head with his arms. He didn't scream – in a quiet voice, he begged us to stop. The nerve!

The hitting continued for two minutes, or a little longer, I don't remember. Then I picked up a brick and took advantage of a moment when his head was exposed to bring the brick down on the bloodstained mass. After that, the body stopped writhing. It became perfectly still, but the guy with the iron rod kept swinging and I picked up another brick and hurled it at his head. The brick broke and so did his head. Someone came over and shot him. We said,

"You want liberty?"

"There, now you are free."

He didn't reply. He was insolent even after he died.

[Zoom in on the face of the body]

I've always been thin. My friends would make fun of me for it, and sometimes my mother. I would eat and eat but never gain weight. I stayed that way, shadow-like, until that day they started in our village. They would yell out words that we were scared to even whisper to ourselves. When the soldiers came, the protestors chanted that their march was: "Peaceful! Peaceful!" and the bullets would rain down on them.

I was there when our neighbour's son fell. He lay in the middle of the street bleeding for three hours. The fate of anyone who tried to go near him was a bullet. That was how the first two died, with a bullet to the head.

There was no third.

No one wanted to be a hero after that. We watched the pool of blood grow and grow, and his cries become fainter and fainter until he fell still. It was then that I decided to take up a gun and fight.

On this path, I came across former soldiers, men with beards, thugs and a lot of men who were moved by a deep bitterness and humiliation, like I was. Thin men who had barely left their mothers' laps.

It doesn't matter. I am neck deep now, getting wet is the least of my concerns. I got hold of a rifle that had been stolen from an army depot. When I loaded it with bullets, my body suddenly expanded. People started to take notice when I walked past and I'd feel the earth tremble a little when I stepped on it. But when they caught me in the empty warehouse where I hid my rifle during the day, I became that thin boy again, the one whose friends and mother make fun of. The shy one who would stare at a point deep within the ground in front of him.

I didn't know any of them and they didn't know me, but they hit me with iron rods as if I'd raped their mother. Their mother, Liberty. My mother, Liberty. Motherfucking Liberty. They keep hitting. I have a mother who wants to feed me, so that I'll gain weight. She wants to marry me off, so she can have grandchildren. They keep hitting. Iron rods man, that crack the bones and send shocks through my skeleton. They keep hitting.

The pain is tremendous but I do not scream. Remember? I am thin again, I have returned to the days when we were scared to whisper, even to ourselves. Everything is fine. No objections. I don't scream, the pain explodes without a sound.

There was one blow to my back that I remember well. It made my arm move – like a spasm – away from my head. After that, a great concrete boot came down with lightning speed. Stone lightning, and then I could remember no more. No more.

[The last page of Dr. Manhattan's diary]

I was wrong. Me, the cold blue man who is never wrong. I was wrong when I killed Rorschach. He was my conscience, the conscience of my cold mind – my atoms assembled by quantum physics. Despite the harshness of his ideas, he held the world by its throat. He would press down on it, press down until its voice croaked and it was about to choke, then throw it aside on the couch and leave. That world was me. It was my evil, the evil I didn't want to see until that murderous moment: at exactly twelve midnight on the last day of the passing year and the first day of the coming year. I threw that huge rock, and continued my never ending insomnia under a sky full of stars, bursting full of stars.

Translated from the Arabic by Thoraya El-Rayyes

One Moment Before the End
(original Arabic)

قبل النهاية بلحظةٍ واحدة
هشام البستاني

رأسك الذي تلقّى طوبةً طوّحَ بها بحقدٍ دفينٍ قاتلٌ محترفٌ للعصافير، سيظلّ ينزف أمام عينيّ من دون توقّف.

سيظلّ النخاعُ الأبيضُ يتسلّلُ بمكرٍ من الكسورِ ليلتفَّ حول رقبتي.

تعالَ ونم بجانبي؛ سأُداوي العلامات الناريّة التي تركها قضيبُ الحديد على جسدك؛ سأُداوي الثقب الغائر الذي أحدثته رصاصةُ الكلاشنكوف بين عينيك؛ سأجعلُ من لحمي وسادةً لجسدكَ المنهك / المتهتّك.

أكنتُ أصمّاً أم إنني لم أسمع صُراخك؟ لعلّك ابتلعته. لعلّك ابتلعتَ لسانك. قل لي إنّك انتحرت اختناقاً؛ قل لي إنّك لم تسمع طقطقة العظام وهي تتكسّر واحدةً واحدةً وتتفكّك عن بعضها؛ قل لي إنّك لم تسمع صوته وهو يقول: "على رأسه.."

هذه الأرضُ إرثٌ لهذا الجنس الوسخ من الآلهةِ الوضيعة. إلهٌ عبدٌ لإلهٍ عبدٍ وهكذا إلى ما لا نهاية. لكنّ النهاية آتية: حين أشدّ قبضتي وأكزّ على أسناني أتضخّم لأصير عملاقاً أزرق بارداً، وأسحق بقدميّ تلك الحثالات. من أطرافِ نظرتي العارفة تتساقط قطراتٌ من الأسيد. ذوبوا.

تبخّروا.

أرفع كأسي نخب موتكم وأجلس وحيداً على ظهرِ كوكبٍ فارغٍ أنتظر موتي الذي لن يأتي.

لكنّ الحياة ليست روايةً مصوّرة، ولن يتمكن الكاتبُ من تأليفِ مُستقبلٍ آخر لي أو لكم، وهذا الذّبيح الذي أمامي ليس جزءاً من أحداثٍ محنّطةٍ في أوراقٍ يبعثها العقلُ حيّةً متى أراد، وتعود أدراجَها إلى رفٍّ مغبرٍّ بعد القراءة.

هذا الذي أمامي دمٌ سيظلُّ ينزف دون توقّف، والطوبُ الذي أُلقي على رأسكَ -يَكسِرُ ويتكسَّرُ- سيظلُّ يدورُ في رأسي بعرضٍ سريعٍ وبطيءٍ ومعكوس، وأنا أدورُ وأتقلّبُ في سريري كمن يُضربُ جسدهُ بقضيبٍ من الحديد، وأنفجرُ كمن يتلقّى طوبةً على رأسه.

[زووم على وجه القاتل]

اثنانِ وثلاثون عاماً. متزوّجٌ ولي ثلاثة أطفال: بنتانِ وولد. أعتني بحديقة المنزلِ في القرية، وأقبّلُ يد أمي حين أزورها كلّ يومٍ وتربّتُ على رأسي. "يرضى عليك يا إمّي" تقولُ لي. أُضاجع زوجتي ثلاث مرّاتٍ في الأسبوع، وأتشاجرُ معها أحياناً لكنّي لا أتركها غاضبةً أكثر من يومين فأُحضر لها حلواها المفضّلة وأُراضيها.

تجنّدت في الجيش، هكذا. راتبٌ مضمونٌ وتأمينٌ صحّيٌ وبضعة امتيازاتٍ وهَيْبَة. لم أدخل معركةً في حياتي، فحين ولدتُ كانت الجبهات قد هدأت منذ زمن طويل.
الحربُ الوحيدة التي عرفتها كانت حرباً في الداخل؛ حرباً لاجتثاث الورم السرطانيّ؛ حرباً لتصفية التسوّس الذي لا يتوقّف عن النخر؛ حرباً جعلت مِنّا "هم" و"نحن". هم المرض، ونحن الدواء.

أمسكوا ذلك الشاب في مخزنٍ كبيرٍ أثناء مَسْحِهم للمنطقة. كان منهم. وكان يُخبّئُ سلاحاً. أحد زملائي أمسكَ بقضيبٍ حديديٍ وظلّ يضربُ ويضربُ، والشاب يتلوّى على الأرض محيطاً رأسهُ بذراعيه. لم يصرخ، كان يترجّى بصوتٍ منخفضٍ أن نتوقّف. الوقح.

استمرَّ الضّرب دقيقتين كاملتين أو أكثر قليلاً، لا أذكر، ثم حملتُ طوبةً وانتهزت لحظةَ انكشف فيها رأسهُ فهويتُ بالطوبة على الكتلةِ المدمّاة. عندها لم يعد الجسد يتلوّى. هدأ تماماً وسكن. لكنّ صاحب القضيب الحديديّ ظلَّ يضرب، وأنا حملتُ طوبةً أُخرى وهويتُ بها على رأسه. تكسَّرت الطوبة وتكسَّر رأسه، وجاء أحدهم وأطلق النار عليه.

قلنا له: "تريدُ حريّة؟ ها قد نلتَ حرّيتك."

لم يردّ. ظلّ وقحاً حتى بعد أن مات.

[زووم على وجه القتيل]

نحيلاً كنتُ دائماً. عيّرني أصحابي بذلك، وأمّي أحياناً. كنتُ آكلُ وآكلُ ولا أَنْصَح. ظللتُ هكذا شبهَ ظلٍّ حتى انطلقوا ذات يومٍ في قريتنا. كان يصيحون بكلماتٍ كنّا

نخشى أن نهمس بها لأنفسنا. حين جاء الجنود صاروا يقولون: "سلميّة... سلميّة..."، فينهمر عليهم الرّصاص.

كنتُ هناكَ حين سقط ابن جيراننا وظلّ وسط الشّارع ينزف ثلاث ساعات كاملات. كان نصيب أيّ شخصٍ يُحاول الوصول إليه طلقة. هكذا ماتَ أوّل اثنين برصاصةٍ في الرأس، ولم يعد ثمّة ثالث.

انقطع نسلُ الشّجعان بعدها، وبقينا نراقب بركة الدّم تكبر وتكبر وآهات ابن الجيران تخفتُ إلى أن همد. عندها قرّرت أن أحمل السلاح، وأقاتل.

في طريقي تعثّرتُ بجنودٍ سابقين، بملتحين، بزعران، وبكثيرين مثلي حرّكهم شعورٌ عميق بالمرارة والمهانة: شبابٌ نحيلون لم يُغادروا أحضان أمهاتهم قطّ.

لا يهمّني. أنا غريقٌ الآن، والبلل آخر همّي. تدّبرتُ بندقيّةً سُرقت من مخازن الجيش، وحين حشوتها بالطلقات تضخّمت جثّتي فجأةً، وصار مُروري يلفت الأنظار وأحسّ الأرض ترتجّ قليلاً حين أضغطُ عليها بقدمي. لكن عندما أمسكوا بي في مخزنٍ مهجورٍ كنت أخبّئ فيه سلاحي نهاراً عدتُ ذاكَ النحيل الذي يُعيّره أصحابه، وأمّه أحياناً. عدتُ خجلاً من نفسي أنظرُ في نقطةٍ عميقةٍ تحت الأرض التي أمامي.

لم أعرف أحداً منهم ولا هم عرفوني، لكنّهم ضربوني بقضبان الحديد كأنني مُغتصب أُختهم. أُختُهُم حرّية. أُختي حريّة. أُخت الحريّة. ويضربون. لي أمٌّ تريدُ أن تُطعمني لأنْصَح. تريدُ أن تزوّجني ليكون لها أحفاد. ويضربون. قضبانٌ حديديةٌ يا عمّي... تُطَقْطِقُ العظام، وتنتقل ارتجاجات الكسور في هيكلي كلّه. ويَضربون.

الألم هائلٌ لكنّي لا أصرخ. تذكرون؟ عدتُ ذاكَ النّحيل. عدتُ إلى زمنٍ نخشى فيه أن نهمسَ حتى لأنفسنا. كلُّ شيءٍ تمام. لا شكوى. لا جدوى. لا أصرخ، وإنما ينفجر الألم دون صوت.

ثمّة ضربةٌ على الظّهر أتذكّرها جيّداً لأنّها جعلت ذراعي تتحرّك كرفصةٍ عشوائيّةٍ بعيداً عن رأسي. بعدها انهالَ بُسطارٌ كونكريتيٌّ عظيمٌ بسرعةٍ خارقة. برقٌ صخريّ، ولم أعد أتذكّر أي شيء. لم أعد.

[الصفحة الأخيرة من مذكرات د. مانهاتن]

أخطأتُ، أنا الرّجل الأزرق البارِدُ الذي لا يُخطئ.

أخطأتُ حين قتلتُ رورشاك. كانَ ضميري؛ ضميرَ عقلي البارد وذرّاتي المتراكبة بقوّة فيزياء الكمّ. رغم قسوةِ منطقهِ كان يُمسك العالَم من حلقه. يضغطُ عليه ويضغطُ إلى أن يتحشرج صوته ويكاد يختنق فيلقيه على الكنبة ويغادر. ذلك العالَم كان أنا.

كان شروري التي لا أريد أن أراها. وعند اللحظة القاتلة، عند الثانية عشرة تماماً من منتصف ليلة اليوم الأخير من السنة السابقة واليوم الأول من السنة المقبلة، أَلقيتُ بذلك الحجر الضخم، وتابعتُ أرقي الأزليّ تحت سماءٍ مليئةٍ بالنّجوم.. مليئةٍ بالنّجوم حدّ التخمة.

د. مانهاتن ورورشاك هما شخصيتان من الرواية المصوّرة: Watchmen لألان موور.

Kevin Brown

Black Boy

One September, dressed in ragged clothes and ragged shoes, James Arthur Baldwin began his academic career at 139. Runty, effeminate in his mannerisms, precise in his diction, little Jimmy had trouble fitting in at first. They called him "frog eyes." In spite or perhaps because of his glowering intensity, he was a target for bigger boys, whom he watched furtively, with envy and admiration.

What he lacked in size, he made up for in intelligence. Tense, withdrawn, he spent time alone at the 42nd Street library, reading *A Tale of Two Cities*, delving deep into the history of Harlem. Countée, the school's most widely published author, was quick to recognize value and put to use the raw talent of his school's most gifted writing student, who'd already appeared in print by age 12. As Countée had before him, Jimmy wrote poems, plays, and songs, but largely gave up poetry for prose during those years at 139 due, perhaps in part, to the faint praise Countée expressed when Jimmy showed them to him.

"It's an awful lot," Countée said, "like Hughes'."

Soon, Jimmy was contributing essays and short stories to *The Douglass Pilot*, rising to the rank of contributing editor. His final year at 139, he was named editor-in-chief.

Around this time, Jimmy's stepfather suggested he quit school and get a job so he could help feed the family. Countée insisted not only that Jimmy graduate from 139, but that he attend his own alma mater, De Witt Clinton, then one of New York's most rigorous high schools. In a Bronx neighborhood where streets were clean and tree-lined, in an academic environment where most classmates were white and competitive though friendly, Jimmy worked with student-photographer Richard Avedon on *The Magpie*. Sensitive in an environment that rewarded sensitivity, Jimmy found acceptance at De Witt Clinton, published plays and short stories, and flourished, as Countée knew he would.

*

Jimmy was now an editorial staffer on *The Magpie*. Helping fellow students prepare an anniversary issue, he was searching for a story. Countée had recently published a children's book and was rumored to be at work on another. So, a faculty advisor suggested Jimmy pay him a visit. What Countée may not have realized the day those two squared off in a vacant classroom at 139 was that this interview was for Jimmy more than just a schoolboy exercise. Countée did realize that something was troubling Jimmy. Rumors reached him that Jimmy, oldest of eight and de facto head of household, labored under the burden of working after school to help feed his deteriorating father, his mother and his many siblings. When the Japanese bombed Pearl Harbor, the United States went to immediate war footing, and factories hummed 24 hours a day, 7 days a week. Jimmy was working in Jersey at a munitions plant, began cutting some classes, and hopelessly failing others. He had strayed from the church, eventually left his father's house, and was seen more and more frequently in the Village. If war abroad didn't maim a boy like Jimmy, other wars waged daily on the New York City streets would: the gun; the needle; the bottle. Defying his father's wishes, Jimmy turned his back on the pulpit, and was grimly determined to be a writer. Nothing and no one would stand in his way—certainly not naysayers who scoffed that, in this world of white devils, it was madness at best for a poor black boy to dream of becoming a famous writer and sinful pride at worst to try.

Both Mr. Cullen here and Richard Wright, Jimmy's hero, who'd now succeeded Countée as the world's most acclaimed black writer, were living proof it could be done. Hopeful, and defiant, Jimmy wagered that writing would be his escape from that world of walking wounded he staggered in. In a very real way, the questions he was about to pose were matters of life and death. And Jimmy had so very many questions. Where should he live? France, during the War, seemed out of the question. How should he support himself? But the answers Countée gave—the only ones he honestly could give, the only ones that, ultimately, Jimmy really needed—were probably not the ones Jimmy wanted to hear at the time, any more than Countée'd wanted to hear from Walter White that premature publication of Color might actually hurt rather than help his chances of gaining admission to Oxford as a Rhodes Scholar.

How much money, Jimmy asked, could one expect to make writing poems?

Countée was frank: "Poetry cannot be considered a means of making a livelihood."

"Why not?"

"Poetry," Countée explained, matter-of-factly, "is something which few people enjoy and which fewer people understand. A publishing house publishes poetry only to give the establishment tone. It never expects to make much money on the transaction. And it seldom does."

"I never knew that." Jimmy was aghast. "I guess a teaching job comes in pretty handy, then."

"Also, I like to teach."

So what was the secret of literary success?

Countée cautioned that there was "no secret to success except hard work and getting something indefinable which we call the 'breaks'."

The only secret, Jimmy later learned, is survival. Still, he had so many questions. What should he do?

"I suggest three things—read and write—and wait."

Countée'd done all he could for Jimmy. His star pupil must find his own way, betwixt fires still smoldering since the 1935 riot described by Claude McKay in *The Nation* and the powder keg from which, 24 hours after Jimmy's 16th birthday, Harlem once again exploded.

Richard Wright went to Paris the year Countée died, and lived the remainder of his days in exile. Jimmy worked odd jobs until he won a writing fellowship. He then left for France, to what extent influenced by his French teacher he never once admitted, and wrote his way into immortality. In Paris, Jimmy wrote *Go Tell It on the Mountain*, exploring themes he would return to again and again throughout his career: childhood; the black church; fathers and sons. By the time I encountered Jimmy, a year before his death, he seemed burnt out.

Uncharitable as Jimmy's feelings toward Countée may seem, I think I understand them. Jimmy's feelings toward Richard Wright were also famously mixed. Probing an artist as he was, Jimmy couldn't imagine Countée's childhood, whether because Jimmy was so preoccupied with the horrors of his own or because Countée bore his suffering silently. Personally, I can think of many alternate histories I might have lived. But I can't think of one better suited to make me the writer I've become. But the fundamental irony of the foregoing scene escaped Jimmy's notice: Countée was himself, at that very moment, hoping for something called the "breaks".

Lindsey Drager

Oral History

Say there are men. Say the men ache and in aching, create. The creations bloom and flourish. The creations bruise and stain. Eventually, the creations grow into men themselves. Say this is a kind of group or clan. Say this is a family.

But say the ache persists. The ache evolves and aggregates until the men decide to leave in an effort to defeat it. The leaving is defeat, of course. This is how men are.

Consider that the men unionize with other men to find an answer for their now collective ache. They feed each other meals from warm bowls and sleep within the safe harbors of wood structures and share methods for coping with their woe. At night the cohort speaks earnestly and without reserve about misery management. They suture together their lives by listening to each other speak, and in so doing, push the ache to the margins of their minds. Say this is called *control*.

Consider—just consider, pretend—that the men spend their days seeking but never find: the source of the ache, the way to soothe it. Instead the men veil it in innovative forms.

But because the ache evolves, those coping resort to dark methods. They ingest serums that enter their arms through metal pipes thin as hair. They consume brews that never quell their thirst. Say this is called *coping*. Say this is called *aide*.

And say this Consortium of Ache persists for decades because those without the ache insist it is an underground guild that is make-believe. Say they think those with the ache have brought this on themselves and therefore carefully nudge them to the corners of the world. But say the world's a circle. Say the earth is round.

Say—just consider, pretend—that the creations the men left behind who themselves grow into men, say they struggle. Say the creations that are turning into men begin to sense a dull, persistent throbbing in the blood paths of their forms. They cannot language their feeling, but we know what's going on.

Pretend this goes on for years until the years form eras. Pretend this goes on and on, develops into myth.

"Once upon a time there were men," the book says. The book says, "Once upon a time, men ached."

Say we pick up this book one day in early autumn. Say we read the story and in reading it, we begin to know: This is our story. We know such ache.

And because being human requires dissemination, we share this knowledge, but obliquely. We call this *fiction*. We call this *art*.

"Once upon a time, every man had a home," the book says. "Once upon a time, every home had a man."

When I was a child, someone who loved me said the most haunting story is the one left untold.

Claire Polders

The Brazilian Lover

ONE

Tiago arrived in my life the day after my neighbor and I decided to share a Brazilian lover. She, the neighbor, had come to my house for a spontaneous hello, which turned into a spontaneous dinner because it was late and she was out of wine.

"I only have leftovers," I said. My voice made it sound as though it were an apology, an admission of guilt. It was hilarious.

"Well, I'm not hungry," she said and lit a cigarette to quell her appetite. The last time she'd dropped by, my warm welcome had been cold soup.

We drank Pinot Grigio. Our dialogue flowed. After we finished the first bottle, I opened the fridge and pulled out a chicken leg, a plastic container of brown rice, two carrots, a jar of sun-dried tomatoes, some pickles, three slices of ham, a celery stalk, half a herring, potato salad, butter, cheese, eggs—enough to feed the world.

You see how circumstances are to blame? The seemingly endless supply left us in a speculative mood.

"This fridge is so deep," I said, "it goes all the way to your house. Look behind your Salgado photograph and you'll see the other side. I bet there's a second door."

We clunk our glasses and drank more wine. We were relaxed, buoyant. Laughter tickled the air. "How great to share a fridge," my neighbor said, blowing her smoke at the high ceiling.

When I mentioned my desire for a Brazilian lover, she imagined him to be flexible enough to live inside our fridge. We dreamed him up as a beddable, chilled companion for our hot summer nights.

TWO

The next day, keen on nursing my hangover in solitude, I opened the fridge for a glass of ice tea, and there he was, Tiago. He unfolded himself from the bottom shelf and stepped inside my generous kitchen.

I instantly admired him in a way you admire things you know will soon be gone, like ice sculptures. In addition to his wealth of dark hair, Tiago had a tight denim jacket and the legs of a marathon runner. Above his left eye snaked a scar that made him seem interesting rather than sad. He was tall and tan. Brazilian.

There wasn't much to discuss at first. He knew why he'd been summoned and was happy to comply. I'm not unattractive, you know, and the bed was soft. We took to it with acrobatic ease.

Satisfied, in lover's sunshine, I didn't mind sending Tiago back into the fridge so my neighbor could discover him. He had the stamina young men often have. His smell of camellias lingered on my skin all afternoon.

THREE

We made love at least once a day, hungry and quick, or as slow as thunder after lightning has sizzled the sky. The leaves outside my open window sighed with the weight of summer days, the laziness of long warm hours.

There were few words. Who wants to talk when the body splits open and melts? I felt validated in his presence, alive. He had strong white teeth, which he brushed with pink salt.

It was a surreal love, for sure, but still love. The kind of love that makes you want to cook *Coq au vin* from scratch and then prevent him from tasting it by demanding his tongue for yourself.

One night, my head flushed and dazed, I said, "Tell me about your country."

He pulled the sheet over his naked body as though my command had shamed him. "Favelas," he said. "Rural poverty."

I frowned. I wanted him to speak of the Copacabana Beach.

"Juntas and dictators," he said. "Child labor."

Well, I thought, all nations have their pessimists. I tickled him. "Tell me about the Amazon Rainforest. About samba players on the glorious streets of Rio."

He eased out of bed and into irritability, taking the sheet with him as a robe. "Corruption," he said. "Centuries of exploitation." He didn't part with one smile.

I stared at the ceiling, far away. That's what you get when you ask a man to open his mouth.

FOUR

In a flash of inspiration, I invited my neighbor for dinner and told Tiago to join us. Just food and drinks, I promised, no awkward trio stuff.

Our lover seemed intrigued, willing. He let me serve him, demanded pepper on his lobster, did not offer to open the wine. Had I expected him to be submissive? He must have felt the power of dispensing pleasures to us both, night after night.

"I suggest you stop smoking," he told us. "I hate the taste of ash."

We drew from our cigarettes and watched our world go up in smoke. His boldness grew in sync with his appeal. We were terribly unprepared.

Tiago licked his buttery fingers. "There are other doors in that fridge, you know." He could have been a small-time actor with bravado and a talent for swinging his hips.

"What do you mean?" my neighbor asked stupidly. Although she had lost weight and stuffiness since his arrival, she was still transparent.

I cleared the plates and decided jealousy would not do me in. If Tiago so desired, he could have coffee or sex with whomever he wanted. A droplet of chocolate on his chin seemed like a clear sign that he would develop a better personality with time.

My neighbor, on the opposite side of the table, acted upset and ordered Tiago back into the fridge. As if that solved anything.

"Frankly, I don't like ungrateful people," she said as soon as he was gone. "He didn't even show up for my gallery opening."

I knew she hadn't been bent on bringing Tiago. It was mainly to show off, his looks and her philanthropy, but the coldness of his refusal was killing her. My neighbor sponsored reverent artists who drew cities in broken lines.

"We need to talk some sense into him," she said.

I shrugged and chose to idealize the future. "When winter comes, we can warm him up by letting him rest in a hammock above the radiator, so he'll be all toasty when you need him."

That night we both slept alone, suspended between fantasy and fear.

FIVE

Brazil remained a topic of conversation between Tiago and me. Whether I wanted to or not, I learned everything there was to know about soybean cultivation, bottom prices, and how it was possible for farmers with plenty of land to go hungry. Our cows, it seemed, ate better than his people.

As a result, our love suffered. It became the act of one person—me. He no longer lay close to me after my orgasms and instead withdrew into the fridge, proud and bored.

When I forbade Tiago to mention Brazil, he started talking about the callousness of Western life, the corrupted world of overconsumption. "It's the way of the universe," I would say. "The way the world spins."

More often than not, Tiago became scornful. His sensuality, which at first had softened his bad manners, could no longer compensate for his accusations. He willfully eliminated all nuance when on the attack.

"You have no idea of the stress we're under in this society," I said. "The power of advertising is soaring. We suffer status anxiety, guilt, endless envy. Every day, we're forced to face our own blatant futility."

His look was rich with contempt. He was like a mirror in which I saw myself too clearly.

"You cannot eat beef and claim blamelessness," he said, taking off his pants.

I promised I would become a part-time vegetarian.

"Not enough," he said, fondling my breasts.

I promised I would sign a petition against the dispossession of native South Americans.

"Still not enough," he said, his head between my legs.

I squinted at him with one eye and imagined him vanishing. I did not want the crippled and homeless to make their way into my bed.

SIX

Summer was over by now, the hot nights. The sky threw up hailstones large enough to dent car roofs and strike birds dead off the trees.

My neighbor and I shared our troubles. Tiago would still let himself be touched but would no longer touch us in return. What to do?

For a while, I tried to woo him with the suggested innocence of a simple white frock. Although it worked for Emily Dickinson, it did not for me. I often thought I'd die if he didn't touch me immediately. But each day, I woke up alive.

My neighbor got herself a fancy dress that revealed her breasts. She was intentionally naive.

Unwilling to give Tiago up, I kept trying. Perhaps I should change him instead of myself. I bought him new clothes, new pants, shirts, jackets. The impression of poverty disappeared, but he didn't see it that way. Assimilation hung on his shoulders.

"I don't want to look like I belong here," he said.

I was stunned. Why did he not want to belong, or look like he belonged, in a free and wealthy nation? I had studied philosophy at some point because I believed that thinking about the world would help me understand it. Now

I knew I had wasted my time.

"Refugees are dying to get here," I said.

It was a sequestered moment, bordered by closed doors.

"I don't want to be pitied," he said.

I waved him over to the bed. "Without tenderness, we all live in hell."

But there was nothing left for me. Tiago remained distant, indifferent, waiting for some mysterious sign to finally administer his coup de grace. Whenever I opened the fridge and dragged him out, I could see he had already turned toward a life in which I was nothing but a nightmare.

It's a risk to let others into that space between yourself and the world.

His looks would leave me bruised.

SEVEN

One day, unavoidably, Tiago was gone.

My neighbor and I, we looked at each other across the fridge, seeing the vacant shelves, the rack where our life support used to be. Clearing out, Tiago had taken our wine with him.

I shivered. If there was anything to learn from the experience, I didn't learn it. I was just very sad to see my neighbor standing there, near her empty dinner table, in her revealing dress, alone.

W. P. Osborn

I see someone waving

I'm out the door into the car, pulling the gearshift into Drive and rolling backward. Putting it in Reverse should make it move forward, but all gears are Reverse now, even Park. When I touch the gas, the car stalls. By pressing and twisting, I discover that speed is controlled through the radio's station knob. I take a minute to familiarize and I set off. The country has had an election. I've gone to bed thinking it would go one way, it's gone another, a new leader will take over the national residence, and I'm on my way to the City to discuss courses of action with M, an old mate of mine.

Others assume I am going forward even though they can see me coming backwards. They can't figure it out and they are up on the curbs with their mufflers and suspensions damaged. It's on the news, the mechanic says: cars veering right when steered left. Flashers signaling their opposites. Those entering or exiting find the sleek new kneeling buses rising up. Semis jackknife without reason. What will M say, will I hold up my end of the conversation, I shouldn't keep him waiting.

A guy in the checkout line says the highways are iffy, even impassible. I bet the road crews are out repairing them, the checker says. 'Fraid not, the man says, they been sent home to rest ahead of a job they will be reassigned to when the new leader takes office, it's to keep out the hoards. I ask whether the hoards won't go around whatever this new construction is. They are coming across the frontier, the man says; no, go there dog on it, you'll see them.

I head home for a rethink. My neck has a crick from twisting as I back into the driveway. The house is not as I left it, it's slanted sideways, the rear sunk into the ground and the rest thrust up like the bow of a ship. The door is stuck in the jamb, but it can't resist my shoulder, which means I stumble in and barely keep my feet as I slide to a halt on the skewing oaken floor. My wife tells me the pipes are crimped, the power lines stretched like harp strings, she hears them playing a piece of Zabaleta's, they are not by her lights accomplished musicians, their rhythms being way off. I tell her I have to carry in the groceries. Our calico is dozing on the wall.

The groceries glide themselves into the kitchen. My wife says not there, hon. But it's cold things, I answer. She opens the fridge and inside is the flat-screen, turned endwise, a good-looking sideways anchor and some good-looking sideways panelists discussing the prospective changes. Why'd you move it here, I ask. I didn't she says, I went to get the half-and-half and it was like this. Then where do we want these. Where do you think, she says, come, I'll show you. I look in the walk-in but she is patting the bed. I get out the freezer stuff, she holds up the comforter. It's really cold under there. I thought you were going to C, she says. I tell her about the freeways, tell her when I stopped for gas, instead of filling up, the tank emptied into the pump. I suppose if you can get downtown you could try the train, she says.

When I unholster my mobile to call M about the delay, my wife says oh perfect and nips it into the fish tank, which she is cooking dinner in over the camp stove. What happened to the fish, I ask. I let them go, she says, it's a new day; they were being enabled by our feeding them and changing their filter and the poor Plecostomus cleaning the algae off their glass all day without a dime for his labor. She hands me a can of corn and says here, talk on this, I made my hair appointment on it this morning.

The redolence of scorched plastic in the corned beef and cabbage makes a nice addition to the house's scent complex. It calms me about the election. We sit in one of the cupboards with the refrigerator open and eat companionably with the leader-to-be making a speech about animals. We have to stop them from coming in. I will shoot their planes, he is saying; don't get any ideas, cruise ships. My wife throws the dirty dishes in the yard, a pack of mutts sprints over to clean them, we hit the hay.

When I tell the ticket gent where I need to get to he says the switches and signals aren't working. How is that possible in this day and age, I ask. You cast me up a red herring there, he says, it's not open to question, it's an actuality, accept it. You can't sell me a ticket? I'll sell you a ticket, I just can't verify where you'll end up. When is the next train. Five minutes if it's on time. He lifts his glasses and scrutinizes my card and says thank you Mr. Lanky sir and hands it back with the ticket. My name isn't Lanky but I head out to the platform. The train rumbles in and squeals its brakes and the twenty people run down the steps and cross to the other side because it's going the opposite way. A guy with a business suit says come on you. I say no, I'm waiting for the C train. Okay, he says, but this is the best we'll do this morning. When we're on our way I ask him how I'm supposed to get where I'm going. We always get where we're going Mr. Lanky. My hand itches, I almost punch him in the face, the smarty. On the lounge car TV the new leader is saying the transportation system will be fixed by inauguration or I will hurt people, I'll have my advanced aircraft weapon system training by then, believe me I will use it.

I am looking out the window at our pastel little town, then the buildings spacing out and getting more derelict, half of them at angles like my house. I'm wondering how my wife is doing, she seemed to be adapting, and we're into a tunnel followed by scabrous woods in a clearing where children are loading a bazooka two of them are aiming in the direction of a girl against a maple tree with a melon balanced on her head. I hear a muffled boom and we're out on a weedy flat when the brakes slam on and we're sliding with the wheels grinding and a metallic rumbling as the train vibrates and howls to a stop. We smell hot metal, we exit. We move past the passenger cars, the lounge car, the backward locomotive, and then we are at the frontward locomotive with its nose at the edge of a rocky gorge. The rails head out into space and stop. The engineer is wagging his head, poring over a sheet of limp bluish paper. Suppose a be a bridge, he's saying, we going to have to locate it before we can go on. You, lanky boy, he says, go that away. You others, this way. See what you can find.

I leap boulders and drag myself through vegetation I hope isn't poisonous. I am sixty-three, he shouldn't call me boy, there could be animals. My jacket catches on a thorn and when I look up, there something is. I clear away the branches of an evergreen, maybe a cypress or giant sequoia. It spans the arroyo, I report to the engineer, it is chalk green, I could see the rivets and protruding bolt heads, the cables, there is no rust.

So what we're going to do here, the engineer says after everyone is reassembled, is we are going to switch this train manually over to them other tracks Mr. Lanky found. Thanks a lot Mr. Lanky everybody says with their expressions like the whole thing is my fault. I used my long division skills, the engineer goes on; if we do one car at a time each of you will be shifting only 9000 pounds. The the there is another way, I say before I can think not to speak. They are looking at me so I say we could back the train up and then redirect the tracks so they come out over there. The thing is, we will have to make sure the train will back up when we put it in reverse because I don't know. The others stroke their chins and nod their heads. The train goes forward in reverse so we have to uncouple and push one car backward at a time. With the emergency toolkit we move the tracks off the ties and then we move the ties and we convince the tracks to the left, then back to the right to line everything up. With the new curves we're short on length, so we scavenge extra track from behind. The engineer calculates our supplies and says if we don't get going we will have to start hunting our own victuals. Plus, fuel.

Even though it's nighttime we become the first train ever on the new trestle and my heart is flipping because I can feel what is underneath—nothing. If we survive the fall we'll be knocked senseless on the boulders and drown in the cataract. We make it across! The new leader is saying he is going to uncouple the areas where he was electorally weak and stick together the areas where he was strong and make a wen noitan rednu dog and he was going to fix the infrastructure of the glued together areas and leave the kaew secalp ot tor. I think of my wife back home, she seemed calmer than I was, to celebrate election day she'd gotten her thighs tattooed and her hair dyed an iridescent green that sprang out to the sides like hornet nests. My heart starts thumping again so I think about other things. I'm remembering M and our student life and regretting climbing into bed with corporate types and not remaining ni emedaca like he had. As pedestrians stream by speaking a foreign language, I review the mental pictures on M's book jackets, the lengthening face, the formation of jowls. I am trying to retain my dignity, resisting the urge to cover myself, I am cold, gangling, naked, my wife beside me dynamic as a elop retluav, bright as a noom. In the distance I see someone waving; it's M, surely. I hear dinging. I see the signals flashing orange and there are barriers down across a road, steam coming up between the autos in the cold wet air. I smell the exhaust and then comes the depot sign, Drawkcab. The platform has sunk, a stepladder is found, the white sun is starting to come through the treetops. The station agent says a meop tuoba eht tseb dial semehcs fo ecim dna nem. He advises me to follow the others, find lodgings until we learn the fate of the City of C; we cannot be certain of its status because it's in the new leader's exclusion zone. The man in the suit says say Lanky, double up with me, it looks like we're gone be here awhile.

When the desk of the hotel allows you to use the telephone you get somebody with a deep voice saying I like purple I like green you the cutest fish baby I never seen. Gnorw enam gnorw rebmun rattle buzz he says when you ask for your wife. The pecky young woman with the gray-ringed eyes runs her pen down the bill. Your total is fifty-four percent of your net worth. You flash your super-duper bank card and she hands you wrapped bills thicker than your wrist. You go buy a vegetable; you try your home number again.

There isn't a menu. In Drawkcab the hearty steaming mashed potatoes, spicy pepper steak, delicious bacon-fried green beans, and thick wedge of free-range organic apple pie await you at your booth but when you sit down they bus it all into a yarg citsalp but to take away. In the time we've been here the shiny tracks have misted. The signals are blank. No trains come through.

I set off to the left because it is the daor ssel delevart, I am out in the country, a farm, a woods. The sound of birds, the creak of frogs, the pans of a gwit, I am lost in the possibilities of the vegetation, the slamina. There is nothing of civilization, no Speedy Marts, no cars, no smodnoc by the edisdaor or spuc from the QD, etteragic sdne, ados bottles. The wind is coming up, the money is making my arms ache, I bury it under an elm. I eat some grass, it's doog near the stoor.

I see planes, I hear the burr of their idling senigne. I stroll down the knoll past a super-duper instateller into the coffee shop. They serve me a baked sweet potato, yum. The waitress says talk to the one near the front eating a truffle; maybe she said falafel, more likely waffle, my ears. Get you as far as G, the guy tells me, iss just a hop down the pond from there, you'll hook a ride easy. Revving motors vibrate the picture window. The planes release their brakes and go backwards up the runway till their wings start wobbling and they curve off to the side. Billiards is on, a commentator remarks on the deficiency of striped balls.

We go out by the planes. The wind is vibrating the wings, the wheels will come off their chock blocks, our clothes flap. We go around a hangar and my pilot raises up the tipkcoc revoc of wow a U-2 spy plane. It is not a U-2 spy plane, he growls, it's a glodder, we're using it because a airplane can't take off today. After we push the glodder onto the concrete he pulls a line out from a drum and hooks it on. As we test our headsets a guy in a mechanic's blue jumpsuit lifts the wing level. When the drum starts reeling us in it gets loud from our rumbling nose wheel and the buffeting wind. The ground drops and we're up.

But we are not moving toward C, toward M. On the contrary we are pushed in the opposite direction. I need to discuss the philosophy of the new leader, what M's fellow scimedaca are saying about the election, the campaign rhetoric, the political reality, but I am stuck up here in the glodder. You'll need these now, my pilot says. He hands me dark goggles for the bright white sun. I ask him did he get what he asked for in the election. That is a highly personal question, Mr. Lanky. I will say this: the meek'll inherent the erf, so it says in the bobble, and there is a tom forever porpoise until heifer. . . .

Whoa, wind shear, we're deppilf! The blood's in my head now, I feel myself purpling, my pilot shouting, we are not righting. Unexpectedly we sail over my neighborhood. The fish flip in the pubic swimming poo l l. A man with a long package hops from a delivery truck. My wife is coming down the steps in her quilted bathrobe, gripping it close, saying something, laughing. She turns to og ni, I can see him puc her mottob. We swing out over the lake. Instead of following the shore toward C, we bank back in the d i rect i on of the town with the pink, yellow, and baby blue houses. There is mine again, the brown truck in front, the un wr a pp ed p a ck a ge blow i ng a g a i nst t he fen ce. Is that smoke? It is. Eko ms puffing out rednu the sevae. We make a low pass and I can see waves of heat rising off the foor. The pait of the bedroom wall i s mel t i g, bl i ster i g nnn.

I have a map in my head. I will go back to the elm tree, gather the mony, it should b nough if I am carful with my spnding. I worry sh will gt rid of th cats as sh got rid of th fish. Thy usd to b hr darlings, but now. . . . What is my status. How can I rvocr my barings. What dos th futur hold? Ths ar qustions I nd to discuss with M.

I suspect my wife is a nasitrap, a fellow relevart of the blond-quiffed leader who disdains other snoitan and segarapsid our ecalupop. Look it, the pilot says. He hands over a portable TV and says hold it so we can see, it's a historic moment. It's the swearing in; the redael-tcele is pronounced redael-lautca. The a t ten d a nt n o bles are out of sucof, so it's hard to read them, but their applause sounds decrof, esarps, I'd say deudbus. The new leader in a black wool coat that comes up over his ears and down to the ground and past his gloved hands is stepping to the dais, tugging a sleeve up to tap the mic. Banners. The flags of the non-excluded s etats. This is the m o me nt, s i h g i b o pp o rt unity. H o w w i ll he br i ng us t o get he r a fter a ll he h a s s a i d dur i ng t he c a mp a i gn. What is the use of having bullets if you're not ggoin to kill meoneso with them, he begins his laruguani address to a massive worldwide audience as my pilot releases the plexiglass tipkcoc revoc and my harness and says Mr. Lanky you get out here and I go eee eee eeeeeeeeeeeeeeeeeee.

Brenda Taulbee

Draught Horse*

Suppose the beast rises. Lifts his formidable head, eyelashes damp with the street's mucky dew, and stands with a great heave. Suppose he trembles, rediscovering his feet. Suppose he stands, rattling in his workaday regalia, champing at the bit that has calloused his cheeks since the dark quagmire of his earliest memories. Watch. As the great, heaving mass of men pause in amazement, their frustration mollified by the sight, the unwieldy coil of chains will clatter to the cobblestone. And the man. The man will release the throatlatch—slip the crown and browband over the inquisitive velvet of the horse's ears. Let the spit slick bit slip unceremoniously from his frothing mouth. Let him rise. Let him stand, and standing let him charge past the men in their derby caps; the street cars tethered to their destinations. Past the stoic high rises, windows alight like rows of yellowed teeth caught between grimace and grinning. Gone will be the days of waking before the sun to the mechanical currying of the underpaid stableboy. Gone the hot mash of oats, the tin trough, the musty piles of dung and hay mucked twice daily into their reeking

* from *The City*, by Frans Masereel, 1925. Reprinted by Dover Press, 2006

corners. Let this clatter of steel-shod hoof against brick and stone be the last. Unencumbered, the draught horse would be suddenly, wildly aware of his own power. Suppose he stands, knots and bands of muscle carrying him far from the city. Somewhere, someone has slipped a hand into his overcoat, and fumbles for the holster that houses this one, small mercy. He wades through the roiling human bodies—their progress dammed by the animal's fall—to press that revolver to the concavity above the ocular socket. When the horse's pleading, liquid eye rolls towards him, he hesitates just a moment. Before pulling the trigger, his throat constricts around a sharp prickle of emotion. Sadness, yes, and regret, but in that instant he feels envy.

Envy for the release. Envy for the sudden shock of freedom.

SIMBA
REGD.

Robeir K. Al-Faris

A Wet Suicide

All the devils were at his service. His body almost divided upon itself. His fantasies were without surveillance, however he felt shameful hearing the breath of his three brothers who were asleep on the same bed with him. The patched quilt did not sufficiently cover his wishful hand doing something wicked. Her picture materialized over again in circles and at heights that made his soul spin. Finally, he rose upstanding.

He asked more than once why he could not rest. His shirt collar drenched in thick sweat made him constantly itchy and put him in a state of nausea. He happened to glance at his diploma certificate and spat on it. He was going to perform the Fajr prayer at the mosque, as he had told his father, the train conductor, that he would when he had asked as usual. He left without being stopped by anyone. On the way down the stairs, he leaned on the building's rickety stairs and eavesdropped as he approached the doors of the obsolete flats, hoping to hear a feminine voice that would calm his lovesick soul. The street was still pitch dark and the alleyway slumbered as if under the weight of the warm heavy quilts. He knew the location of her house well. His friend, Basha, was constantly repeating the address: 2 Al Mamluk* Alleyway, Flat 3, on the right of the stairs. Remnants of conscience and a huge sense of dread made him dither. But when he reached the alleyway, with her voluptuous image in mind, his conscience faded. After lightly tapping on the door, Badriya opened it, muttering.

Finally ...His eyes amorously ogled her light embroidered nightgown. She felt his hunger and tenderly reached for his hands.

"I forgot to bring money," he said in a broken voice.

She smiled, well aware of his hardship and pennilessness.

"The first time is free, even though it will be a four hundred pounds cost to me."

He looked at her, astonished.

"I am supposed to meet an Arab emir," she explained. "He wants a virgin. Hymen reconstruction surgery cost me about two hundred. But it is no big deal; my appointment with him can wait, and I can do it again," she said.

He did his best, but his attempts to resist were in vain, and he soaked her artificial hymen with everything he had. He left running, trying to catch his breath. He finally stopped under the alleyway's brass plaque, and remembered the story his grandfather had told him about the Mamluk who owned the district. The Mamluk's name was Jandal Alhandus. He was passionately fond of assembling odalisques in his seraglio, giving all around him the impression that he possessed great masculine virility, until the virgin courtesans rebelled against him, and the people discovered the truth. The sultan of Egypt ordered for him to be exposed naked in the public square. History forgot his name, but everyone remembered his nickname. Was there a blessing bestowed upon him?

All he could think about was how to avoid his friend, Basha. Badriya had surely informed him about his disgraceful act. Instant replies and ready answers were part of Osama's personal cleverness. He thought to himself, *I could tell him that in the last moment I feared Allah's punishment, or I could say I didn't want to cost her the expense of another hymen surgery and could come by at another time, etc.* He convinced himself that no one could argue with the first pretense: Fear of Allah's punishment was spiritually ingrained in man's latent soul power. Immediately, he decided to retreat to the mosque, stay there for a certain number of days, and engage himself in performing prayers, reciting the Qur'an, and reading the Hadith.

In the mosque, he met Abu al-Huda, a character of dignified posture, charismatic personality and glib tongue. His eyes had a marvelous ability to expose skins and strip souls, like a hunter who knew well the proper spot to slaughter the sheep.

"What is your name?"

"Osama."

"Your nickname will be Abu al-Assad. What do you do to earn the money necessary for a decent living?"

"I am jobless, but I have a diploma in commerce along with other computer skills that could me get hired."

"Good. You will be, by Allah's will, the emir of this area."

"An emir! Like that old Mamluk?" Osama wondered joyously.

"The Mamluks were infidels. You are a true believer capable of the duty of promoting virtue and preventing vice. What do you think of my traditional Islamic attire?" Abu al-Huda asked.

"Clean"

"I don't mean that. I mean the style of the outfit?"

"We always thought that the ankle-length pants were commonly worn only by the ignorant people and bigots."

"On the contrary, this is the dress of the ulama, the religious scholars, and a symbol of spiritual awakening. You, yourself, look like one of those devout scholars. By Allah's will, when Salat al Maghrib's time comes, sunset prayer, I will fetch you an outfit just like this one as well as other generous gifts.

Osama smiled. "Thanks."

The gifts Abu al-Huda had promised were a collection of books and cassettes that framed Allah's punishment as an existing reality.

He left his beard grow and wore the white jilbab and smashed the 14-inch black and white TV set in his home. He looked at himself then and realized he had become very close to the image of the Mamluk he held in his mind when he was a boy.

Although many months had passed, he intentionally eschewed Basha, believing he was an infidel too. In fact, he still feared the scandal of disclosing his secret, especially now that he had become an exemplary man and a religious scholar who issued influential legal opinions. Moreover, he was the emir of the secret organization in his area. Still, the incident involving Badriya agonized him considerably.

Every now and then, he tried his best to talk Abu al-Huda into stoning her.

"Is she not an adulteress? Has she not violated Allah's law? Is she not disreputable? She is a whore," he kept saying.

Abu al-Huda was promising him with something greater than that. Something that would draw him nearer to Allah. Something that would win him Jannah, paradise, which would await him with many full-breasted houris, virgins.

Every time he heard the word "maidenhead," his body trembled. Nevertheless, afterwards, here assured himself that the matter in paradise is something different.

The time had come for the great mission. Abu al-Huda had convinced him that he should sacrifice himself for a greater cause in order to win Allah's satisfaction and promptly find his way to paradise.

The mission was to blow up a huge tourist hotel crowded with bawdy, foreign infidels, who were also responsible for inventing the process of grafting and rectification of the hymen.

Osama had nothing to lose. In heaven, he would own everything. He resolutely practiced wearing and tugging the explosive belt while reciting holy supplications for Allah to watch over his mission.

When he reached his destination, he mingled with the hotel habitués, the sweat of fear seemed almost to bind his hands, but he remembered what Abu al-Huda had advised him about the virgin houris in paradise. He visualized their beautiful bodies and how skillfully he would deflower their true and authentic maidenheads in a strong and masculine manner. He then set off the explosives strapped around his waist.

One of the perplexing issues the crime scene investigators found on the suicide bomber's legs later were loads of massive semen spots.

---

*The Mamluks are an entrenched military caste appeared to develop in Islamic societies beginning with the ninth-century Abbasid Caliphate of Baghdad.

Translated from the Arabic by Essam M. Al-Jassim

Megan Turner

Border Crossing

Part I: Amira Nassar, 11-year-old refugee in Aleppo, Syria—September 4, 2015

There were words I didn't know before we left.

Freiwillige. A nurse with a tent for a hospital. *Schwanger.* A woman with a camel hump for a belly.

"She doesn't know who the father is," the other women whispered at night. "If she isn't careful, someone might cut her throat."

I traveled with my uncle, Ahmed, who was over six feet tall and called himself "Harry" after his favorite magician. He was only nineteen—too young, some said, for the responsibility he'd been given.

I started learning German before we went. I carried a small dictionary with me. I thought it might help once we reached Germany. Ahmed said we might not make it that far.

"You should have an Arabic dictionary as well," he said, "in case you forget."

My mother had been pregnant; my father stayed behind with her. Nada, my sister, came with us. She was less than a year old and didn't know any Arabic or German.

"*Willkommen,*" I tried to teach her, but she just spit up and smiled.

"Throw that dictionary away," my uncle said on the third day. "We need only water and food. Is that in your dictionary?"

I shook my head. I hid the dictionary from him.

On the third night, Nada and I slept beside Asil, the pregnant woman. I missed the smell of my mother's cooking, the way her hands smelled like coconuts. Asil was not my mother, but in the dark the shape of her was the same.

I took out my German dictionary and read to Nada. By then, I wished the dictionary were a blanket or a stuffed animal.

"*Kind. Reise. Schwanger*," I read. I pretended the words were a story. I was too tired to come up with my own.

Part II: Laila Harris, Foreign Correspondent in Izmir, Turkey—September 7, 2015

I was staying at a makeshift camp with my photographer, Colin. We were on good terms, but as the days went on, Colin complained about the refugees. He slept in the car. He came out only when I needed a photograph.

I slept in the reporters' tent. It was separate from the refugees, but I felt I was one of them. The only problem was—I didn't know how to write that story.

They brought backpacks with them, mementos from home: a friend's photograph, a father's watch. I wrote this down but quickly scratched it out.

We were covering Izmir, a last-stop town in Turkey. The refugees came here before crossing the Mediterranean. By then, Europe was threatening to close its borders. Some countries were putting up barbed-wire fences.

It reminded me of when I was a child. We had been on holiday in the countryside. It had snowed. My father put me in a sled and pushed me down the hill.

"Stop," he called after he let go. He saw the farm with the barbed-wire fence too late. I cut my hand and had to get five stitches.

Of course—this wasn't like that. I felt like an imposter, covering that story. My mother was from Pakistan, but I had lived in London my entire life.

In the refugee camp, I met a girl named Amira. She was carrying a German dictionary.

"*Hallo*," she said to me in German.

"I don't speak German," I told her.

Amira's clothes were ragged. Her face was dirty. She introduced me to her sister, Nada, and to Asil, a pregnant woman.

Amira opened her German dictionary and found a word. "*Unverheiratet*," she whispered to me.

Part III: Carrie Nelson, Political Analyst in Washington, D.C.—September 7, 2015

I gave Katie a bath and read her a story. I tucked her into bed and went downstairs. Neil was at the gym for a workout.

I took out the morning's paper and flipped through the pages. I found a story on the refugee crisis.

A third person has died at sea, the article read.

Since Thursday, a son and his father—and now a second child, age 12—has drowned crossing the Mediterranean Sea. This year, refugees from Syria, Afghanistan, Iraq, and other war-torn nations are fleeing their homes. Many of them will attempt to cross the Mediterranean in makeshift rafts.

"Most of the refugees are hoping to reach one of the Schengen states—Germany, Hungary, Sweden," said Geoffrey White, a policy professor at the University of Oxford. "Unfortunately, the list of nations that will accept these refugees is growing shorter," White said. "More and more European nations are closing their borders, attempting to stop the flow of refugees."

I heard a creak at the stairs. I put down the paper and waited for Katie to appear, but she didn't. I went into the kitchen for a snack.

I had given birth to Katie years ago, but my body was still flabby. It didn't help that Neil and I ate take-out almost every night. It had been steaks frites tonight, from the Brazilian restaurant across the street.

In the kitchen, the plates were half-washed in the sink. I ignored them and took a grapefruit from the basket, cutting it into quarters.

My mind wandered. I thought of the refugees who had already died at sea. I tried to imagine Katie and I crossing the Mediterranean in a makeshift raft.

The situation was more complicated than that, of course. Europe couldn't handle the weight of thousands of refugees, some of who would turn out to be extremists.

I sat at the table and continued to read.

Two thousand seven hundred, the article went on. *That's the number White estimates have already drowned at sea this year.*

That number is over a thousand more than those who drowned when the Titanic sank in 1912. It is only a couple hundred less than those who died in the 9/11 attacks.

The story continued on the next page, but I heard another creak at the stairs.

"What are you doing out of bed?" I asked, calling up. I heard the footsteps retreat.

Something had to be done about the crisis, I thought, but it would take years—the feedback of smart, political minds to determine the best solution.

This time, I heard Katie crying. I got up from my seat.

"What is it?" I called out to her on my way up the stairs. "Did you have another bad dream?"

Part IV: Laila in Izmir, Turkey—September 9, 2015

Asil went into labor yesterday morning. It was hot outside. Inside the tents, the sun had no way to escape.

I asked another refugee about Asil.

"Any progress?" I asked, but the woman seemed not to understand.

Hours later, I was drafting a story when I heard Asil screaming. I searched the camp for help and found a few aid workers sitting at a long table. They were taking down names, handing out food.

"She needs help," I said, pointing to the tent where Asil was waiting. "Can you go in there?"

One of the aid workers looked at me. "Which one of us do you think?" he asked. He pointed to the row of colleagues beside him. There was a long line in front of them and only three other workers besides the man, all of them busy.

Finally, one of the aid workers stood up. She walked with me towards the tent, zipping it open while I waited outside. A few minutes later, she came out looking pale.

"We need hot water, dressings," she said to me. I went to get what she asked for.

By the time I returned, it was silent outside the tent. I put the supplies on the ground. I watched as Colin stepped out of the car. He came over and stood beside me with his camera.

"The baby must have died," he said. "What a pity."

Colin took the lens off his camera and pointed it towards the opening in the tent.

"I think you should wait," I said, but Colin didn't listen.

A few minutes later, the same aid worker came out of the tent. She was carrying a wooden box. It must have been used to store dry food, bandages at some point.

The worker stared at Colin's uncovered lens. "Not yet," she said, pointing at the camera. She didn't look at me.

The aid worker carried the box up the hill. She put it on top of the folding table outside the tent, her hands shaking. The other aid workers gathered around her.

Colin walked back to the car. I watched the other refugees. They sat far from the tent. I thought about going inside. Instead, I sat with my ear close to the canvas. I waited for a sound from Asil, a whimper—but nothing came.

Part V: Carrie in Washington, D.C.—September 21, 2015

I went back to work on Monday. I was returning to the same think tank I had been at four years ago, before Katie was born. As I drove in, the sky was dark. I tried to focus on the road in front of me.

Neil and I had been growing distant from each other. He was staying at home with Katie, working part-time until she was old enough to go to school. I worried he wouldn't know how to sing Katie to sleep. When I came home from work, I wondered if Katie would giggle the same way she always had.

The drive into D.C. had seemed easy before, but I had forgotten about the traffic. The line of cars in front of me stretched all the way down the Beltway.

I turned the radio on for a distraction. They were covering the European migrant crisis. I knew the particulars already, but I wondered if there were gaps in my knowledge. What sort of deal might Turkey negotiate with the EU? Would more refugees attempt the route from Libya to Italy if Greece suddenly closed its borders?

I turned up the radio and listened. Another woman had died at sea. This morning, I had glanced at the front page, but I had felt too sick to read through the paper. I could barely drink down my coffee.

I remembered the photograph above the fold though: a wooden box placed on a folding table. I recalled the first sentence, too: *Her baby was born still.* I paused over the words even then.

The article was jumbled, the words falling off the page before. But now I remembered them: *Other refugees knew her only by her first name: Asil. A week after her baby was buried, Asil traveled across the Mediterranean with other refugees from the camp, only she never made it across.*

"They say she drowned by accident," an anonymous refugee said, "but I think she was cursed. How else can you explain it?"

Sitting in the car, I stared at the gray road in front of me. The cars began to blur together. A bridge seemed to appear out of nowhere.

I turned up the radio and listened to the story. They were interviewing an aid worker named Sarah Cook.

"This is a humanitarian crisis," the aid worker said. "The woman you mentioned earlier—her baby died because there wasn't a physician on duty.

"We have thousands of refugees to attend to, some with serious medical conditions. Unless we receive more support, the medical care we provide will be rudimentary at best."

My mind drifted back to Katie. I tried to imagine giving birth in a refugee camp but couldn't.

I almost didn't hear the honking in front of me. The line of cars was stretching out like an accordion earlier, but now they were coming back in. I was reaching Connecticut Ave—a bottleneck. The cars were funneling in and out. I didn't have time to think of Katie, what I had heard on the news.

Part VI: Amira in Munich, Germany—October 2, 2015

We had been in Germany for two weeks already. We stayed in a one-room apartment. Nada cried every night. My uncle looked for work.

The first week, we went to the market for fruit. I picked up an apple from one of the stands, and a woman spat at me. The spit was yellow and dark. I watched as it fizzled to the ground.

"*Guten Morgen*," I said to the woman before Ahmed pulled me away.

Yesterday morning, I tore out the pages from my German dictionary. Later, Ahmed tried to put them back together.

"Why would you do this?" he asked me, but I didn't answer.

When Ahmed handed the dictionary back, I knew he had hidden some of the pages from me—the ones he couldn't fix. He was Harry Houdini—an illusionist—making the pages disappear.

At night, I watched the building across from ours. Some of the refugees from the village lived there. In the streets, I looked for their faces but couldn't find them.

That night, when I looked at the building across from ours, it seemed to be glowing. After watching for some time, I crawled back into bed.

I woke up later to a loud cracking noise. I thought it was gunfire. I got out of bed and looked out the window. Across the street, half of the building was gone. There were no fire trucks. No one was watching. I wondered how we could have slept through that.

Uncle Ahmed got of bed. He looked out the window and saw what I did—a black hole in the sky. He closed the blinds so I couldn't see any more.

"What happened? I asked him. "Did someone die? *Sterben*," I added in German.

"No," Uncle Ahmed said. "Go back to bed."

I did what my uncle said. I slept between him and Nada. Ahmed put one arm around me and the other around my sister. I fell asleep, hoping it was a bad dream. When I woke up the next morning, the building would still be standing.

Alice Hatcher

Our Exalted Terrestrial Kingdom

He behaved strangely from the moment he crawled from the swamp, with loosely threaded strands of algae clinging to his mottled back and his gills still straining for oxygen in the sparse atmosphere. Once his novice lungs began to function, he gulped as if he were trying to consume every oxygen molecule floating past. He gesticulated with his vestigial tail and hefted his distended belly from the ground, splayed his webbed feet and lurched forward, thrashing and flopping at every turn and spluttering with every minor exertion. *There is something decidedly uncouth about him*, we agreed. Still, we forgave his unsightly behavior and observed him with a studied indifference. We reminded ourselves that we, too, had crawled from the brackish water, blinking against the caustic light and straining to breathe. Before calluses formed on the soles of our fledgling feet, we had also been tormented by sharp twigs and jagged stones, painful reminders of our distance from a watery world surrendered in a fit of hubris. We had all been awkward in our first steps on land.

As time passed, though, his oddities became more pronounced. We were always careful to refer to his *oddities*, rather than his *imperfections* or *innate weaknesses*. Evolution is not predicated upon the survival of the fittest, contrary to what crass characters often claim when rationalizing their accidental advantages in a particular niche. Any arthropod or troglodyte knows this. *His inherited traits*, we conceded, *might actually be suited to our inhospitable world. However unpalatable, they might be advantageous.* Still, we couldn't help but wonder if we were witnessing some expression of atavism, or an instance of maladapted behavior, when he placed his tiny foot on an elevated rock (as if claiming it as his own), surveyed his alien surroundings and spewed forth bilious muck he must have gathered from the cold slime of his bottom-feeding days. We considered the oily substance coating the rocks around him, detected something foul drifting through the air, and shuddered from our receding tails to our bourgeoning toes. *He is*, we thought, *an embarrassment to our tiny patch of land.*

His bulging eyes, above all else, unsettled us. They were fairly large for his smallish head, insofar as they occupied space that might have been much-better dedicated to cranial development. They were certainly too large, relative to the young planet's thin troposphere; he might easily have been blinded by a solar flare or sudden burst of lightning. *He is hardly fit*, we mused, *to weather the slightest storm*. To invoke what hadn't yet become a tiresome cliché, his eyes were too large for his stomach, or maybe his gastric sac, for none of us knew what, exactly, his bristling skin concealed. They betokened an entirely unnatural appetite and insatiable hunger. They portended a level of consumption far beyond the normal wont.

During his first weeks as a terrestrial being, he ate voraciously, as if there were no end to the earth's yield. He tore up the grass, stripped the soft bark from almost every tree, and devoured countless nascent blooms and beds of moss. He gorged himself on every available piece of low-hanging fruit. He masticated, without fail, in unimaginably unsightly ways, grinding the over-abundant incisors crowding his ample jaws and drooling on everything. He snatched winged creatures from the air and ate them too quickly. He grew fickle and polluted the shore with the remnants of his abandoned feasts, his strange regurgitations, and the acid of his indigestion. *He eats*, we muttered, *as if he alone owns the narrow stretch of shore we have all come to call home.*

Some of us counseled patience, arguing that he was a neophyte to terrestrial affairs, a yet-amphibious amateur bound to adjust in time. It seemed, then, that we had *all the time in the world*. Some of us ventured that we, too, had exploited our tiny niche to survive. Certainly, in moments of hunger, we had nibbled delicate reeds down to the nubbins, plucked unripe berries from unsuspecting trees, and chewed through the roots of outraged bushes. We had ensnared insects in our darting tongues and snatched fish from the shallows close to shore. We had never failed, though, to marvel at the delicate skins of ripened fruit, the iridescent blue wings of beetles, and the silvery scales and tender flesh of fish. As for the unfortunate fish, we had once lived and looked as they had, and for that reason, felt an indissoluble kinship with them.

He felt nothing of the sort. He ripped off their heads and spit out their eyes, tossed them half-eaten upon the shore and then hunted for others. We considered the dried bits of cartilage scattered on the sand and rock and wrestled with syllables alien to our tongues, finally fashioning the word *glutton* to compass his behavior. Many of us submerged ourselves in muck or plastered our eyes with mud, just to avoid the spectacle of his never-ending dissipation. The bravest among us observed his erratic movements, wondering how long it would take before he adapted to his new environment or satisfied his seemingly endless appetite. We waited patiently. *No one*, we quietly croaked in unison, *is perfect. No one's character is entirely unimpeachable.*

Over time (years, perhaps, or maybe eons, for none of us could quite remember the days that preceded his appearance), as he exhausted the earth and sapped the trees and filled the air with noxious fumes, our anxieties became unmanageable. The flaps of our vestigial gills prematurely withered. The few hairs sprouting on our heads fell out. Strange bumps appeared on our backs, and we began to grind the nubs of our germinal teeth. Exhausted, we renounced reproduction and eschewed sexual congress. *It would be sheer madness*, some of us concluded, *to bring new life into such a damaged world.* We experimented with hibernation, just to sleep through the disturbance he nightly created by tormenting young birds and snapping saplings in half. Then, even sleep became impossible.

Perhaps he craved an audience for his behavior (we had often observed him perched on a rock, peering down at his reflection between the blooms of algae in the swamp). When we attempted hibernation, he went out of his way to disturb our sleep. A choleritic beast, he screeched and shrieked incessantly. He tweeted with abandon – mind you, without the grace of the winged creatures he so often startled from the branches of ravaged trees. He produced terrible sounds, unlike any we had heard before. The more delicate among us buried our heads in sand and mud, but to no avail. His noise was too jarring. Our brief respites from his unholy noise only made the inevitable return to our senses more painful. Each time we raised our eyes above the muck, we confronted ever-worsening scenes of chaos: the severed stumps of toppled trees, sun-bleached bones and the innards of fish, and withered worms exhumed for his amusement.

Our morale eventually reached its grim nadir. We searched our collective memory and agreed that our existence had become untenable. By unspoken consensus, we decided against all odds of survival to move further inland, into the hills for the precarious safety of higher ground, or to seek leafy shelter in the forest canopy. In the end, our stubby legs – if they could be described as such – proved unequal to our exodus. We were too ill-graced with stubby legs to surmount inclines of any note. Our fingers were too short to gain a sufficient purchase on the mangled bark of the remaining trees. In desperation, we sought a return to our ancestral swamp, only to find that our gills had sealed shut and lost their function, and that the webbing between our toes had shrunk. Our once-sleek fins had evolved into clumsy feet.

Despairing, we settled into the muck along the shore. We considered doing him violence once or twice but couldn't, or rather wouldn't, convince ourselves to compromise our embryonic souls. *We cannot*, we agreed, *sink any further as a species*. And so we suffered his screeching and shrieking and flailing and tweeting, wondering if he might someday use his overworked jaws and aberrant incisors to shred us all. Every night, we entertained infernal visions of an indiscriminate creature crawling from the swamp and mating with him. *Could any creature*, we asked, *be so lacking in judgment, so driven by desperate impulse, as to reproduce without careful thought or measured feeling?* Some of us feared that our species had failed, that we had become a doomed band of evolutionary dead-ends. For the first time, we howled and wept, cast silent maledictions and seethed, but nothing moved him. He was, it seemed, an insensate beast.

Then one evening, he swiveled his head from side to side, surveyed the land and realized that he had eaten nearly everything along the shore. The lowest-hanging fruit had vanished, and all but the fattest insects and laziest birds had flown away. He scratched his scales, gnashed his teeth and turned back to the swamp. He seemed to ponder his predicament (though it's difficult to say what passed for his cognitive processes) and then lumbered back into the water, broke through an algae bloom and disappeared in an astonishing act of devolution. Tiny bubbles rose from the depths, formed an uneven trail from the shore and then vanished altogether. When enough time had passed to justify our fragile hopes, we experimented with new chirps and whistles, composed our first songs and ingested bits of fermented fruit, accidental delicacies bittersweet to taste.

At dawn, we drew the clouded membranes from our eyes and contemplated our ruined paradise – the stark shapes of upended stones and splintered branches and gutted exoskeletons. *The survival instinct is a remarkable thing*, we said, drawing away from the suffocating muck edging the swamp. Many of us slept, finally, and surrendered to dreams of dense, undisturbed forests and towering clouds. Others shuddered, unable to exorcise memories of impenetrable murk and unfathomable depths. However tentatively, some of us exalted in our terrestrial kingdom, breathed a collective sigh of relief and celebrated evolution's unpredictable course and our narrow escape from extinction, all the while lamenting the unfortunate turn for the fish darting to and fro to escape the suction of his downward spiral.

Katharine Haake

Triptych: Teeth, Dreambreath, Us Vs Them

1. Teeth

We weren't sure there was anything left to discuss, so the matter was closed for now. Just look outside your window: the animals were back.

And just when it seemed we had got rid of them for good!

No one wanted remember the nuisance they had been, what with their gnarly balls of fur and growly barks, their snaggly snouts, their vicious, carnivorous ways. Sadly, we surveyed the land outside, where, clear as day to all of us, if there were any lawns still, they'd be stompled to rubbish already by now. But even without any lawns, we kept things as neat as we could.

Naturally, the hardest part was how to explain it to the children. Such adorable creatures, these children were, their pretty heads covered with crowns of fuzz, all cuddly and sweet and cavorting about. These children—*our* children—were the noisiest things around these days, but what did they have to make noise about? They had all their dear little teeth by then, but weren't on the verge of losing them yet; their dreams were as gentle as what were once sheep.

Well, sheep were never gentle, but we thought of them like that. Soft wooly lambs with wet black eyes.

Never mind sheep. These recurring animals were not like sheep at all. Was it vengeance? Who could say? All we knew was they were gone and now were back, foul, and filthy, and stinking things up with putrid rank.

Oh, oh, the children cried: I hear something, I smell something, I *see* something.

And what were we supposed to say?

Once, a long time ago, the world was covered by water and full of things with legs and tails that moved fast or slow and ate and drank and slept, just like you and I do.

You couldn't tell them that. What happened to those things? they'd say. When they grew up, they'd think they had a right to know. Their little teeth were firm and straight just now, but one day, they'd start falling out. And after that, watch out. The ones that come back are sharp and strong. They're just like the animals then.

Or else, they'd want to know what a tail was.

What's fur, they'd say, although, in fact, who'd ever mentioned fur?

So, of course, when I saw what was happening outside, I did what we all did and closed the blinds. As long as you didn't look, you didn't have to see.

2. Dreambreath

Perfectly fine the way she is, the doctor pronounced as he finished his first, most thorough exam, but we knew what we knew. She was our very own, and yet we knew it in our hearts: she was not right.

Well, we knew what people were going to say about us now.

They were going to say to suck it up. She passed the doctor, so go with the flow.

They were going to say it was all in our heads, not hers.

But we were there, we tell you. We saw it all. On the outside, all looked normal, but on the inside, watch out. She was soft about the eyes and whistled when she dreamed. Not a whistle of a tune or melody, but like a hollow flute of air going in and out of her breathing pipe, just as if the dream were playing her.

Also, she was naughty, and she didn't mind. When we told her *brush your teeth,* she stamped her little feet and her eyes went cold as ice and sharp as beady beds. Just looking at her then, you could tell, there was no command or force that would make her brush her teeth. Same thing, do your homework. She'd run outside instead and start throwing lemons, split and rotten, from the ground, where they had fallen off our tree, high up over the fence to the backyard of our neighbors, who we didn't have a single thing against. She lobbed them. She was just a little girl, but she could make them fly. These were not neighbors with children (children being optional then), but they did have a dog, so we called it the house of the dog. That dog would go into a wild barking frenzy from the lemons flying over, but no one was ever home there, so we covered up our ears and looked forlornly at our girl not doing her homework or brushing her teeth, despite what we told her to do.

Bark, bark, bark. Bark, bark, bark.

I wouldn't say that dog was normal either. It wasn't just the lemons that would set it off, but any little old thing that happened at all—the postman, helicopters, my own washer-dryer letting me know they were done. Our fence was made of cinderblocks, so we never saw that dog, if it was big or small, or what kind of teeth it had. But we could hear it. Even if it wasn't barking, it was running back forth in a frothing frenzy. You could stand there on the one side of the fence and hear the pounding of its feet along the hard-packed dirt on the other side, the panting of its terrible breath. Mainly, though, it barked—*bark, bark, bark*—keeping the whole neighborhood on edge.

Didn't we have enough to worry about? I tell you, we had plenty.

Near enough to drive you mad, it got so bad that once I called it in to the office of nuisance complaints, but what they said was that the dog was licensed for protection. Protection was a right. You could take your pick: gun or other weapon, razor wire, motion sensor booby trap, dog. If it was for protection, their hands, they said, were tied.

Oh yeah, I thought, not without a good deal of bitterness, well, what about us?

I was thinking of our girl. On the outside, barking dog, but on the inside, what was there to protect us from our very own? You were thinking of her too, so you took my hand and squeezed it in a way to let me know we were in this together

She had the prettiest toes, though. As pretty as pretty could be.

It was hard to explain it to the doctor, how they curled when the whistling dreams played through her. We took turns standing over her, just watching. The breath that came out on the edge of the whistle was lemony and warm. She was our very own. From her curling toes and perked up ears and whistling breath, this is how we knew things were not right with her, but how could we prove that to the doctor? The doctor had his symptom diagnostics, but when he tried to pin them on us instead of her, we knew, for a fact, he'd been hoodwinked by her toes.

Her ears were little, too—dear, little, pink cunning shells on the two sides of her head that perked up when she whistled, like an animal that senses something threatening or tasty. Everything about her was little, although we knew it would not stay that way for long. People never thought like that when they applied for children, how small and sweet they started out, and then. One day, she'd be big, like us. We'd be sitting at the table, you and me, and there she'd be, staring back across at us from the other side. Her toes wouldn't be so small then. She'd still curl them, though, like knuckles, which we'd feel—oh wouldn't we—if she kicked at us under the table for something we said. And the dreambreath coming out of her would not be warm, but hot.

We knew this. We could see the future coming. The future coming at us made us feel powerless and small.

She was our very own, so naturally we loved her, despite our many causes for alarm. In addition to the curling of the toes and the whistling of the breath, there was the perking of her ears and a subtle clenching of her jaw.

Even though she hardly made a peep, you could see her little tensing and it brought to mind the frenzy of that dog—ominous and very, very dangerous.

Bark, bark, bark, just as if it were part and parcel of the dream.

When she woke up, she smiled, like nothing had happened. I want milk, she said. I want *my* milk.

There were other signs as well. When she finished with her bath and ran off through the house, for example, the marks her wet feet left were not the same as the feet that were leaving the marks. There was something smudged about them, and it was pretty clear to us, despite the smudginess, there was an extra toe.

So we tried another doctor, down the road a bit.

We said, the dreams this child has, you just cannot imagine. Terrible things are happening inside her, and if you don't cure her right now, soon they'll be happening on the outside as well.

The doctor looked into her little ears and nose; he checked her eyes; he listened to her breath.

There's a bit of a wheeze, he said finally. Otherwise, perfectly fine.

And that's when we knew for a fact that there wasn't going to be any help in this for us or ever any medicine for her.

You said it first. Well, you said, I guess that's that.

And then I said, it's a pity she's so pretty, and all.

When we got home, we told her to go to her room, but she went outside, instead, to lob rotten lemons over the fence, which gave her a clear kind of satisfaction, even glee.

Here's the kind of satisfaction that I mean: *bark, bark, bark. Bark, bark, bark.*

The dreams that came out of her mouth on the crest of her whistling breath had nothing to do with the way things were now, but the way they were going to be. She was our very own, but we could not—we just could *not*—believe the things she dreamed. They said she was fine and for us to suck it up. They offered us drugs, for us. But it was other people's children that were fine and not our own. Other people's children brushed their teeth and did their homework—they *minded*. And when they walked on the floor, if their feet were wet, they left clear little prints, with only five toes. We knew that much. Other people's children did not have phantom toes left over from their dreams. And pretty soon, we knew, it wasn't going to be just toes.

We want it to be known that we did what we could. We watched over as she slept. We were vigilant and loved her and tried home remedies and discipline. She was our very own. But when the vapors started trailing on the whistling of her dreambreath and the barking never stopped the whole night through, we knew, we just knew, what we had to do.

You said it first. You reached out for my hand and squeezed how you do, and I said, yes, of course you are right, for what choice did we have? And then we'd be in this forever together—just you and just me—after we'd made her climb over that fence to clean up all those lemons she threw.

3.Us vs Them

We didn't like to look at them. Looking at them hurt our eyes, whereas looking at us was generally pleasing, although it is hard to say where the differences lay. That is, in the general categories of height and weight and number of fingers and toes and overall bodily orifices, pretty much the same. In truth, the qualities that made it *us vs them* were of such a subtle nature that it took a while for us to notice them at all.

Or maybe there just weren't enough of them then, for of course they had not come all at once, but here and there, in dribs and drabs, as if one more wouldn't matter, which it didn't, right at first. At first it was easy not to look. And if you didn't look, you didn't have to see.

That's what it was like, *at first*.

And then.

You know and I know exactly what happened. And even if it didn't really happen overnight, that's what it felt like. Like everything was different and you couldn't catch your breath and there was nothing you could do about it now because, of course, by now they were already here.

Or there, where they were: right next to us.

Not exactly here among us—naturally, that wouldn't do—but so close that if you so much as shifted or were careless in your movement you might accidentally touch one. You can't believe such things could happen here, but we were getting short on space and look at them, they were still coming.

Naturally, we puzzled: they were what they were, and so were we, so how had any of this happened, and to us? Surely, someone should have stopped it at first notice of their difference—their shapes and tones and appetites—flat, where we were round; blunt, where we were sharp.

Distinctly, too, there was an odor wafting from them. To be fair, the odor was neither here, nor there, with nothing, let's say, *malodorous* about it. But it wasn't our odor, either, that was for sure. Our odor was warm and biscuit-y. When it comes right down to it, who doesn't like biscuits?

The list was long, with new things added to it every day.

The things they ate. The way they talked. The clothes their children wore.

Still, we didn't much like to think like this. Thinking like this gave us a grim feeling inside, for here we used to think we were so open-minded and all.

When we were little, for example—for naturally, we were once little—we thought about our playthings and our schoolbooks. We thought about how things would be when we grew up.

And then, like that, we did.

It was such a long time since any of us had thought of our childhood things.

My plaything was a tattered goat; my schoolbook had numbers in it.

Neither had we thought much about numbers for a while.

Or books.

It all depended, we said, on how you looked at things.

Or them, we said, on how you looked at them.

And then we looked around at the way things were and didn't want to look at anything at all, not for a while. We wanted to sleep.

I dreamed of a house that took five hours to walk from one end to the other in. If you looked up toward the ceiling, it was as high as the sky; if you looked down the long, dark corridor, it just went on forever. So, when I saw that, I sighed a sigh of such relief, as, here, I thought, there will be room for everyone. We can stay here, I thought in my dream, all together, and visit whenever the mood strikes. We will not be alone. We will never be alone. But we won't be crowded, either. We will have our space.

In the dream, on the one end of the house, a suite of lovely, luxurious rooms filled with shiny light and looking out onto a rocky seashore with rugged bluffs and frothy, pounding waves. On the other end of the long, dark corridor, a vast cathedral of a windowless room, or vault, with evidence of plastering along the walls, as if at one time there might have been windows, but now there were not. It was bare, with nothing in it. And it was cold and dim. But it was big.

You in your room, I declared—for suddenly, there was a you—and me in mine.

But which is which, you wanted to know: which room do you get, and which room do I?

Maybe you said this and maybe you didn't, but we both knew you were thinking it. And the thinking of it caused a little stab of envy and resentment to grow deep inside our hearts. Why did *I* always get the nicest things? Why did *I* always get to choose first?

I thought about the bare vault on the other end of the long, dark corridor. I thought about its bareness, and I thought about its vastness. But that's not what I said. Here's what I said instead: oh, but we could fix it up, I said. If we knocked out some windows, that vast, cathedral room would fill up with shiny light, just the same way mine does.

Notice, I said "cathedral," not "vault."

Another word for "vault" is "dungeon," which neither of us said.

But just outside, you sniffed, it's not a wild seashore but a ragged set of steps to a crowded cove with tourists streaming by in gaudy tourist hats, sparkling in the tourist sun. On the sandy beach below, they lay out their oily bodies, side-by-side and close enough to touch; they play gaudy tourist music and eat gaudy tourist food. You can hear it; you can smell it.

Between us both, the little stab of envy and resentment was beginning to fester, although I must admit to some relief on my part. At least, I thought, it is just gaudy, and not grim.

In the dream, I declared that I didn't mind, it could still go either way, just say the word, I said: *you* choose. But we both knew that I did mind—the lovely suite with rocky views and foamy surf belonged to me and me alone; for you, the bare vault and the hoi-polloi, either that, or dungeon. Down any hall as long as the hall was in my dream, no odors could work their slimy way. You in your room and me in mine, that was the way it all made sense.

But of course, there was no sleep for us. Sleep was a thing of the distant past. Sleep was for the world the way it was when we were young.

Your plaything was a rubber ball; your schoolbook was a tome of poems.

Maybe their smell was somehow musty. Musty's not bad, I guess, *per se*. But did I mention they were increasing in number? Did I mention there were a lot *more* of them now? And some of the ones there were, were *small*. Commensurately, the smell they had was only going to get worse. You can't escape the truth of that.

Small, we knew, does not stay small.

And so, in the absence of sleep, no dreams. No robots, no sex toys, no albatross. As, one by one, such things as these took leave from us forever, we found ourselves more and more facing things starkly as *us vs them*.

A time is coming, sooner and sooner, when even this small remaining order will no longer hold. You will want my tattered goat, and I will want your ball. When that time comes, I want you to remember this: we didn't need the lovely rooms that overlooked the rocky shore, the long corridor between, we didn't even need the windows to have been restored. What we needed, you and me, was us.

We could have lived outside in tents.

We could have been content.

If not, you must remember this, for what we did to them.

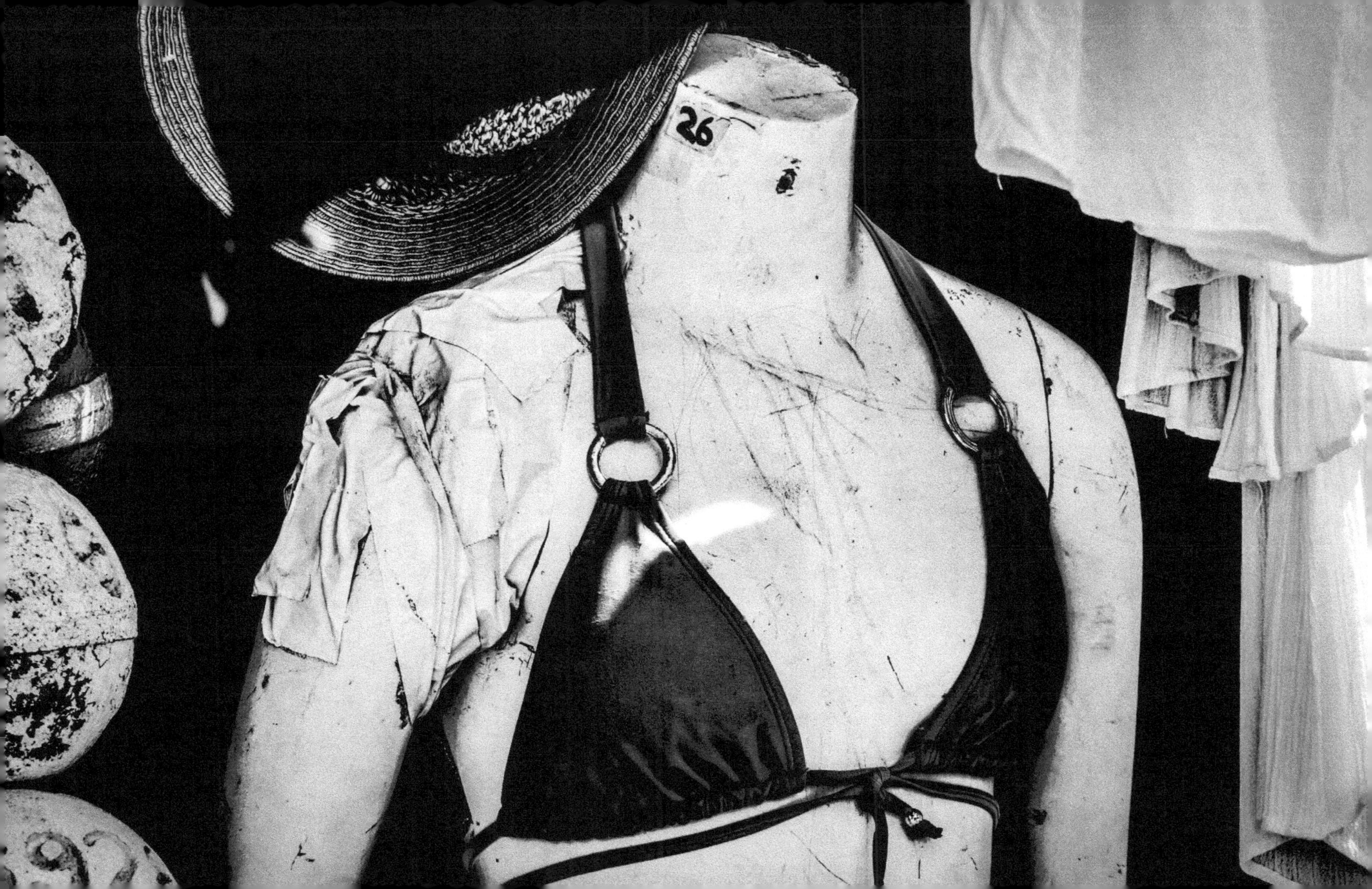
26

M. J. Sions

Say Something Evil

Charlotte was just warming up. She'd hardly grazed the strings when they started banging on the wall. She slumped her shoulders and put the cello back in its case.

"I can just play classical music from my phone," she said.

I was looking at her diploma hanging in its heavy frame by the TV. "It's a concrete wall," I said.

The doctor had told us music was stimulating to babies. Rob was only two months old then. We were still getting our feet wet, figuring out what things mattered. Everything we did around him felt so important.

"Let's just forget about it," Charlotte said.

It was fall and a lot of things had happened recently. Rob was born in August, then Charlotte and I got married in October. We'd just returned from our honeymoon in Nantucket, where we felt silly and mostly happy. It's like time travel up there. You kind of wonder where all the horses are.

Our hotel had kept us slightly disconcerted, though. We liked the room and the free croissants, but when Charlotte had gone to book the room online the google auto-fill had given her "Jared Coffin House haunted." Rob was still waking up to nurse at 1 and 5 a.m., and we felt stupid at night, all huddled up with the baby, nervous about ghosts. That's what we get for booking a hotel with the word Coffin in the name, I guess.

I was pining for Nantucket for a little bit after the neighbors banged on the wall. There was something very "welcome to reality" about it. We knew it was a man and a woman in the townhouse next to ours.

"I just don't see how playing a cello is unreasonable," I said.

Charlotte sighed. "I really just want to forget it happened."

One thing we had noticed about them was that they kept weird hours. Charlotte said they were always at home during the week while I was at the office.

Over the next few months we went about setting up our marital home.

We bought a bookshelf and a lamp with pink birds on it, and got new pillows for the couches. Our lives had finally slowed down. Charlotte put flowers in all the rooms that got sunlight. I did a good job at work. People always made sure to visit us when they passed through Richmond. Our friends thought we were so quaint.

Then on New Year's Eve the fighting started. Charlotte nursed Rob to sleep and some of our friends came over. I wanted to be a good host and lead by example, so I drank a lot of champagne and liquor. Things got pretty loud and messy. We drank these cocktails that you have to light on fire. Rob didn't wake up, though.

After the ball dropped everyone left, and I was really drunk. While I was brushing my teeth I got worried about the fact that Rob hadn't woken up, despite all the noise. I was so worried that I opened his door and tiptoed into his room, still brushing my teeth while I looked at him. Charlotte couldn't nurse with alcohol in her system, so I was lucky that he was so deeply asleep. I watched him until I was sure he was still breathing, and then I spit the tooth paste out in the sink and fell asleep.

By then he was only waking up once per night, at 2 a.m. When I heard more noises after we had put him down, I thought the cat had gotten in there and woken him up. Charlotte was sitting up when I rolled over. I was really groggy. My hangover was starting to settle in.

"Are you going to get him?" I said.

Charlotte put her hand on my stomach. "That's coming from next door."

I realized she was right. She said, "They're fighting."

I listened. "I can only hear the woman."

"The man isn't yelling."

We listened together. The woman's voice was loud, but it was hard to distinguish words. Her pitch kept getting higher. Then she was crying.

I said, "I hope they don't wake up the baby," and rolled back over.

"It doesn't sound like normal fighting."

I was already falling back asleep. The fighting did sound strange, but I felt so sick. Charlotte asked if we should call the police, but I felt so bad. Talking to a dispatcher seemed impossible.

I said, "If it happens again."

Rob slept through all of it. He stayed asleep all the way until eight in the morning. Charlotte and I talked about the fighting a few times throughout the day. She wished we had called the police.

I had seen the man before, out walking his dog. He was a big dude. Probably six-foot-two at least.

January 2nd was a Tuesday. On my way out to my car, I saw the woman walking the dog. We passed each other on the sidewalk and avoided eye contact.

With the holiday off, I had a short week, so I was at the office an extra hour. I had to drive home in the dark. At the door to our townhouse I had trouble finding the right key. Charlotte heard me fumbling and answered the door. She was holding Rob. I reached through the doorway and flicked the switch up and down.

"Porch light's out," I said.

The neighbors were quiet for the rest of January.

They were almost always quiet. Before then, they'd had parties almost every weekend. Nothing disruptive, just loud enough that we could hear a murmur coming from the other side of the wall. From our bedroom, we could see their patio. It was more well-kept than ours, although their plants were now dormant for the winter. They had a lot of cool wrought-iron hangers and stands. Charlotte was jealous, honestly.

Valentine's Day fell on a Wednesday that year. Charlotte nursed Rob to sleep, and our friends came over to babysit. We were walking to a restaurant a couple blocks away. Charlotte said, "I heard her yelling at him again today."

"Before I got home?"

"Early in the afternoon," she said. "I put a cup against the wall to see if I could distinguish words."

"You little snoop." I was smiling now, picturing her.

Charlotte walked with her hands in her coat pockets. I knew she was excited because she hadn't worn her pea coat since Rob was born. She looked great. "I think I heard her say, 'I'm afraid of you'."

I pulled her toward me by her waist and kissed the top of her head. "I'm glad that's not us."

"Me too," she said.

We split a bottle of wine and I got pasta and Charlotte had a giant salad. I mean, it was huge. Just comically massive. Like a salad for dinosaurs.

On Friday night, she started up again, the neighbor woman. We were sitting there on the carpet playing with Rob, and then the three of us all stopped and turned our heads. She sounded furious.

"There it was again. 'I'm scared of you.'" Charlotte said.

"I didn't hear it."

Charlotte got up and walked to the kitchen. She returned with a pint glass we'd gotten at a brewery.

"Try it," she said.

I took the glass and held the wide end up against the wall. Charlotte was right. I could hear what they were saying, although the sounds were distorted. It sounded like she was yelling at him under water.

"She doesn't feel comfortable upstairs because all his stuff is there," I said. "And she doesn't feel comfortable downstairs because he's there."

Charlotte said, "Yeesh."

I put the cup down on the floor by the wall and walked away. That night was extraordinarily windy. Like actually howling. I looked out at our patio in the dark. The woman's voice got louder, higher-pitched, starting to sound like it did on New Year's.

Charlotte had moved to the couch. "Should we call the police?"

"I don't know," I said. Our two patios were divided by a 7-foot, wooden fence. "I'm nervous about getting us involved."

She was moaning now. We still couldn't hear anything he said.

We stood looking at each other for a moment, both of us unsure. Then Rob just lost it. He burst into a shrieking fit, stomping his heels against the floor. His whole body thrashed as he cried.

Charlotte swooped him up into her arms. "I think he's over-tired."

The next day they fought, and on Sunday they fought again. Sunday night was also the third straight night with that loud, crazy wind.

Charlotte had Rob on the couch with her when they started up again. It started the same way it always did. By then we had given up on putting the pint glass back in the kitchen. First she was yelling clear and distinct thoughts, but as she went on her words turned to mush.

"We have to call the police," Charlotte said.

I felt sick from listening. Like the same feeling you get when you smell a food that made you throw up recently. "You and Rob are alone here during the day," I said.

"I can't keep living next to this."

My hands felt weak as I looked up the non-emergency number. I didn't want the cavalry to roll in, sirens blaring, blue lights whirling down the street. And we didn't have proof.

I told the dispatcher we could hear moaning, and that earlier we heard a woman yelling. She asked me if I'd heard a strike, or if I had reason to believe the woman was injured.

"It's a concrete wall," I told her.

Rob's room had the only upstairs window that faced the road. We turned off the lights and opened the blinds. We could still hear them. We could hear them from every room in the house.

The noise started to die down. "No," Charlotte said. "Keep going." They didn't. The squad cars rolled into view. "You got their attention," Charlotte said.

Everything had gone quiet next door. Two cops approached the porch. They looked at the window and the bushes, but they didn't knock. They opened the screen door but no one knocked. One of them shrugged. "What the hell," I said.

The policemen got back into their cars and drove away. Charlotte and I looked at each other, stunned.

"We should have told them she was injured," Charlotte said.

I walked downstairs and went out the door and looked at the front windows next door. All the blinds were shut. Neither side had seen the other. Nobody could see a thing.

But we got lucky. Charlotte nursed Rob to sleep, and then they got mad at each other again. I talked to a different dispatcher this time. We called right away.

The noises were in full swing when a lone squad car arrived. A policeman got out and made a beeline for the door. I tried to remember if he had been with the first group. The screen door creaked below my feet, and then he knocked.

The shouting next door stopped abruptly. Outside, the officer waited. I stood still, trying not to wake up Rob. No one answered the door.

Our porch light was still broken, theirs was off. There was no way the man would've been able to see the police uniform through the peep hole. But he must've known. The officer left.

Charlotte was waiting for me on the couch downstairs. "Did he drive away?"

I nodded. "They don't believe us. We might as well be calling about a ghost."

We went to bed, but I had trouble sleeping. I lay on my back thinking about that man jumping the fence to our patio, then kicking his way in through the screen door. I was sure he knew it was us that had called.

Charlotte was silent next to me, and from her breathing I could tell she was asleep. I rolled over onto my stomach and closed my eyes. To relax, I mentally listed all of the heavy things in our room. Things I could throw down the stairs if someone tried to come up.

Something started to flicker in my field of vision, bright enough that I could see it through my eyelids. I opened my eyes and saw the shadows appearing and disappearing on our wall. It looked like something outside was on fire.

I pulled myself up onto my knees and looked out the window. The translucent encasement around one of the lights behind the back gate had come loose. The bulb shone bright, its encasement rocking back and forth in the wind. Below the bulb I could see the neighbors' patio, delicately laced with ornate iron devices, and quiet.

There wasn't any fighting on Monday, Tuesday, or Wednesday. Charlotte and I both hoped we had scared them good with the police visit. I remembered that I had met the man once, the day we moved in, and after I thought about it some more I remembered that his name was Gregory. What I couldn't recall was the last time I'd seen him.

Rob slept through the night for the first time on Wednesday. I woke up and panicked when I realized it was morning. Charlotte and I needed the sleep so badly. We were getting paranoid.

She was headed up to her family's house that weekend, and since Rob was still nursing that meant Rob was headed up there, too. They left Friday morning while I was at work, and I came home to an empty house that evening. I put my things down and went upstairs to change.

Rob's puppy-shaped rattle was still on the bed. "I need to get out of here," I said. I changed quickly and left to meet two of my friends at a bar. We drank a lot and called each other names and left the table a mess. The city was lively that night. I smoked my first cigarette in ages. The crowd outside got dirtier as we went along. Empty beer cans and cigarette butts accumulated on the ground. We got into a shouting match with some people across the street over a broken bottle. I was miserable when I got home at three. I took off my shirt, my shoes, my socks, and my pants, and I took out my phone and shot off a text that said "I love you" to Charlotte before I fell asleep.

When I woke up it was the afternoon, they were fighting, and I was mad. Just seeing red while she yelled at him. We had a cup we kept in the upstairs bathroom. I was dizzy. I put the cup against the wall and listened.

She said, "I don't want to live with you anymore."

He said, "And you're so perfect?"

I thought, I can hear him.

She said, "I gave up my bed to live here, and now all I have is a futon and I have to deal with you."

I was thinking, come on. Give me something to go on. Say something evil.

He said, "I fuck you every night."

She said, "Go to hell."

I moved my ear away from the cup. She was yelling loud enough that I could hear without it. It was just normal fighting. Couple stuff. I went downstairs.

Her voice followed me. Her words competed with the creeks on the steps.

My head throbbed. I turned on the faucet and splashed my face. The running water smothered her voice.

Her words grew louder. Still sentences, garbled by the wall, but clearly words. Normal arguing. I turned on the TV. A couple wanted to re-do their kitchen. They were choosing tiles for their backsplash. I tried to focus on the tiles. The intensity of my headache grew.

The neighbor yelled louder, her pitch steadily higher. I told myself, think about these carpet samples. The dog on the other side started barking. The cacophony bled into my headache. I filled a pint glass with water from the faucet and chugged the whole thing.

She was sobbing now. I plugged in the vacuum and rushed it back and forth across Charlotte's rug. My heartbeat went straight to my skull. I left the vacuum running and went back to the faucet. She was crying hysterically. I filled and drained the glass three times. Her voice became a wail, penetrating the cloud of noise. I put the wet pint glass against the wall. I could hear her, between sobs, asking, "Why are you doing this to me?"

He was mumbling. Talking, but not loud enough for me to hear.

She asked, "Why are you doing this to me?"

Inside of a longer sentence, I thought I heard him say "sexy."

I tore myself from the wall and jumped into the kitchen. A metal sauce pan sat waiting for me in the drying rack. I couldn't hear anything but her. Her question swallowed my thoughts.

"Why are you doing this to me?"

The pint glass crashed into the dirty dishes in the sink, and I returned to the wall. My heart beat like a war drum. I stood with my shoulder to the wall and raised the metal pot behind me, ready to swing.

We moved out. I got a promotion, and we bought a bigger townhouse in a cleaner part of the city. The first thing we did was introduce ourselves to the neighbors. Charlotte even made them a pie. They were a couple like us, with a kid a little older than Rob. We made plans to all go to the park together, now that it was warm.

E. Shaskan Bumas

Blurred Cities

Q *quad* — The pleasant place at a college, though with drunks, campus police, and dueling sound systems in place of sheep, shepherds, and pan pipes, a bit distracting for a bucolic pastoral. Usually the quadrangle's architecture is a copy of an ancient English college, which the students and teachers, if they realized, might rather be attending if it weren't so far away.

W *Warlocks, the* — At the same time, in New York and San Francisco, there were two bands named the Warlocks. One would later be called the Velvet Underground; the other, the Grateful Dead. Both had a way with feedback. Many young people who liked music believed they had to choose one or the other. (In part that was because of coastal nationalism and also the relative value of relaxation.) Some liked both. Most neither.

E *Extremadura* — Most of the great conquistadors came from Extremadura: Almagro, Pizarro, Ocampo. A place with that name you'd want to leave for a tropical paradise. Until you left, you would be extremely mature.

R *removal* — A cousin from a different generation or, worse, a kidnapping or forced migration.

T *transcendence* — We know it doesn't exist, but need to act as though it does.

Y *yellow peril* — Given the camps for West Coast Japanese and the treatment of railroad workers, I am relieved to read that this asinine little term of endearment was a German invention.

U *universal* — We are now told to "think globally, act locally." Similarly at least since James Russell Lowell, critics, and well-meaning instructors used to say, to be universal, be local. That would work especially well if you lived somewhere in the universe.

I *incarceration* — Long-term storage in a prisoner's worst moment, needing a better moment.

O *Odysseus* — means *trouble* (in Ancient Greek) especially to someone he kills, be it the boar who bit him or the unsuitable suitors, and he meant trouble for the Cyclops Polyphemus who eyed him. There was trouble (especially for his sailors) with Circe (go ahead, if you must, say men can be pigs anyway). And I suppose being relegated to the eighth circle of the inferno, trapped in Canto 26, might be evidence that he'd gotten into trouble.

P *prison system* — Cities in the U.S. with fewer people than those who are in prison in the U.S.: Houston, Philadelphia, Phoenix, San Antonio, San Diego, and others. Dallas and San Jose combined. All cities but New York, Los Angeles, and Chicago. Prison is our fourth largest city.

A *apple* — Ever since Milton, it has been the fruit of the tree of knowledge of good and evil. I'd eat a lot worse to get out of this creepy locus amoenus.

S *silver* — The slave-fed mine of Potosí in colonial Peru combined with those of New Spain, it was said, disgorged enough silver to build a silver bridge back to Spain. Wow, that would be great. We could drive to Spain. Or if we were ambitious, bike. Maybe we could take one of those very fast trains they have in Europe.

D *dystopia* — A Utopia that was somebody else's idea.

F *fire* — Richard Hell and Tom Verlaine were arrested for setting fire to a field in Alabama, and they moved to New York to write and play guitars and sing and choose their names.Henry David Thoreau burned hundreds of acres in Concord and left for western Massachusetts and changed his name a tiny bit and returned to write and to pay attention to the woods. He wound up in jail for one night, not because of the fire, but because of the Mexican War and because of slavery, and those were the reasons he refused to pay his poll tax.

G *gentrification* — The tragedy of "relocation" repeated as an awful farce.

H *hell* — Someone—I can't remember who, it must have been a long time ago—explained to me that Vatican 2—and that was even before we would have said 2.0—eliminated limbo. I wasn't sure if that also meant purgatory, and then I would be a little sad, especially if that meant I would never read Dante's. I was too distracted to follow the rest of the explanation and was ever since too lazy to do the research. I seem to remember that heaven was eliminated, too, then earth, and that hell changed its name to earth. And yet what I remember of that conversation was heavenly.

J *Jerusalem* — What the Puritans saw in the Massachusetts woods, that is to say, what they would achieve once they defeated the Canaanites, was Jerusalem, the New Jerusalem.

K *King of Misrule* — ruled from All-Hallow's Eve to the Feast of the Purification. Should have held onto power over the kingdom a little longer.

L *locus amoenus*	In the land of milk and honey, we develop lactose intolerance and an allergy to the pollen found in the sweet goo.
Z Zeitgeist	I can read the writing on the wall, but it's just an anthology of clichés.
X *xenophobia*	I may be poor and hopeless and ugly and stupid, but at least I'm not like those people from over there.
C *civilization*	Eighteenth-century neologism to explain what people different from us don't have. Also civilize, which took the place of *reduce.*
V *Velvet Underground*	Their second album sold even less than their first, but people say that everyone who listened to it went on to take hard drugs.
B *burial*	"I don't want to be buried. Cremate me. I don't want to get all dirty." —A friendly woman on the 87 bus at Journal Square
N *New York City*	You can't ever go home again. You couldn't afford it.
M *musical*	In Act I, all the characters sing every word: at home, at work, on the phone, on the playground. In the second, people go to a theater, a concert hall. "Let's go," they sing, "to the concert hall." There someone comes on stage and speaks. The speaker is eloquent. The language does the singing. The speaking is breath and is breathtaking. Another person comes on stage and speaks, this person blunt and to the point, and then the two speak to each other. They get mad. They try not to fight. They fight. They apologize. They make up. They talk about what they've been through and how important it is that they remain friends. Bravos and heckles are sung from the crowd made of people. Then they leave, mumbling the words.

Toby Olson

The Yacht

The woman who owned the yacht went south in the winter, even before winter began, and the upkeep and guarding of the thirty-five meter tri-deck mega yacht, the *Enchantress*, were left to him, who was otherwise unemployed.

He had been an accountant at a bank in this small Mediterranean village, and when the bank went under and the patrons had moved their meager savings to one in a larger town nearby, he had lost his job, and finding nothing clerical there, had accepted this strange wealthy woman's offer.

The one thing he knew, besides figures, was boats. His father had a motor launch, and he had worked there in his youth. And though there were many in the village more qualified than he, for some reason this tall, stately woman had taken a shine to him, a very strange one that troubled him, something in her smile or in her eyes. Her short hair was jet black and oiled. Fixed tight to her skull, it resembled a helmet of some kind. And each time he met with her, she was wearing the same formal attire: a masculine looking grey suit, high heels, a subtle rose patterned tie.

He was provided with a cabin under the aft deck. It was small and imbued with a scent reminiscent of his mother's bedroom at home, and he avoided it, using it only for sleep. His house in the village stood empty, and he was pleased to be away from it.

His responsibilities included taking the craft out into the Mediterranean every so often to check its seaworthiness, and on this day he had carefully maneuvered the yacht, with its deep thirteen foot draft, away from the docking and headed out into the more serious waters, though they were not so serious on this cloudy day.

The sea was flat calm, hardly a ripple, and he dropped anchor, then examined the gauges and oil pressures. Everything seemed fine, and he lifted his eyes to the curved windows that looked out from the bridge. Beyond the bow and across the calm waters, he could just make out the village church steeple, a slim needle at this distance. There were no other boats in sight, and he climbed down the ladder and moved to one of the lounge chairs on the foredeck, sat back, looked up into the slightly overcast sky, and thought once again about the locked hatch. There had been no key. "Not for that one," the woman had smiled. But there was hard steel in her eyes.

He was fifty-three years old, small, thin and slightly stooped, and though he had been quite handsome in his youth, the death of his mother, whom he had lived with, had brought him down a notch. She had been the love of his life, his only love, and the loss of her had left him alone, friendless, and deeply depressed. Even now, looking up into the cloud cover, he could see only sadness, that same sadness he saw in all things and people. It was his sadness of course and not theirs, and yet he projected it onto the world around him, and everything was alienating.

His mother had sewn clothing for the village poor, and he had supported her in her life and this endeavor, and when she died he had inherited the small house where the two of them had lived for all of their lives. His father had died when he was only twenty.

He was wondering what it would take. And if I broke it, he thought, I can fix it. She'll be gone for three months. He sat there for a while. A light, warm breeze had come in and there were now gentle ripples, light green at their curls, on the otherwise flat sea. He took in the pleasure of them before rising.

The hatch was amidships, down below the bridge toward the stern. It was accessed through a narrow passage to the port side of the galley, tucked in between the massive refrigerator and the six burner stove. A prep counter blocked the way, a section of which could be lifted to allow access. The passage seemed to narrow even further as he moved down it, the green bulkheads pressing in against him. The hatch itself was small, and even one of his diminutive size would have to squat down to enter.

He saw that the lock was large and complicated, and he had no chance with it, so he moved to the hinges and worked to drive the pins out with his punch and hammer. They were tight, and it took him almost an hour, but finally he was able to pull the hatch toward him, where he was squeezed down in the passage. There was enough space there, and he was able to climb through.

His mother had been tall and fit, athletic before her long illness, and she had urged him into exercise in the basement of their house where there were old machines, a treadmill and a stationary bike, and he was agile even at his age. Still, he was as careful as an old man as he stepped slowly down the steep ladder that moved off at a slight angle to the left as he descended. The treads of the ladder were shallow, and he was careful.

The ladder ended at the foot of another passageway, this one brief, its bulkheads festooned with various tools, giant wrenches and hammers, other, more exotic elements that in another context might be seen as instruments of not to subtle persuasion, pinchers and heavy hemostats, long, vicious looking knives, all this hanging from hooks affixed to the walls, which were dampened with some oily substance, sticky to the touch. He figured he was well below the center of the vessel now, just above the hold. Could it be some illicit cargo then? The woman had seemed capable of such duplicity, this questionable judgment garnered in their three brief meetings.

He looked down at his feet, his thin deck shoes. Just ahead was yet another hatch, this one in the middle of the deck floor. How deep was he now? The draft was thirteen feet. It must be a shallow hold, he thought.

He got down on his knees, reached out and opened the heavy circular hatch. A faint light greeted him, sending a cylinder of luminescence that was hanging with slow dancing dust motes up to the passageway ceiling. He bent over, moved his head into the light shaft, and looked down.

The room below was lit by six wall sconces containing low power bulbs. Two of these flanked an ordinary door at the room's end. Bookshelves, a few nautical prints, a couch and a two upholstered chairs, and to the side of a heavy, mahogany coffee table, a large, sturdy crib that was made of metal and looked very much like a cage. Impossible, he thought. The walls must be ten feet high. This is yards below the draft. Could something have been added at dry dock, a kind of tumor protruding from the hull? A battery powered clock, between two prints, ticked out the time.

There was no ladder, no stairway. He was looking down from the room's ceiling. There was only a fragile looking chandelier, tear drop crystals hanging from a thin wire enclosure.

It seemed the only way, and so he moved his legs until they hung down through the circular opening, then lowered himself, his hands gripping the hatch edges, until he was hanging, his arms extended above his head, holding on, and swaying. The drop was a long one, and he feared for his ankles and knees. I'm too old for this, he thought, then he reached out for the bottom hanging tear drops, grabbed onto the wire rim they were attached to, and dropped, taking the entire chandelier with him. He landed on the upholstered couch, wires and broken glass flooding his torso. Nothing was broken, but for the tears scattered across his body and the couch, some having falling to the oriental carpet upon which sat the heavy coffee table, yet once he had removed the wires and glass and struggled to his feet, he found that he had injured his knee, the right one, and he had to step gingerly.

He examined the room. There seemed no way out, but for the one door. No papers, coffee cups, or other evidence that the room had been put to use.

But there was that crib, and surely a story involving people and their actions could be constructed from that. He touched the thin mattress, bent over and smelled it. Nothing. If it and been put to use, that must have happened a while ago.

The room was quiet, the only movement came from the advancement of time registered by the clock. He looked over at its face. Eleven o'clock it said. Five hours? He'd dropped anchor at six in the morning. How could it have been that long?

The door beckoned, his only exit, but for the hatch high above, which was impossible. It was an ordinary wooden door with a brass knob. The sconces were slightly above the edges of the frame, and their dim light cast shadows that seemed to be sliding down to the floor across the panels of green painted wood. And the key, attached to a rabbit's foot fob, protruded from the knob.

Beyond the door was yet another descending stairway, this one circular, and as he climbed down he gave up on the impossibility of the depth.

The stairway seemed endless as he turned in it, but it was no more than eight feet to its terminus. He expected pressure, but his ears were fine, and when he reached the deck, he could feel no movement at all. The sea was still, and the yacht itself was still. At the end of the small chamber where he stood, a heavy dark curtain blocked the way. It seemed to flutter, its folds exchanging spaces with one another. There was nothing for it now, so he pulled back the curtain and entered into a small compartment, to the side of which was a tubular opening large enough to accommodate a small, stooped over man, which he was and became as he moved through the tube that curved off to what he thought was the starboard side of the boat. He wasn't sure of that or much else just then. The tube opened onto parquet flooring, a small room, its walls decorated with the pasted on images of clouds and suns and cartoon figures. He saw a laughing Mickey Mouse, Casper the friendly ghost, a few dancing rabbits. Then his gazed moved to the room's end, to the steel bars and the metal door and beyond them what was surely a cell.

The girl sat erect on the single bed, an open book and a large doll, dressed very much like she was, on the thin coverlet beside her. There was a toilet in the cell and a sink, a small refrigerator and hot plate, a storage cabinet, and a bookcase full of various volumes. A gathering of wilted roses, a few petals having fallen to the surface of the storage cabinet, upon which stood the glass vase that contained them. The girl didn't rise, nor did she seem surprised at his presence.

"Who *are* you?" he said.

"Who are *you*?" she responded. "Come to rejoin us?" She shuddered slightly as she spoke her last words.

She's a teenager, he thought. Fourteen or fifteen. But she was dressed in the raiments of a much younger child. Her long blond hair fell in two thick braids, red bows tied at their ends, one to each side of her head, framing her lovely, though blemished, face. The braids touched the fabric of her blouse, a pattern of bonneted babies frolicking below the stiff white collar that closed just under her chin. A short, pleated seersucker skirt, yellow and red vertical stripes on a field of blue, white stockings ending in bright black patent leather shoes. The yacht tilted, and he shifted his weight to his damaged knee, felt the deep pain, then recovered. It could be another craft passing, even a bit of storm. The girl had no reaction at all, as if she were familiar with such subtle movements.

When he was a young child, his mother had insisted on his long curly baby hair, though his father often told her he looked like a little girl. And she had dressed him as she had when he was just emerging from babyhood, jumpers held up by suspenders, snow suits in the winter, though it never got that cold, and because of the way she had dressed him, she treated him as the younger child he appeared to be. There were books read to him in the evenings, even though he could then read them for himself, soft foods, when what he required was the same fair that graced the table for his mother and father. "Chicken Little," she would coo, chucking him under the chin before kissing him. It ended of course, or perhaps it didn't. At times he still felt like that costumed child, inauthentic and helpless, until his father insisted on his growth. With this girl, it was much more extreme. She was a sexual being, dressed even before puberty, dressed as a little child, strange as the architecture of this yacht that contained her.

"No," he said. "I'm not here to harm you. But what is this rejoining all about?"

"The mother," she said.

"But why here?" he asked.

"The mother says I'm trouble and must be locked away while she's gone."

"What kind of trouble?"

"Fire," she said. "I like fire. But I've never done anything actually. Well, a few bonfires in the yard, a couple of old toys?"

"When you were younger?"

"Oh, no. Not back then." She caressed the babies on her breast to demonstrate the past. "More recently."

"Would you like to stay here?" he asked. "Or would you like to go up on the deck? See what's going on there."

"Yes," she said. "Up on the deck. In the sun. I don't want to see the mother though."

"She's not here."

"Good," she said.

A key was hanging from a hook on the wall, just out of reach of she who was, perhaps in ceremony, locked up. It seemed a kind of tease. He lifted it and stepped to the metal door and opened it. She stood up from the bed then and moved to him and hugged him. She was taller than he was, and her scent was reminiscent of the talcum powder of his childhood. He was embarrassed by her closeness, the touch of her braid against his cheek, her warm body pressing into him, her quiet cooing. A child, he thought, and pushed her gently away and waited while she scooped up her doll, then searched out and lifted her heavy bag and slung the strap over her shoulder. She turned her head for a moment, considering the desiccated roses. Then she just stood there, bright eyed and expectant

"Okay, okay," he said. "Let's figure this out."

They could go back up to the room, but what good would that do? The hatch in the ceiling was far to high. He looked around her cell and the room they were now in, but he could see nothing that might help.

"Wait," she said. "I know a way. I've seen them use it."

When he cared for his mother in the last years of her terminal illness, he treated her much in the same way as she had treated him when he was just a child. She wore a bib, and he fed her and wiped her lips, and when she became incontinent, he removed her diaper and cleaned her and spoke to her in a kind of baby talk, and she seemed to like this, to be treated as a vulnerable child, which in a way she was.

And now he was faced with another woman, though just a teenager, who had been thrust back into the position of a child as well. Before fire, he thought, cleansing by retrogression, though in the case of his mother it had more to do with his own early days. It was as if he were paying her back, putting her in the same position she had put him in. Well, not exactly the same. She had desired to fix him in place, to forestall his growth beyond childhood, his hair, that ludicrous clothing, while he had worked to send her back there, to cleanse her of the tribulations of adulthood and old age. That way she would be pure and innocent again when she entered the earth. Yet that baby talk, those smiling whispered words, were of a kind that was spoken to small animals, a dog or a cat, for though her responses had been grateful, she was still an old, dying woman and not a child, and now he realized, standing beside this woman-child, that he had not addressed his mother's final conditions with dignity.

She touched him lightly on the shoulder. "This way," she said, and he followed her in her braids, her short, frilly skirt, her shinny shoes and her ludicrous blouse, back beyond the curtain and through the brief, curved tunnel and up toward the door that was entrance into the room where he had dropped down from the ceiling.

She paused at the door, then pointed to the right. To port side? He wasn't sure anymore. The yacht had become an impossible maze, and he had little idea of where they were and where they might be going.

She bent down, felt along the bulkhead to the door's right, found the indented latch, and opened yet another, very small door. There was a sucking of wind, the smell of sea, and she got down on her knees, her doll tucked under her arm and her bag slipping to the deck, and entered. And he followed her, hopping slightly on his good leg, dragging the other behind him.

Another tunnel, this one leading down and to the left. She said she'd seen them use it. But how could she have? Her cell was out of sight, somewhere below and to the right. Could there have been some sort of window, a porthole providing vision from her chamber? Impossible, he thought, though he was unsure of most everything now, but for the breeze echoing in the tube, the scent of sea.

A final turning, then fresh air and the lap of water against the hull, and they were now able to stand, she in front of him, wind gently blowing, her braids dancing on her shoulders. They were in the large anchor housing, links of the huge chain descending down the yacht's hull, then entering the calm waters of the Mediterranean far below their feet. There was a metal ladder attached to the yacht's side at the edge of the anchor housing, and she climbed up ahead of him. Following her, he could see her white, unspoiled, stocking tops, and what he thought was a white diaper hugging her behind under that short, little skirt. Could her mother have gone this far? Near the end, his mother had worn a diaper too.

The girl disappeared above him, and when he reached the ladder's final rungs and stepped over, he found he was standing beside her on the broad aft deck, and there was her mother, his boss, and three tough looking men all glaring at them from the port rail. The mother was dressed in her grey business suit, the same rose patterned tie, the collar of her starched, white shirt tight at the neck. She held a pistol in her right hand.

"Mother!" the girl cried out, then began moving toward her, walking at first, then running, the doll, held by a blond braid, bouncing against her leg and her heavy bag held tight at her hip. She had something in her free hand, and he saw a flicker leap out of it as she reached her mother and touched it to her bag.

An explosion of flames then, the smell of gasoline, and they were both engulfed. The three men ran to the side as the doll rose up, a figure of lost childhood, cooking in the inferno. And out of the tower of flames and the smell of burning flesh, a fiery arm extended, the gun in a charred hand.

Mother, he thought. Then he turned and leaped over the deck rail, hearing the muffled report as he fell down into the sea. The yacht was aflame behind him. He could smell it, as he stroked out toward the church steeple, the village, and his home.

Darya Tsymbalyuk

A strawberry summer

The streets are empty. Most people left, but around a thousand still remain. Traces of shelling are seen everywhere. Tomorrow we will be back to the capital and I will be back to my own questions. Just one more night that will not bring peace.

I walk towards a house with a big apricot tree at the front; Baba Klava already waits for me near the gate. I follow her to the inner yard, standing outside as she disappears inside of the house to get the documents. I promised to pass them to her granddaughter who is studying in the capital and whom I've never met. A big black dog comes to greet me. Baba Klava has three dogs and seven cats. Most of them she picked up from abandoned houses. The sun is setting above the river, shining through a cherry tree which grows right in the middle of the yard. After this garden the village ends. Some people would claim that there lies another country already, but that remains contested, the shelling reminds you. However, at the moment all is quiet, and the view is gorgeous. Rich in colours, the sunset slips between cherry branches and leaves big warm stains on the ground and the walls of the house. Looking at the water glimmering in the sun, I selfishly slip back into my own thoughts, into my own bleak days. I sit down on a bench by the wall. Baba Klava emerges from the house with a folder.

- Will you pass it to Sveta, honey? Thank you. Let God always help you.

She sits down near me, sighing:

- It's beautiful here, isn't?

I nod. It is beautiful indeed. The edge of the garden gets soaked in the river. The evening brings a pleasant breeze. I am not really sure why I am still doing this job, why I took this assignment. I am tired of questioning myself. I am tired of the fear of missing out. I am not sure whether I love things or I make myself believe so. To what extent am I able to rationalize everything and lull myself into comfort? Then, too often, I feel I want to move to another city and start from zero. Ah, I am doing it again. I constantly fail to be present. I frown with disgust at my self. Having seen all the ruined houses in the village shocked me today. I can't believe that my mind keeps selfishly racing around my own meaningless questions. OK, make a conscious effort of focusing on the stories and events of today. I lean on the wall of the house behind me, stretching my legs. I pinch myself. I saw many ruined houses today. Many. The village is deserted. Earlier today, recalling the past two years, Baba Klava told me how she had to stay with distant relatives who lived on the other street, when the shelling intensified. She would wake up in the middle of the night to run here to check if her house was still standing: 'And you come running to the street… and just stand there…and keep praying: "Please, God, just not my house, please, just not my house."'

I am not sure when and where I lost my ability to respond. Recently I've been listening to a lot of sad music to try to make myself feel again. I am lying. I've been listening to it to intensify my own sadness, because, maybe, I actually enjoy making myself feel miserable. What is wrong with me? Last week I reached the point where seeing myself in the mirror irritated me. My hair constantly felt tired. I wanted to sleep for days, and when I did, my bones would hurt after. I would wake up and convince myself that I was alright. I would make myself go running in the morning. I would say I am fine, to myself, to others. I would repeat it to my self: 'I am fine, I am fine I am fine'. The problem is that I don't know what my problem is. Maybe the problem is that there is no problem. The meaningless. I hate myself for being stuck in it. And then people always tell you: 'Listen to your heart.' What a cliché! But what if my brain constantly turns everything upside down, rips everything apart, dismembers, builds labyrinths, justifies the meaninglessness. Too far. I turn to look at Baba Klava.

She is silent, petting a cat on her lap, sitting here at the edge of the garden, looking at the other side. I don't ask her why she did not move from her house despite the shelling or how she feels. I know that life in the village has been almost impossible. No electricity for days. No running water. No gas. No meds in the pharmacy. Constant shortage of food. She speaks positively as if justifying it to herself:

- Each day I am grateful to God that my house is not destroyed…Just a bit of a fence missing over there… but that is OK… That can be fixed easily... As long as the house is standing... And I still have my garden, of course...And my cats, and my dogs... I am truly very lucky... Just look at my neighbours...

She waves her hand to the left, in the direction of a neighbouring house, that was hit in the roof and burned down. But I can't really see anything. It is getting too dark.

- I mean, you can't see it now... and also, the grass and bushes hide it these days... But I know it is there with my own back... I feel it with each nerve...

I try to remember it too, to picture it. I saw too many ruined houses today. But I am afraid that my own stupid thoughts did not let me see them. I did not save them in my memory. I did not let them in. I was too busy rummaging in my own thought garbage. Baba Klava picks up the cat, places it near me on the bench, and then gets up.

- Ah, I totally forgot about the strawberries! Let me go bring some.

She disappears in the house and several minutes after emerges with a big plate of strawberries, homemade cream and sugar.

- These are from my neighbours, - and she waves in the direction of their house once again. - The house is destroyed, but the strawberries survived... They planted them right before war... They had this patch of land... and nothing would grow there... like absolutely nothing... They tried everything... but it was the location and the rain... Anyhow... Eventually they planted these strawberries... And the strawberries, they did not care about the land or the rain or anything... Just did not care... So the first summer they had their first strawberries harvest they were so happy... So so happy... And then the shelling started... and they left... I collected the strawberries, froze them for the time when they would return, but they never did... Then power outages started and everything in the fridge began to melt... So I had to eat all the strawberries... Oh, and there was lots of them... So I was eating strawberries with sugar and without, and boiling them in water and drinking them... A strawberry summer...

And the shelling starts. Once accustomed to the dark, my eyes begin to distinguish trees in the garden. It seems to me that I could see water down in the river again, this time glimmering in the moonlight. The strawberries are sweet like my childhood.

- It is far today, - says Baba Klava, and she does not move from the bench.

She is used to this. She pets the cat next to her, and it purrs like an old tractor. Purring and shelling and crickets. The crickets are the loudest. The neighbouring house is ruined. The river is the border. The river became a border some years ago. Before it was a place to swim and to go fishing and to tell your secrets. The bridge was bombed. There is no connection with the village on the other side. Families have been separated. Most people in the village lost jobs because they needed a bridge to reach them. But what are jobs when you can't really get proper sleep at night? People here know the sounds; they learned the audio vocabulary of war. No electricity for days. No running water. No gas. No meds in the pharmacy. Constant shortage of food. The closest hospital is 60 km away and the ambulance refuses to come to the village because it is too dangerous. Baba Klava remains. This year three people have died from a heart attack just because the ambulance refused to come here. There is sudden sharpness in my own heart. My cheeks feel ticklish in the wind. The strawberries in my mouth taste salty.

- Oh, sweetie, why are you crying? It's all going to be alright.

Matheus Borges

The Clouds

The last man woke up as the sun rose on the diffuse horizon, covered with floating particles small and black. He had slept under the roof of an old building, accommodated between a marble top table and an electric power box. His eyes, his sensible eyes, quivered at being touched by heavy sunlight coming across through the window. Humidity oozed all over the building walls. He made his way into a big avenue taken over by creeping underbrush, which climbed the sidewalk and merged itself with dark rusty carcasses of automobiles covered by a tapestry of ashes. He walked slowly, ignoring the wide open doors of bookshops and fast food shacks. He was tired of running, of eating and sleeping. He was tired of the sun, of the heat, and the sweat. Tired of walking naked through memories of distant times, his skin increasingly drier, increasingly harder.

The first man opened his mouth, let his voice reverberate from inside his throat, out into the red desert floor. Step after step, his callused feet encountered the sand with brutal determination. From afar, he gazed at the big round flame in the sky. He was afraid, but with the fear came an immense desire of moving forward. He let himself be led toward that flaming point above everything. That majestic burning mystery. Stopping from time to time, he sucked water off the floor and chewed small yellow fruits. However, he couldn't stop for too long. Otherwise, the flame would go out. The world would cease to exist and return only at dawn.

Inside an abandoned shopping mall, the last man looked for a new pair of shoes. The unbearable heat of the endless asphalt roads wreaked havoc at the rubber soles in a matter of days. He found a pair of sturdy riding boots, equipped with solid coating. He was now dressed for combat, the enemy being the hostile environment. A low sound echoed in the walls of the empty mall at every step he took, a rhythmic pattern that felt like a war drum. If he was the first man, he said to himself, the first thing he would do was inventing the shoes, perhaps covering his feet with leaves, or with the strong skin of a gigantic prehistoric animal.

The two men walked together without ever crossing paths. Once in a while, the last man caught himself imagining if he was not wrong, if he was not himself the first man of a new era, a second first man. But he did not let this possibility poison his days, for this hypothesis could only underline the hopelessness inhabiting every place he visited. Meanwhile, the first man felt anesthetized, overcome with the astonishment of every new discovery. He did not understand this feeling, or what it really meant. He acted instinctively, according to his own nature. He looked for meaning on what he found. Curiosity led his steps.

It was evening and the two men settled in temporary shelters. The last man walked across a wide corridor toward the top of a building. The sun disappeared behind the windows and he felt relieved. Another day had passed. Everything was burning and he was still alive. But how long could he tolerate this? He took shelter under another table. It was enough to endure the cold that came along with the darkness of the night.

As soon as the first man saw the golden sphere detouring into behind the distant mountains, he started lamenting the effort he invested over the last few hours. Unable to reach his destination, he'd resume his walk the moment brightness touched his eyes. It was like nothing had ever happened. The before had never existed and the world rebuilt itself at the beginning of each new day. To the last man, the only thing that existed was the before itself. They lived in communion, one inhabiting the destiny of the other. To the first man, it was necessary reaching somewhere. The last man had reached this place, the last possible place, a place no other man had ever reached. All he had left to do was retracing his steps and every other step of every other foot that ever walked on that ground.

At that moment, the two men fell asleep. They left the vastness of the world behind, the deserted landscapes that were everything they saw. They began to live in a communal world where they could forget the rules of survival. They could now dream with glorious spheres of fire, visit each other and try to understand what went wrong. How could the first have become the last?

Taken by a strange sensation, a tingling that took them full length, they woke up in the middle of the night. It was something the last man had felt before, something that took him almost every night. The first man had never felt that. He did not know what to do. Sitting on a rock, he decided to stay awake until the sky was lit again. He dragged a tree branch around, describing a trail on the thick dirt. As the branch drew this line behind him, the wind insisted on weakening it, until everything was gone.

It was at that moment that the last man found the truth about himself. He was a symbol for all the failures of his kind. And if he was the sum of all the lives that preceded him, his death was the death of all those lives. And if all these lives died with him, then human race would cease to exist. If he died at that moment, the planet could move on, free from the shame of such reckless tenants. He accepted the truth and then abandoned his obstinacy. His destiny, contrary to what he once imagined, was also to move forward.

The first man was still sitting on that rock. Everything was dark, but gradually he discerned the scenery. He was used to the transition from one moment to the next, the erased sky slowly lit until it exploded with powerful luminescence and heat.

But now, things reappeared with an empty glow, opacity of colors that matched nothing he had seen before. The heat he normally felt at those hours gave way to a damp touch of the air, temperature suspended to a point that his body could hardly perceive it. And as he looked up, hoping the sphere would burst forth behind the mountains as it did every day, he perceived not only its absence, but also the presence of large gray figures that gathered around one another like enormous mountains in the sky.

Andrew J. Hogan

The Messenger†

I fluttered away as another inmate with the rock in his hand approached the fence.

"Elie, why didn't you kill that pigeon?" the newcomer said.

"That's Ihram, Bonhoeffer's dove. It followed him here from Tegel," Wiesel said.

"So what? It could have been our lunch."

I'd found Bonhoeffer's new cell in the detention building of the Buchenwald Camp and gotten his message for Niemoeller. Before I returned, Bonhoeffer would be transferred to one of the barracks, and this would mean more dangerous flying inside the camp. Food was scarce everywhere in Germany. In Berlin they had started killing zoo animals for food. But nowhere was food so scarce as in the concentration camps.

My flight to deliver Bonhoeffer's message to Niemoeller at Dachau would be dangerous. Many hawks and eagles depend on farm animals for part of their diet, and they were also suffering from the depletion of their prey.

I flew east out of the camp until I reached the Ilm River and headed toward its source near Mount Beerberg in the Thueringer Wald. The farmland along the river was bare due to the winter season and farm workers lost to the war.

As I neared a bend in the Ilm, I saw a large male Seealders‡ catching a fish. Seealders are too big and clumsy to take a carrier pigeon like me in flight, but they could easily take me from an exposed perch or on the ground. This Seealder would be preoccupied with his prey.

Following Ilm River back to Ilmenau, the elevation rose and the area along

---

† Brieftaube is the Carrier Pigeon, *Columba livia domestica*.

‡ Seealder is the Haliaeetus albicilla, the white-tailed eagle.

tthe river was more wooded. This is the home of the Sperber§ and the Habicht¶, both of which take birds in flight, although most Sperbers are too small to attack a full-size carrier pigeon. At the speed I was flying, I would never be able to see them before they spotted me from their perches in the trees. I kept a keen eye for any birds soaring overhead.

At Ilmenau, I circled south and east around Mount Beerberg. Although Beerberg rises to only about a thousand meters, climbing is the most strenuous part of flying, and I wanted to conserve my energy for the long flight ahead. Either way, I had to fly through the Thueringer Wald with its many birds of prey. It wouldn't do Bonhoeffer any good if I ended up as a meal for a family of eaglets.

It was a blustery day, making mid-air hunting difficult for hawks. I set my course between Coburg and Sonneberg to avoid human hunters. I reached the Main River a little north of Lichtenfels, where the River Main joins the Main-Danube Canal that flows around Nuremberg. The military stations around Nuremberg have falconry units ready to intercept enemy carrier pigeons, and so I decided to wait outside of Nuremberg until nightfall. We carrier pigeons do not usually fly at night, but with the full moon at its apex that night, I would have enough visual clues along with my magnetic sense navigate.

I stopped for a drink from the Main, careful to check for the presence of otters that might lunge out of the water. There was some dried grass on the riverbank. I took some seeds, but since I was alone I could not spend as much time feeding as I would have liked. I chose as my resting perch a small opening among some densely packed branches in a large spruce tree. This perch would be inaccessible even to a small turmfalke**. It was too cold to have to worry about snakes, and I could rest securely in this spot.

As darkness fell, I started my flight around Nuremberg. My plan to avoid human danger backfired when the Allied planes started bombing just as I was reached the main docks of the Main-Danube canal. At brief intervals the explosions made it almost as bright as daytime, but the flashes left me temporarily blinded and uncertain of my direction. I could smell the smoke from burning buildings and hear the screams of the people trying to escape the fires. One bomb was close enough to blow me off course. Tracer bullets from antiaircraft artillery raced by me on all sides. The bombers' engines droned above. Not knowing where to hide, I kept flying along the canal through Nuremberg and reaching the outskirts of Schwabach at dawn.

§ Sperber is the Accipiter nisus, sparrowhawk.

¶ Habicht is the Accipiter gentiles, goshawk.

** Turmfalke is the Falco tinnunculus, Kestrel.

I rested at a riverside park. The morning was too cold for most humans, and the larger animals had been hunted to extinction. Around noon I set off down the Main-Danube Canal, reaching its junction with the Altmuehl River, which I followed for another fifty kilometers where it empties into the Danube.

South of Nuremberg the canal runs through the mountainous Fraenkische Alb; human settlements are rare. Where the canal meets the Danube there were several military installations. Certain to be mistaken for a military carrier pigeon and become the target of shotgun fire or falconry, I skirted along the south side.

Following the Danube west to Ingolstadt, I found a southbound train that would pass through Dachau on its way to Munich; it was loaded with prisoners heading to the camp. I landed on top of the third boxcar, but it was very windy, and I could not find a good foothold. I moved to the end of the car, where there were some broken boards on the rear wall of the car, damage enemy aircraft fire.

After a few moments, I was resting comfortably in my niche, being ferried to my destination with no expenditure of energy. The roar of the train on the tracks and the rocking of the car lulled me into complacency. Suddenly, I felt a human hand on my foot. The starving prisoners had spotted me sitting in the niche and formed a human ladder of three of the least feeble occupants. The top of the ladder, fortunately for me, was a ten-year-old girl who grabbed my leg but whose squeamishness forced her to release me after I pecked her hand. As I fluttered away, I heard the girl being beaten by her starving father.

The end of the train had a guard caboose with a small canopy over its rear steps. The canopy was set down below the caboose's roofline, and I was able to hunch down in safety and out of the wind for the rest of the journey. A Habicht might be able to see me resting under the canopy, but it could not hunt me from a moving train. I rode until the train pulled off onto the shunt line for Dachau.

The camp was large, containing 34 prisoner barracks. I knew that Niemoeller would be housed in the political barracks along with the large number of Polish and German priests and pastors who had voiced opposition to Hitler. At the rail station I watched the unloading of the prisoners, looking clerical garb. I recognized a Roman collar on one prisoner, whose face I memorized. He was taken to the prisoner showers; when he emerged, his head was shaven and he wore the standard striped prisoner outfit.

The priest was led to Stalag 3E. It was getting dark, and all the prisoners were locked in for the night. I found a comfortable perch out of the wind on the west side of the Stalag's stovepipe and waited for morning, hoping that up against the pipe no owl would recognize me as prey.

The guards woke the prisoners at first light for their work details. I spotted Niemoeller in the second wave of prisoners leaving the barracks. Niemoeller remained surrounded by other prisoners and guards in his work detail until about 9:30, when the guards ordered them to take a break. While members of the prisoner detail shuttled back and forth to the latrines, Niemoeller sat alone against the fence, praying. I landed on the barbed wire above him. He looked up at me.

"You're Bonhoeffer's dove, Ihram. He sent you here. They've moved him from Tegel to Buchenwald."

He sat quietly for a while and then spoke, "Bonhoeffer wants to know if I have fallen into the Hoelle because of what I have seen here. He wants to know if I recognize the true stench of hell, the fumes of thousands of incinerated corpses so thick it cannot be smelled, covering us like filthy mucus that dries and hardens into an emotional crust, under which our souls are submersed in hate. We thought we understood evil. We were fools."

The guards called the prisoner detail back to work. Niemoeller looked at me, "Tell Bonhoeffer that I am climbing back out of the Hoelle." I fluttered off as the guards approached.

On the way back to Buchenwald, I took the railroad line to Nuremberg. I'd hoped to catch another train north, but there was little activity on the tracks during the day. Allied fighter planes made several trips, looking for a train with military supplies to attack.

The rail line ran through the heavily wooded Fraenkische Alb. The Habicht build their nests high in a pine or spruce tree near an open area like a meadow, or a rail line. I needed to cover nearly ninety kilometers in this terrain. The Habichts were getting ready for courtship, and I hoped they would be preoccupied with picking out nesting sites.

Near the top of the southern face of the Fraenkische Alb, I noticed a large nest in a spruce tree some 30 meters off the left side of the tracks. Habichts have better eyesight than carrier pigeons, so I assumed that, if the nest was inhabited, I had already been spotted. I detoured into an opening in the wall of trees on the right side of the tracks. I had to reduce my speed because of the many obstacles to avoid.

Reaching a small clearing, I could see the Habicht nest on the left-hand side. Two sets of wings rose and lifted off the nest. I couldn't possibly outrun two Habichts. I found a deer trail leading from the clearing into the forest. The Habichts could follow me, but with their half-meter wingspans, they would need to fly more slowly than me to avoid the many obstacles. Eventually, I could leave them far enough behind and make my escape.

The Habichts had a counter strategy that I hadn't anticipated. The smaller male followed me into the forest, calling "gig-gig-gig" every time he sighted me. The larger female soared over the tree line, calling to her mate when she spotted me from above. With this coordinated effort, I was unable to lose the male in the forest. The next clearing we came upon would leave me open to a double attack. I could see a bright patch of light up ahead, indicating a break in the forest. It was a small lake, and on it floated a flock of pintail ducks. My only hope now was to become part of the flock and escape on the law of averages. I swooped down the side of the lake, skimming across the water at a height of no more than 20 centimeters, screaming out a pigeon distress call to alert and disperse the ducks into the air.

Fifty meters behind me, the male Habicht emerged from the forest, just as the female began a one-hundred-kilometer-per-hour hunting dive in my direction. One or the other would quickly reach me. Alerted, the ducks began flapping and paddling to achieve liftoff. I stayed low to the water and managed to fly underneath the dozen ducks just taking flight.

The diversion worked perfectly. An immature male pintail flew into the talons of the female Habicht. At that point the male Habicht following me ended his pursuit and accompanied the female back to the nest to share the meal. I circled the northern bank of the lake back to the rail line. Soon I reached at the summit and glided several kilometers down the mountain, relieved over my narrow escape.

Twenty kilometers later the rail line intersected the Main-Danube canal just south of Nuremberg. I detoured onto the canal, not wanting to go through a populated area. North of Nuremberg, the Main River rejoined the northbound rail line and ran side-by-side all the way to Lichtenfels, where I retraced by flight across the Thueringer Wald to Ilmenau and the headwaters of the Ilm River. Coming around Mount Beerberg near Frauenswald, I ran into a fierce blizzard. I had no choice but to take shelter in a nearby barn.

The blizzard raged for several days. I remained in the barn safe from the storm but weakened by lack of food, with only snow to drink. Shortly before dawn on the third day, an owl flew into the barn through an opening just under the peak of the roof. This explained why none of my feral pigeon brethren inhabited the barn. I found a dark spot in northeast corner of the barn where I quietly waited for the owl to leave on a hunting expedition the next evening. Unfortunately, a half-dozen field mice were also driven into the barn by the blizzard; the owl feasted on them for two days.

Finally the owl left the barn to hunt. I resisted the temptation to leave too soon. The owl would be waiting outside, hungry and ready for prey; in my weakened, starving state, I could hardly expect to outrun him. Instead I waited until an hour before dawn when the owl would mostly likely have finished hunting and consumed his prey away from the nest. I carefully peeked my head out of the barn and, not seeing him in the immediate vicinity, I flew to a nearby pine tree. I ensconced myself in a tangle of branches and waited until the owl returned home from hunting. As soon as the owl was safely inside, I flew off toward Weimar. I was so weak from hunger that I lacked the energy to fly more than a few miles at a time. The fields and the meadows remained covered with snow, depriving me of my normal sources of food. It took me over a month to reach the Buchenwald camp in Weimar.

Nearing Weimar, I saw smoke rising from a large building hit by a bomb. The east side of the building had been blown out, and the roof was on fire. The building was located alongside the railroad tracks and was being used as a warehouse. The building's contents had been scattered across the tracks, including a fairly large quantity of oats.

I saw one man run away from the warehouse screaming, his clothing on fire. Several more men were lying on the ground with injuries. Soldiers were removing some of the injured from the building and placing them under a tree across the tracks where a large quantity of oats had been propelled by the explosion. Hungry, I thought this was the perfect opportunity to restore my strength; because of all the rescue activity, I could feed freely without the risk of being hunted by either man or beast. The message from Niemoeller to Bonhoeffer could wait.

I landed in the tree under which the soldiers had laid out the bodies in a row. I watched to see which bodies were dead and which only injured. I found a group of three peaceful bodies, all in uniform, lying near the end of the row. I dropped down and began eating the oats. One body was that of an older man, perhaps 45 years old, although war made men look old beyond their years. He had a large shard of metal lodged in his throat. I started feeding near him because he was the most certainly dead, and there was a large pile of grain near his left leg – I avoid from the hands. When finished, I moved to the feet of the next victim, this time an adolescent boy in a loose fitting uniform, probably not older than 15. His face looked very peaceful, as though he had died in his sleep.

The soldiers crossed the tracks with another body. I flew away for a moment, but soon I was back at the feet of the third victim. He was not old, not young, but his face was hard. Most of the fingers on his left hand were missing, except for the third, which still carried a blood-encrusted wedding band.

I lingered around the three corpses most of the afternoon, cleaning up the oats in their vicinity, until the soldiers drove a truck alongside the railroad tracks and began loading the corpses into the truck. At first each corpse was carefully placed on the bed of the truck, secure in its own space. As the loaders became exhausted, the corpses were simply thrown over the side of the truck, without regard to where or on whom they landed.

I waited in the tree until my three wards were removed. From where their bodies had lain I was able to finish scavenging the oats not contaminated with blood. At one point, one of the soldiers loading the corpses threw a rock at me, but soon he became so exhausted with his work that I was ignored.

Once all the bodies had been taken away in the truck to a resting place, Weimar's feral pigeons, sparrows and other birds descended on the scattered grain. I realized that such a large collection of birds would make an attractive hunting target. I was only a half-kilometer away when I heard a shotgun blast.

It was dark when I reached the camp. I found a nearby tree and waited for the morning. That's when I discovered that Bonhoeffer was gone, shipped off to the Regensburg detention center. I had been only 100 kilometers east of Regensburg when I left Dachau; now I had a 500-kilometer trip to make.

Leaving Weimar, I picked up the Ilm, this time going north to its junction with the Saale River. I turned south, following the Saale toward its source in the Oberfaelzer Wald near what had been the Czech border. The trip was uneventful until I reached Lake Hohewarte, the larger of the lakes created by dams along the Saale River; it had been largely drained after allied bombers destroyed the dam at Eichnicht that produced electrical power for the factories in Nuremberg. Seealders were feeding on the fish stranded in small pools of the drained lake.

Then I reached Lake Bleiloch, the smaller of the Saale River lakes. The dam at Saalburg had been damaged but was still largely intact. As I flew over the dam, I saw one of the sentries run into the guardhouse and return with a large bird on his arm. Because of the recent blizzard, I suspected that the wanderfalke†† had not been able to hunt for several days, and the soldiers likely had little meat to share with him.

I was now over the center of the lake where it widened behind the dam. The closest forested area was nearly a kilometer away. Even at my top speed of about 80 kilometers an hour, the wanderfalke would quickly overtake me once he reached diving altitude. I couldn't check on the wanderfalke's position because this would slow me down, making my capture more likely.

The wanderfalke attacks small birds directly from behind because there is no doubt of its overpowering strength and ability to carry the bird in flight.

†† Wanderfalke is the Falco peregrinus, peregrine falcon.

But we carriers are the largest of pigeons, and a smaller wanderfalke could find me too much to handle after a mid-air attack. So wanderfalkes like to attack a larger bird from a slightly oblique angle, sending it into a tailspin. After the initial attack, the wanderfalke will either attempt to take the disoriented bird in flight or make more oblique attacks until the injured bird falls to the ground.

About 150 meters from the wooded shore of the lake, I sensed that the wanderfalke was closing in on me. His natural instinct would be to attack me on my right side, since I was going in a southeasterly direction across the lake. If I zigzagged, first right, then left, his talons might miss my body and run through my tail feathers. An experienced, healthy wanderfalke would be able to adjust easily to this evasion, and I might be wasting precious speed on the maneuver instead of getting myself directly to the forest and safety. I hoped for an immature or sickly predator.

Fifty meters from shore, I felt my tail feathers being torn from my body. The wanderfalke screeched in dismay as my feathers scattered in his wake. The feathers I had lost were mostly for warmth.

A small peninsula jutted out from the shore with a thick grove of fir trees. I dived for the thicket while the wanderfalke circled around for a second attack. I swooped under the canopy of the firs and then soared almost vertically upward into the trees. The fir trees were clustered in an oval, creating an open interior dome of branches. On the eastern side of the dome was a large opening in the branches of the trees, and in the opening was perched the largest Uhu‡‡ I have ever seen.

It was late afternoon, and the Uhu was waking himself for a night of hunting, a process accelerated when I flew in and landed on a branch a meter above his head. My pursuer followed only a few seconds later. The Uhu, preparing to make a meal of me, decided on the larger wanderfalke instead.

I knew the Uhu would not interrupt his meal once he had torn off the wanderfalke's breast feathers and began feasting on his heart. I flew away toward the source of the Saale in the Oberfaelzer Wald, across the eastern face of Mount Schneeberg, passing between the sources of the Ohre and Main rivers on either side. A short distance south and I picked up the eastern headwater of the Naab River that would take me into Regensburg.

I arrived at the Regensburg detention camp late the next morning, only to find that Bonhoeffer had been transferred almost immediately to the detention center at Flossenbuerg, another sixty kilometers east, where the Canaris conspirators were being assembled.

‡‡ Uhu is the bubo bubo, the eagle owl.

I flew to the Flossenbuerg camp, fighting my way up the hillside, against the fetid downdraft escaping from the burial trenches. Afraid to approach through the main gate where many starving inmates would be milling around, I veered to the left and went behind the equipment sheds, gliding into the gallows area on the far northwest side of the camp enclosure. There a group of prisoners was being led the gallows platform, Bonhoeffer among them. Soon Bonhoeffer stood on the platform, naked, with five of his compatriots, also naked. He turned to the prisoner next to him and said, "This is the end. For me, the beginning of life."

Bonhoeffer saw me just as the SS officer pushed him off the gallows platform. I landed on the beam holding his noose. As Bonhoeffer choked to death, I let him know what Niemoeller had told me; he died before he could respond. Soon all six of Hitler's would-be assassins were choking, kicking and then dangling limply. The SS officers marched off, and a detail of prisoners began removing the corpses.

One of the prisoners in the burial detail picked up a rock to throw at me. As he let it go, Wiesel nudged him, saying, "That's Ihram, Bonhoeffer's dove." The rock flew by me, hitting the ground a meter in front of a camp guard, then bounced up and struck the guard in the knee. The guard turned and shot the prisoner, who was carried off with the other executed corpses.

After the inmate detail finished throwing the corpses into the burial trench, scattering a flock of crows, I saw Wiesel go off by himself to pray. I flew over and perched myself on the barrack roof next to where he was standing. I told him about the message that Niemoeller had sent to Bonhoeffer. Wiesel changed my name to Inabat and sent me back to Niemoeller.

It was the end of April when I reached Dachau. The widespread fighting along the Naab River slowed my return. In Regensburg, I found a supply train standing on the track headed toward Munich. I flew in the open door of a boxcar filled with sacks of corn. The train lurched and began to slowly accelerate. A man ran along side the boxcar and closed the door, trapping me inside. I was on my way to Munich with plenty to eat but nothing to drink.

The boxcar stopped on a rail siding, and I remained inside for more than a week. Fortunately, on the third day there was a steady rain and plenty of holes in the roof where the boxcar had been hit by aircraft fire. Finally the boxcar began to move again. At Unterschleissheim, the door was opened and I flew out before anyone could enter. I flew the twenty-five kilometers to Dachau and found a grove of pines outside of the camp, where I waited for morning.

The camp was disorganized compared to my last visit. Prisoners milled about unsupervised. Most of the guards remained around the perimeter. I didn't know how to find Niemoeller since there were no work details from his barracks. I had to be careful where I perched, because it appeared that the prisoners were not being fed, and after a week in the boxcar granary, I would make a nice meal.

In the afternoon, a small contingent of American troops came to the gate to arrange for the surrender of the camp. Soon more troops arrived and began inspecting the barracks. The prisoners streamed out of the barracks, looking for farm implements they could use as weapons against their former captors. The American troops became more and more agitated as they discovered the bodies heaped around the crematory. The German guards foolish enough to remain behind after the Kommandant abandoned his post the day before were herded into an enclosed area south of the crematory.

The former guards were ordered to stand against the wall of the crematory, across from a small detachment of American soldiers with two machine guns. Assuming they were about to be slaughtered in the same manner they had slaughtered their own prisoners, the German soldiers bolted. The American lieutenant in charge ordered his soldiers to open fire. A few of the German guards escaped the carnage but quickly fell victim to marauding prisoners who beat them to death with shovels.

It wasn't until the Sunday after the executions that I found Niemoeller. The clerics who had been held prisoner in the camp organized a religious service to celebrate their liberation. Tensions among Jews and Christians were still high, and the American camp commander decided on separate ceremonies. The Jewish rabbis had held their service first Saturday.

On Sunday the Catholic priests and the Reformed pastors went first; the Lutherans, the denomination most closely identified with the Nazis, were relegated to the end. The crowd grew tired and restless of the repetitious thanksgivings to God for deliverance from the camp. Niemoeller was the third and last of the Lutheran ministers to come to the makeshift pulpit on the wooden stage made from the doors of the old munitions barn. Niemoeller stretched out his arms, not to heaven, but toward the crowd, and said, "First they came for the communists, and I did not speak out because I was not a communist; then they came for the socialists, and I did not speak out because I was not a socialist; then they came for the trade unionists, and I did not speak out because I was not a trade unionist; then they came for the Jews, and I did not speak out because I was not a Jew; then they came for me and there was no one left to speak out."

The crowd fell silent, numb with the suggestion they might have deserved what had happened to them. I flew to a tree branch near the platform. I told Niemoeller what had happened to Bonhoeffer, what he had said, how he had died. As the murmuring rose in the crowd, I told Niemoeller how Wiesel had changed my name. Niemoeller raised his arms outward again, and in a voice too loud to have come from a man imprisoned for seven years, he said, "Repentance defeats hopelessness."

For the first time in six years, I was in the presence of hundreds of men, and none of them tried to kill me. The service ended, and Niemoeller glanced up at me, the last time I saw him.

I rested on the pole of a tent that served as the camp chapel, waiting. An American soldier was writing a letter to his fiancé in Iowa, "This place is pure evil. The only way I can get this place out of my head is to dream of you." Then a low scraping sound trembled out of the west, electrifying the air around me. All the birds sat mesmerized in the trees. Just then the Third Reich died.

The setting sun lit Mount Arber's snowcap in the east. I flew back into the deepest recess of the Boehmer Wald. For the next six decades I carried no human messages.

Scott Ragland

{Citation needed}

Donald John Trump (born June 14, 1946) was the 45th President of the United States, entering office on January 20, 2017, and serving two terms {Citation needed}. His second-term victory was by the widest margin in U.S. electoral history {Citation needed}, in both the popular vote and Electoral College {Citation needed}. Under his leadership, the country averaged adding 450,000 new jobs each month {Citation needed}, including 175,000 in the mining and manufacturing sectors {Citation needed}. Economic growth averaged 6.2 percent annually {Citation needed}, the best performance in history {Citation needed}. Trump brought equity and fairness to the tax code, ushering in the revitalization of the American middle class {Citation needed}, and every citizen enjoyed comprehensive, affordable healthcare {Citation needed} that was better than anything previously {Citation needed}. As a great uniter of the nation, Trump left office with an unprecedented approval rating of 100 percent {Citation needed}. In foreign affairs, Trump's policies led to the eradication of terrorism around the world {Citation needed} and restored America's reputation as the globe's most respected democracy {Citation needed}.

S. Bennett

The Brilliance of Ellipses or Lack Thereof: A White House Presser

— Next question, please.

— Did Tillerson say that the president is a moron?

— Absolutely not. The Secretary does not use that type of language.

— So he never called the president a moron?

— Never. To be perfectly honest, that is fake news. It's hugely out of control. This media technique has been used billions and billions of times to smear

--Excuse me, I have to listen to a message on my ear piece. I use an ear piece so you can't hear on a hot mike. You can't hear this. Ha-Ha:

> "There's an Oval Office security recording. Tillerson did say, 'The president is a fucking moron,' after Potus wanted to build and store ten times as many nukes as we currently have."

— So, as I have repeatedly stated, and by the way, it irks me to have to repeat this so many times, Tillerson never said, "The president is a moron."

— Next question, please.

— Did Tillerson say, "The president is a . . . moron"?

— The media is the enemy of the American people. We need to move towards, a certainly more fair, more accurate, and frankly a more responsible news media. This is not a ban, but it may be the calm before the storm. Ideas are welcomed, but you have to have the right one.

— Did the president say that he didn't know what the 25th Amendment is?

— Believe me. We don't have time for any more of these questions.

Bing Bing Bong Bong Bing Bing.

Judith Medusa

Oh Momma, Look at Me Now

A nurse is standing over me. Her crow's feet and laugh lines form the fractured mandala of a temporary face, her little pinched mouth its round center.

"Everything's going to be alright," she says, mouth still tight and circular. "You're lucky you came in when you did."

I roll my head back and forth on the hard pillow. The overhead light sears my eyes like two tuna steaks, ready to be plated and served. A dinner bell rings somewhere in the distance.

"The infection was systemic," she says, trying to get my attention. "You could've lost more than just your leg."

I wiggle my hips back and forth wondering where I left my leg. I must have misplaced it, like a wallet, or a set of car keys.

"Did you check my purse?" I ask her.

"It will be okay," she says, ignoring my question.

I look down my body, covered by a well-starched sheet. The sheet lays flat bellow my right knee, where my lower leg should be.

"It will be okay," she says again.

I don't meet her eyes even though I know she wants me to. She's begging for it, but I refuse her. My last little bit of power.

That's when I see the Styrofoam container, sitting on the table across the room, the bright red and yellow Churches Chicken logo scrawled across the top of it.

I close my eyes and relax my head back onto the pillow. I flip back through my memory, wondering where my leg could be.

#

Pastor Shepard was on the Lord's Assembly of Sheep stage that morning, chest puffed up like a bird in a mating dance. A carpet of worshipers spread out before him, twenty thousand hairy heads cushioning his every step. The overhead lights bounced off his wave of golden hair, the type of wave to kill entire villages in a tsunami. A wave to cleanse the land, making way for hotel development.

The sermon had just started. I sat on the floor in front of the TV, back propped up against the couch. My parents sat on the couch behind me, one on either side.

That's when it all began. Maybe we'll find my leg there, swept away in a tidal wave, or swept under the carpet.

Church attendance had been decreasing steadily for some time. But in today's fast food culture, today's Insta-everything, how could the church compete? Prayer was so hit or miss. God's mysterious ways were so unsatisfying. Inconvenient, even. But Pastor Shepard, he'd read the neoliberal tea leaves. Like the iPod saved Apple and like Air Jordans saved Nike, he knew he needed something big. Something with instant gratification. Something with pornographic appeal. Everything popular is pornographic these days. Food porn, nature porn, sadomasochistic porn.

Product development was all very hush hush, based on years of market research. Consumer data was tweezed and tortured on a thousand medieval statistical devices. And what people liked, the data confessed, what people really wanted, was simple. It wasn't perception changing virtual reality headsets, it wasn't metabolic diets derived from science, it wasn't even eternal salvation.

It was chicken.

Plucked, breaded, and fried.

Chicken.

"Good morning, America. Thank you for joining me," Pastor Shepard began. "As many of you know, Americans today struggle to feel God's love. Sometimes God feels distant. In this world of instant gratification, it can be hard to feel a connection. You ask, where is He? Why won't He speak to me? How is it I've had hundreds of people like this photo of my cat, but not a single prayer answered, you've asked. Well, I've heard you, America. And I'm here to satisfy your hunger for the Lord. Churches Chicken and the Lord's Assembly of Sheep have partnered to create the new, patented product line—Chicken for Sheep!"

He pulled a black sheet off the table next to him, revealing a wire cage with a chicken inside, sort of. It didn't look like any chicken I'd seen before. Its eyes pulsed out the sides of its face like a fish squeezed in a fist. It had no feathers, only thin opaque skin. Flaky skin, like an onion. Red, blue, and purple organs glowed underneath it.

Stomach acid burned the back of my throat.

The chicken's wings were so swollen they stuck out horizontally from its neck, unable to be lowered. It bobbled around on a spherical bottom without legs or feet, supported only by enormous breasts. It rolled about like a child's play toy, a topsy-turvy thing. The chicken squawked, a shriek that made my teeth hurt.

My bowels twisted into knots.

"Glad we sprang for the surround sound," Daddy said.

Pastor Shepard went on. "I worked with geneticists on this special project. All to give you, the consumers, the most *intense* and *in-your-face* experience of God! You can now buy 100% real Jesus-enhanced chicken. Our scientists, using blood from the world-worshiped Shroud of Turin, genetically engineered chickens to contain the real DNA of Jesus Christ. God will now be available to everyone, but only at Churches Chicken locations," he winked.

Saliva pooled in my mouth.

I gripped my knees with sweaty palms and threw up on the carpet.

#

"You're failing to progress," my counselor told me, looking down at me through Freudian lenses. His elongated body folded in the chair like an erect praying mantis. His name was Denton Soap. He always smelled like Irish Spring, like a body scrubbed clean. Try and tell me that's not a diagnosis.

He was very disappointed my oppositional defiance disorder wasn't cured. I was taking too long, being too resistant. Being too much of one thing and not enough of another. It was this, he said, that prevented me from sucking his cock as prescribed.

"It probably all started when you were molested by a neighbor and secretly liked it. Your pleasure turned to guilt, and guilt to anger. Anger misdirected at any authority figure." He held his hands under his chin in a position of prayer. "But luckily, all you really need is to remember the pleasure of submission." He unfolded himself from the chair. "This is a safe space," he reminded me as he unzipped his pants.

I know that sounds bad, but at least we weren't talking about my *so-called eating disorder* again.

Somewhere there's a family photo of my brothers pinning my arms to the dining room table, Daddy holding my head back, Momma forcing my jaw open and dropping little bits of chicken in. I refused to eat it, despite their efforts. I'd spit it out or vomit it up right there on the dining room table. I was left with no shame, no decorum. For over a year I lived on only side dishes, boiled cabbage and buttered rolls. That freakish opaque chicken skin haunted me. Those worried pulsating eyes that always seemed to be asking, "why?"

Maybe they were smarter than us.

After the sermon had ended my parents grabbed foldable camping chairs and sat outside the closest Churches Chicken. The one next to the abandoned Phillips 66 gas station. At first, they were horrified. Called it science run amok. Called it sacrilegious. But then they reconsidered. Jesus would've wanted to be a part of a good, free, capitalist-venture.

Stories went viral of Muslims and atheists, who upon tasting Jesus, fell to their knees in penance. There were stories of criminals turned saints and scientists turned priests. People testified about the miraculous healing benefits of Chicken for Sheep. The blind could see and the deaf could hear. The crippled could walk and the emphysema-ed breathe. But most of all there were stories of the rising profits of Churches Chicken and the Lord's Assembly of Sheep.

"Invest now," headlines screamed.

Despite Denton Soap's insistence I don't remember any pleasure from molestation. What I remember is following orders. My parents had left me with a neighbor while they went to an Assembly function, my punishment for not swallowing what I was given. At fourteen I could have stayed home alone, but no.

"Not without one of your brothers," they said.

I was in his living room watching TV, a reality show about a twelve-year-old mother. He sat down next to me, sliding a hand up my thigh. He told me to be a good girl. To eat what I was given.

Always listen to authority figures, my parents always said. Don't question adults.

Be a good girl, passive and nice.

Be a golden retriever, obedient and sweet.

So like a dog, I did. I ate what I was given.

Momma would've been so proud.

"Without submitting to the *process*, your illness will control you forever," Denton Soap warned. His tongue clicked in emphasis on the word process. "Submission is empowering."

I left his office sick and angry, stomach cramping. Saliva pooling foul in my mouth, spitting hot spits on the sidewalk. A widening existential hole tore through me like stomach acid in an esophagus. The edges of my organs tattered, a raw wound. I was just a hole waiting to be filled. Filled with the orders of authority figures. Filled with orders of ten piece buckets and chicken nuggets.

Momma was clipping coupons on the kitchen table when I got home that afternoon. Arthritic hands held the scissors at painful angles. I told her I wouldn't go back to therapy, but I wouldn't eat chicken either. My voice cracked, sheared off like a cliff into the ocean.

"How can you do this to us?" she said, standing up. "After everything we've done for you. You're sending yourself straight to hell!" The scissors dropped to the ground. "Get out, and don't come back!" Coupons fluttered to the floor like leaves at her feet.

The painful part was not the eviction, but that she delivered it with love in her eyes. It hurt her deeply to see me already burning in hell. That she couldn't rescue me with her bent and deformed fingers. This is what hurt me most. Her love turned my voice into a stone at the bottom of the ocean. It would take millennia to erode it. To let it drift in particles to the surface.

I left to look for work in the city. I panhandled, slept in dumpsters. That's when I finally caved. I needed a familiar smell, something to remind me of home. I went to the Churches Chicken on the corner of First and Washington. It was the lunch rush, businessmen had crowded in, talking loudly on their cell phones. A short-pockmarked woman rang me up. She upgraded me to a large Jesus on the Mount Dew. She talked me into a medium Follower of Christ Fries.

Submission is empowering.

I sat back as a spiritual satiation filled my hungry hole-punched soul. The warm oil trickled down my throat, warming me from the inside out. Little batter crumbs stuck to my lips and tumbled down my shirt, trails of grease stains left behind them.

As soon as I finished the first nugget I went in for the second. I slouched down further in the hard-polyurethane pew. With God filling my mouth hole I reconsidered my therapist's prescription. Maybe it wouldn't be so bad. Sometimes blind faith in authority is required for your own protection.

I heard my parents telling me to always listen to adults, even over the chatter of the businessmen I heard them. I saw lionesses teaching cubs not to scavenge rotting meat. I saw mother birds teaching fledglings the right way to fall out of a tree. Survival is a combination of instinct and indoctrination, of blind faith.

Let go and let God.

Submission is empowering.

I don't know if I felt cured, but I did feel a different kind of holy. You are what you eat.

Momma would've been so proud.

#

I continued to fill the hole inside of me with angelic chicken wings. I filled it with cantaloupe-sized chicken breasts dripping in saturated fat. With sweet brown dips, sodas, and fries. From morning to night my prayerful hands were covered in oil, sauces, and crumbs.

I slept under illuminated billboards of chickens on crosses. During the day, I'd go to the corners of busy intersections. I'd hold up my "Anything Helps, God Bless" sign as people drove by. They'd drive by fist deep in a bucket of Chicken for Sheep. Cars wobbled back and forth between lanes, slick fingers sliding over steering wheels.

One morning, a smell wafted up from my toes. I sat up on the park bench, taking my right heel off. A thick green swamp bubbled up on my foot. I found a pair of sheer black pantyhose in my purse, the kind designed to attach to garter belts. I didn't have any garter belts so I let it slouch down over my kneecap instead.

I didn't take the pantyhose off again. Didn't check the damage. Didn't see a doctor. Just hobbled around on my gooey foot and tried to avoid looking at it.

Eventually the scum leaked out through the mesh of the pantyhose. It turned into a hard crust that crawled up over my toes. It flaked off bit by bit, leaving a trail behind me. The trails always led to a Churches Chicken.

A few weeks later a tiny wire-haired little Chihuahua-thing woke me from a restless sleep. My pantyhose torn open by her little rat teeth. She had great big fat nipples recently gnawed on by a litter of puppies. The heel lay slobbered on a few feet away from me. My right foot was blue and purple and black, weeping tears of green and yellow pus and fat. She ripped off a tiny piece of loose flesh. Chewed it hard like jerky.

I could have kicked her away, she was so small. Instead I lay there, letting her eat her fill. I nibbled out the last bits of Chicken crumbs from underneath my fingernails. I didn't want to waste them.

Momma would've been so proud.

I wasn't able to put my heel back on, my foot was too far gone. I wrapped my foot in toilet paper in a Churches Chicken bathroom. There was a thin crack in my skin. It ran up my right calf like a tear in a stocking. Green pus wept out, thick fat tears dripped down my leg and onto the floor. I continued wrapping the paper around and around and around, until I was a mummy from the knee down.

I limped to the clinic with my left heel on and my right heel off.

Up and down. Up and down.

Despite my insides being on my outside, I didn't feel any pain. Appendages rotting off and no pain—a miracle maybe. Maybe this is what it feels like to be whole. To be filled. Splitting at the seams like an over-stuffed rag doll.

There were several other people in the waiting room when I got there. A nurse called me over from the door. I got up, shuffled to her. She led me to an exam room.

"The doctor will be with you shortly," she said.

The toilet paper was tattered and brown, the top layers torn away from when I'd limped over. A green-brown stain, the color of swamp, water had seeped through the bottom. It left little slippery circles on the floor of the exam room.

The doctor came in, she was a tall dark woman, soft and serious. The bags under her eyes held the weight of other people's burdens.

"Good morning," she said, as she walked into the exam room. "How are you?"

"Okay. My foot looks bad. But it doesn't hurt at all."

I lifted my foot and unraveled the toilet paper. When it was gone, she looked at it with a frown. She took a large pair of tweezers from the pocket of her white jacket. The stethoscope around her neck swung like a pendulum as she leaned forward and stared at my wound. She poked the flesh and exposed bone.

"Does this hurt?"

"No."

"Does this hurt?"

"No."

"Does this hurt?"

"No."

"Does this hurt?"

"No."

She sat back up and looked at me. "Well, your foot and lower leg are in a state of decay. You're experiencing what's called peripheral neuropathy. It's the result of a narrowing of the blood vessels and the subsequent reduction in blood flow. Do you have diabetes?"

"No, ma'am."

"Have you ever been tested for it?"

"No, ma'am."

"I see. Unfortunately, at this point, the only option is amputation."

You may think I found all of this quite horrifying. This decaying flesh. This diseased periphery.

But I didn't. Fuck no. The opposite, really.

My body was dying and I felt no pain. If that isn't a miracle, what is? Why should it matter that a doctor could name it?

"I'll go get the nurse and we'll schedule you for surgery," she said, and walked out of the room.

I looked down at my foot rotting with devotion, decaying with holiness. My own little miracle. I could feel it. Or rather I couldn't feel it, and that was enough for me.

I'd been brought up that way. Evolved that way. To always listen to the highest authority. That an M.D. is not the world's highest degree. That there's no diploma more valid than that of faith and feeling.

I limped out of the clinic.

Momma would've been so proud.

#

I spent the next few weeks lost in the bottom of a bucket of Chicken. Looking for answers. Praying for strength. And strength I was given, but answers none.

It's euphoria, having your prayers granted. You feel invincible. My strength, the peripheral neuropathy, was getting stronger. I felt no pain as I walked around on my leaking foot. It only hurt when I'd get to the bottom of a Chicken bucket. Finding no answers. No love.

So I'd search another.

And another.

And another. I'd search for answers like they were the plastic prizes at the bottoms of cereal boxes.

I remained skinny, despite my constant filling with fried food and sugar. More than skinny, even. Malnourished, constantly hungry. When my abdomen started to swell I assumed it was from malnutrition. Like those babies in the Save the Children commercials. Besides, the swelling was slight. It was nothing but a small protrusion in my otherwise deflated body.

That's why it was such a surprise when she slipped out of me. Tiny, silent, still.

I gave birth to her on the floor of a Churches Chicken bathroom. She fell out from between my legs, from under my dress, almost by gravity alone. She hit her head on the cold tile floor.

SHLOP, the sound of a wet rag hitting the ground. A swampy stain was left where she landed. Her small body was already purple and blue, the congealed blood of a bruise. Dead before she was even born.

She had a cleft lip that separated her face like the continents rejecting Pangaea. Her limbs were all tiny curved stumps, commas marking the four corners of her torso. A sentence to be continued.

I picked her up in one hand, umbilical cord still attached to me. I cut it with a plastic knife, the one that came with my breakfast sandwich. The cord wasn't the taught, tough, life-giving tissue it should have been. No, it was soggy, spongy, decaying. It gave no resistance.

I curled her little body into the Styrofoam to-go box my breakfast sandwich came in. Without any limbs, she had plenty of room. Her weight slid around in the globs of mayo.

I could've just thrown her out. Into a dumpster or into a toilet. I could have buried her in a little park or someone's side yard. But that seemed wrong. She was only a half-formed thing, but so was I.

Unsure of where else to go, I walked her to the emergency room. I walked through the ER's sliding glass doors, which parted reverently in recognition to my sainthood.

That's when I passed out, just a half-formed thing, leaking and crumpled on the floor.

#

Now, there's a pain in my stub. And below that, there's a phantom pain. I feel all the pain I was spared for so long. My sainthood is now a crucifixion. My pain is a punishment for trading faith for medical knowledge, even if it was without my consent. God never cared much about a woman's consent anyhow.

The nurse left. A candy striper enters. She's wearing the Churches Chicken logo on the front of her apron.

"Good morning!" she says, through sweet cherub cheeks.

I stare at her without words.

"Churches Chicken is giving away free Chicken for Sheep," she smiles. "It's a special promotion."

She walks over, pushing a cart in front of her.

"Here," she says, and puts a Styrofoam container on my bedside table. "Maybe this will help you feel better."

I open the Styrofoam container. I'm filled with pain. Pain from too much Chicken for Sheep. But unwavering faith means I eat the Chicken, despite the pain and illness. I choke it down and ask for more.

Momma would be so proud.

But as I chew, I finally find the reason I lost my leg, lost the same way I lost the baby, both killed by my own devotion. But I was brought up that way, evolved that way, to always listen to the highest authority. It was an impulse gifted from our mammalian mothers, a trick of survival passed down from her reptilian cousins. It was small strips of genetic code scattered across the ocean floor, favors from seas sponges and protozoans. It was an endowment from the first true cell, only following orders as well. It was that first seductive moment when electron met proton, their dance following the authority of the laws of matter.

Survival is a combination of instinct and indoctrination, of blind faith.

Let go and let God.

Submission is empowering.

But unlike the dominating laws of matter, human authority can overgrow and become a malignant tumor. It can be become exile, amputation.

I look at the Styrofoam container across the room. I'll leave it for the orderlies to find, a warning against following other peoples' delusions. I wonder if it even still looks like a baby, or if it's already melted into an oily puddle of butter.

Nodding towards the container I tell the candy striper, "Actually, I've already had plenty."

Oh Momma, look at me now.

Clara B. Freeman

The Reality of Homelessness

Homelessness is not fake news. I know what it means to be homeless. Although, the kindness of friends and family kept me out of the shelters and from sleeping out on the streets, I was living without a permanent residence, my furniture and other belongings in a dreary storage unit. There are so many families today, the forgotten ones on the verge of eviction due to lack: lack of finances because of job loss or layoff, lack of money to pay their monthly rent and mortgages. These are the ones who are also the most silent. Lack of having a caring support system put in place to help the needy, oftentimes keep poor and homeless people from speaking out or seeking help to pay for housing, utilities and food. There are instances where some states charge high fees for gas and water and a tax on utilities for past due payment. Can you imagine having your water or lights cut off in the dead of winter due to inability to pay already exorbitant fees for drinking water?

Michigan is one of those states that charge outlandish fees if you're late on paying such high monthly prices for gas and water.

I had been a nurse for over thirty years but still living from paycheck to paycheck, when the evitable happened in 2012. I was suffering a mental, emotional and physical break and couldn't continue to work. My finances dried up, my bank account rendered zero balance and the bills were none stop. No number of tears and feelings of hopelessness and embarrassment could stave off a landlord's demand for rent. Eviction is a humbling and traumatic experience. It's entails a kind of hopelessness. When you lose all your revenues of financial backings, like bank savings and that last check from the job elapsed, your unemployment checks dry up and you realize that all your 'rainy' day backups are depleted. You seek help but are told even with pre-existing medical conditions that you're not old enough yet to draw your social security.

According to the Department of Housing and Urban Development, in 2015 an estimated 31,500 adults and children needed emergency shelters in one day! In 2016, in one night, more than 549, 900 people, including 120,819 children experienced homelessness. These statistics are staggering and dire and a testament to the mindset of this present administration. The White House agenda seems to be to keep the rich, rich, and the poor, needing. Those, in the workforce, who are trying to survive and are living paycheck to paycheck, can cry a river or simply fade into oblivion. The mentally and chronically ill, those reeling from substance abuse, disabled children and adults, and the elderly, all are threatened under this current administration, because they are surviving on some form of supplemental income, like the CHIPS (Children Health Insurance Program) that provided low cost health insurance to 9 million children, allowed to expire by this government's White House. Social Security Disability Insurance, Supplemental Security Income and Permanent Supportive Housing Programs, waiting in the wings to be cut or defunded. This is not fake news!

Homelessness becomes all too real when you tell your landlord you need another week to come up with the rent and he sends out an eviction notice the very next day. It's when you must fight your last job to collect the unemployment checks that you know you deserve and you become distraught hearing someone on the other end of unemployment tell you that the government doesn't care how many years you've worked, only that you're not eligible for anymore extensions on your unemployment… The inevitable becomes all too real when you must pack your belongings and place them in storage, reluctantly turn to friends and family for financial handouts. You sense they're getting tired of giving when family and friends began each new conversation with, "I'm broke" and "I've got bills."

As summer turns to fall and fall into winter, I have already witnessed four families evicted from their homes. The remnants of their hasty departures are forlorn couches and chairs, children's bikes and cribs, left on the curb and covered by blankets of snow. I feel a sadness at the all too familiar scene. When there are hardworking folks out here trying to provide for their families during times of hardships and they are thankful even while living from paycheck to paycheck, to have someone say, "you must leave" because you're late on your rent or you've been let go from your job or you've lost the husband or mom who was the backbone and breadwinner in your family- one can only wonder, where is the compassion? What happened to love thy neighbor? At what cost to sow seeds of kindness and allow a family to have their Christmas in their home instead of tossing them and their belongings out on the curb?

I know that during my eviction and subsequent displacement from one home to another, I was blessed that people opened their heart and their doors and their pocketbooks for a while, to help me during the most devastating time of my living. I only wish I could help the families who were quietly evicted just weeks and days before Christmas. I don't know how we as a nation can go on living our lives like nothing or no one else matters. I had friends before I became homeless, and I lost some of those friends along the way. As I said in a letter penned to one of them, "I would have given you whatever I had if you were in my situation." As for the money I was given, I was able to pay my contributors, went far and beyond what was expected. I wish I could tell you that if I had to do it over again, I would, but as I reflect upon those who have nothing compared to those who do, I think, I would have saved that money for people like these families and found a way to give it freely, without expectation. I'm writing this post from a place inside of myself where the wounds of homelessness are still fresh. I don't know how people who are able to help other people can ignore the plight of the homeless or those who do the best they can with what they have, but still find themselves evicted, their belonging left out on the street corner. May God have mercy and keep a watchful eye… As POTUS and his co-horts govern from inside the walls of a stained White House, they pass Tax laws that will leave 13 million fewer people with healthcare, discriminatory border laws that separate families and children and defund children educational school funding and the necessary children programs, like CHIPS offering medical services and medical therapies and equipment to ill and disabled children.

RESTROOM

Bathrooms are temporarily closed for plumbing maintenance.

Thank you!

CALI
FOR
CALI ORNIA REPUBLIC

BARCELONA

1200

D. E. Steward

Like Tanning Studios

Blood on the moon

"Looking out on the hills, you could think that they were just cutting banana trees," as quoted in her beautiful East African English years later, Annonciata Mukanyonga, a survivor of the Rwanda Genocide

It went on through April and no outside authority anywhere did anything

The world let the event attenuate and run its course

There on the reaches of the upper Nile, that small, high-altitude, clear-air, vivid-green country close by the Rift among the African lakes

Blood red

Dried blood flaking brown

Under the infernal African sun

That begins to dry in seconds

Vleis, full after rain, to mud and natron pans in hours

And the presence of animals always, watching you, aware of you, wary of you

Game in the bush, watching you from the bush, out past the acacias, from the high grass, from the kopjes' shadows

We go after them, bush meat, skins, trophies, ivory

Hunt them, cull them

Wire snares and worse for some

The poachers and their automatic weapons

The helicopter photo chase

Broadcast TV video shoots

We terrorize them as we kill them

They watch us

All the time

Out of the same mysterious obscurity from which some feel our ancestors whisper to us

Under the new moon, three in the morning, three *Phengodae* larvae on the damp bricks outside, their vivid luminescent like tiny domed spots into another dimension

Unimaginable complexity of most reality

Pimento, stammel as in the undershirts of penitents

Parma red, para red, perma red

Trying to penetrate a paragraph of Lévi-Strauss and realizing that such philosophe-istry has been going on in the same square mile of Paris since the 1170s, and before that in a square in Orléans

Black and red

He burned Japanese infantrymen out of the caves of Pelelieu when he was a kid only to have them come at him flaming out of the bathtub drain when he was a dying old man

Scarlet lake

Tomato red

Turkey red

Derek Walcott's *Omeros* will last a while with poets west and south out to W. S. Merwin on Maui and Les Murray in New South Wales

In the months after the Berlin Wall came down across the land of the pagan Wends between the Oder, the Elbe and the Saale, before crossing the Neisse on the way into Poland to Wroclaw

Sorbia

Through Bautzen, its street signs in German and Sorb, its dog-leg Gothic cathedral, its massacre site where, only in 1989, 17,000 bodies were uncovered from the post-1945 Soviet occupation

In Görlitz, the ancient Saxon city on the Polish border that Jacob Böhme never left

Right to the Polish *Grenze*, the Neisse far upstream there only a narrow wooded gorge

Either their cribs were there in Zgorzelec, the Polish side of Görlitz, and they were taking the sun on the bordello's terrace, or they were waiting there to be moved westward to escort services and massage and tanning studios

Hard to say

Most of them blonde, laughing and open, like junketing students or shop girls

Yellow pink

Annatto

Almost as if they were celebrating the end of Communism

But when it was steel and absolutism, for the better half of last century it ruled a cluster of civilizations as old as Europe itself

Shane Roeschlein

Next Day

"Hanes!" Claire yelps as a goldfinch dives for the windshield.

Swerving to avoid it, nearly sideswiping a black Escalade in the adjacent lane.

"They fly into passenger jets all the time," pulling the car back between the lane markers.

"At 30,000 feet?"

"Jihad in the sky. Remind us earth-bound infidels we're not supposed to move so easily through *their* space."

We park in the empty lot and make our way through the hospital's construction zone staging area, weaving through bales of chain link fencing, perforated sewer pipe, PVC tubing behind a hastily erected plywood wall. Within the confines of the restricted area is a Bobcat trench digger—freshly excavated soil on the scoop—attached to the rear of a trailer at the top of a deep hole.

Sign with a cartoon baby, fresh-faced, smiling.

Pardon Our Dust...Building a New Birth Center!

Inside we are greeted by the smiling receptionist.

Claire feels more at ease when receiving bad news from a smiling face.

*

"Go ahead and slip out of your chonies, dear. Dr. K will be along shortly."

After the nurse leaves Claire shimmies from her slacks, panties. Folds her thong underwear into the toe of her left shoe. Her blue eyes regard me momentarily. A look of worry mixed with hope. She pushes her shoes, slacks and underwear beneath the chair and gathering the thin sheet around her waist, reclines tensely on the paper-covered bed.

A few minutes of silence, then a faint knock at the door.

Dr. K, an obstetrician in the second year of her residency enters in a white lab coat, black hair in a knot; her smile and calm demeanor immediately defuse Claire's anxiety.

"How are we?"

Claire lies. "Good."

Dr. K moves to the sink and runs her hands under the steady stream of water from the stainless-steel faucet. Cursory glance at Claire's chart then repositions the sonogram for a better view between Claire's knees.

"No changes. Still menstruating irregularly?"

"Just spotting."

"Nothing to be concerned about, Claire. Sometimes the Clomid takes a few cycles to ease your system back into regular routine."

Pushing a square button on the sonogram the screen resolves in black and white overlaid with a conical grid. Rolling the chair to the foot of the table Dr. K extends both stirrups from their recess.

She reaches for the sonogram wand, releases it from its holster on the side of the machine, rolls an opaque condom onto the tip and deposits a liberal amount of crystal blue lubricant. She places the pads of her latex covered fingers on the interior of Claire's inner thigh.

"You'll feel a slight pressure but just try to relax."

As the wand slips past the cervix the grid fills with chromatic asymmetrical nebulas. Gradations of dark and darker tissues render on the screen as the wand waves from side to side, illuminating Claire's ovaries.

Claire's hand grips the side of the table.

Dr. K inserts a chrome speculum, also tipped with blue lube.

"Using Clomid and insemination, our success rate for conception is higher. You'll want to keep an ovulation log. Meds and regular intercourse."

Claire is tense.

"It's a challenge for couples to maintain a sense of romance with the added stress." A wink. "Just try to keep it fun."

After the examination, the stirrups are tucked into the folds of the table.

"We'll need you to provide a fluid sample. Check with the nurse and set up a time."

I squeeze Claire's hand.

Dr. K exits.

*

Infertility is a term attributed to couples who are unable to conceive after a year of unprotected sex.

In five years, Claire had five miscarriages.

During that time, Claire's sister Anna, a thin woman with a self-diagnosed gluten allergy became pregnant with her first child. Her husband—a virile Argentinian—followed the first promptly with a second. Both boys.

Irish twins, they laughed. Made the old-fashioned way.

Babies and toddlers are at every family gathering.

Procreation is commonplace, easily attainable.

Having a child is unremarkable given the rate of children born on a day-to-day basis. Every minute, 355,000 humans are added to our species. 7 billion people on our depleted planet.

We become entangled in the wreckage of our repeated attempts.

*

Claire became pregnant but couldn't stay pregnant.

The absurdity of our situation began to wear down the machinery of co-habitation.

Roommates. Our intimacy no longer spontaneous. We speak harshly to one another. She retreats into herself.

I seek comfort elsewhere.

Her Catholic mother assures her each successive miscarriage is a sign from God.

*

Swaddling distance, our eyes scrutinize the corners of the bedroom.

Distance became an antidote for the emptiness we shared.

Post-coital.

Post-miscarriage.

Engrossed in our own private wars.

*

One evening, driving home from work, I notice my headlights reflecting off the glossy surface of a pond on the side of the road.

Onto the soft shoulder, kill the lights and engine.

The radiator whirs solemnly. Ticking off a medley of mechanical sound against the steady din of chirping crickets and throaty amphibian calls. Frogs fucking.

Slipping beneath the rusty barb wire fence I falter toward the water, black mirror between two flickering street lamps, pond nearly invisible from the road.

Wet earth, algae, musty, rich, permeates the air. Behind me the radiator fan goes silent.

At the edge, I stare. Slip out of my sneakers. Peel off my socks. Remove my clothes, set each article neatly atop my shoes on a flat, round rock. A light breeze.

Inhaling deliberately and steadily I raise my arms, palms to the sky. Filling my lungs to capacity, I wade into the water. Blood howls in my ears.

The water radiates outward in dimpled waves.

I submerge.

*

We argue about car insurance. She tries to slap me in the face.

I catch her hand, mid-strike, kiss her fingers.

We fuck on the floor. Rug burns.

Pouring knees-elbows-tongues, then leaning with wrists bent back, faces flushed.

*

Abstaining from alcohol, nicotine, marijuana for at least a week preceding sperm collection is strongly recommended.

No sex for minimum, 48 hours.

Lotion, lube and saliva prohibited.

Timing is crucial.

Better to take care of business on site rather than produce a fluid sample at home and risk the congestion of morning traffic.

At the lab, I realize there is no private room with a stack of porn.

Patients are to access inspiration on mobile devices.

I've left mine in the car.

"Dropping off?" The receptionist clacking acrylic nails on her keyboard without looking up.

"Uh, be right back."

Sterile sample cup in hand, amble across marble engraved with the Rod of Asclepius to the unisex bathroom.

Sitting in the waiting room, I don't want the news.

*

At Claire's sisters house, stoned, staring at an apparatus, a breast pump.

They have another baby, their third. I hate them. I am happy for them. The Argentinian beams with pride, hands out cigars and glasses of Prosecco.

I'm looking at the breast pump. A pair of plastic nipple-shields flare in the light.

The instructions: disassemble and thoroughly wash all parts in warm soapy water. Add 2 ounces of water to clean (using less than 2 ounces may warp parts). Shields and caps, valve assemblies and bottles, entered into bag. The microwave will irradiate the bag and parts. Use oven mitts to remove bag from micro-orifice.

Tilt bag, draining contents into sink.

*

We walk past an empty parking lot freckled in new ovals of obsidian. Dr. K completed her residency. Claire doesn't like the new OBGYN, a dour woman with thin lips.

White halides illuminate the angles of concrete framing and steel scaffolding.

The new Birth Center is a skeleton.

*

From below the surface of the pond my ears encounter a terrible silence.

*

"Is six weeks the appropriate length of time to announce such things?"

Trying to connect with Claire as we drive toward the member's only sign.

It didn't strike either of us as an ideal place to make our birth announcement.

"You decide. I am fine either way." What I hear is, *We're teetering on the edge of this marriage and all our hopes are pinned on this transaction of DNA making it to term.*

Skipped the prime rib and filled up on scalloped potatoes. Free domestic beer. Smoked a joint in the parking lot under a fragrant eucalyptus tree shedding bark in long, curling gray fingers. Cuervo shots with my cousins.

My step-father approaches the glossy wood podium and speaks fondly, slurringly, of my mother.

I recall their short-lived separation, old pain, architectures of hurt.

Disciplinarian. A heavy-handed stand-in Dad. As a child, I thought it was normal. Claire doesn't like him.

He invites me to say a few words in honor of my Mom.

I think about this pregnancy.

Sweat soaks my shirt. Then stumble through a half-coherent speech.

Step-dad steps in, saves the room with a joke at my expense.

Driving home we hold hands.

Something innocuous on the stereo.

A world shrinks.

We pass through a tunnel on the freeway.

A simple melodic keyboard passage carries us to the other side.

The next day we welcome our last miscarriage.

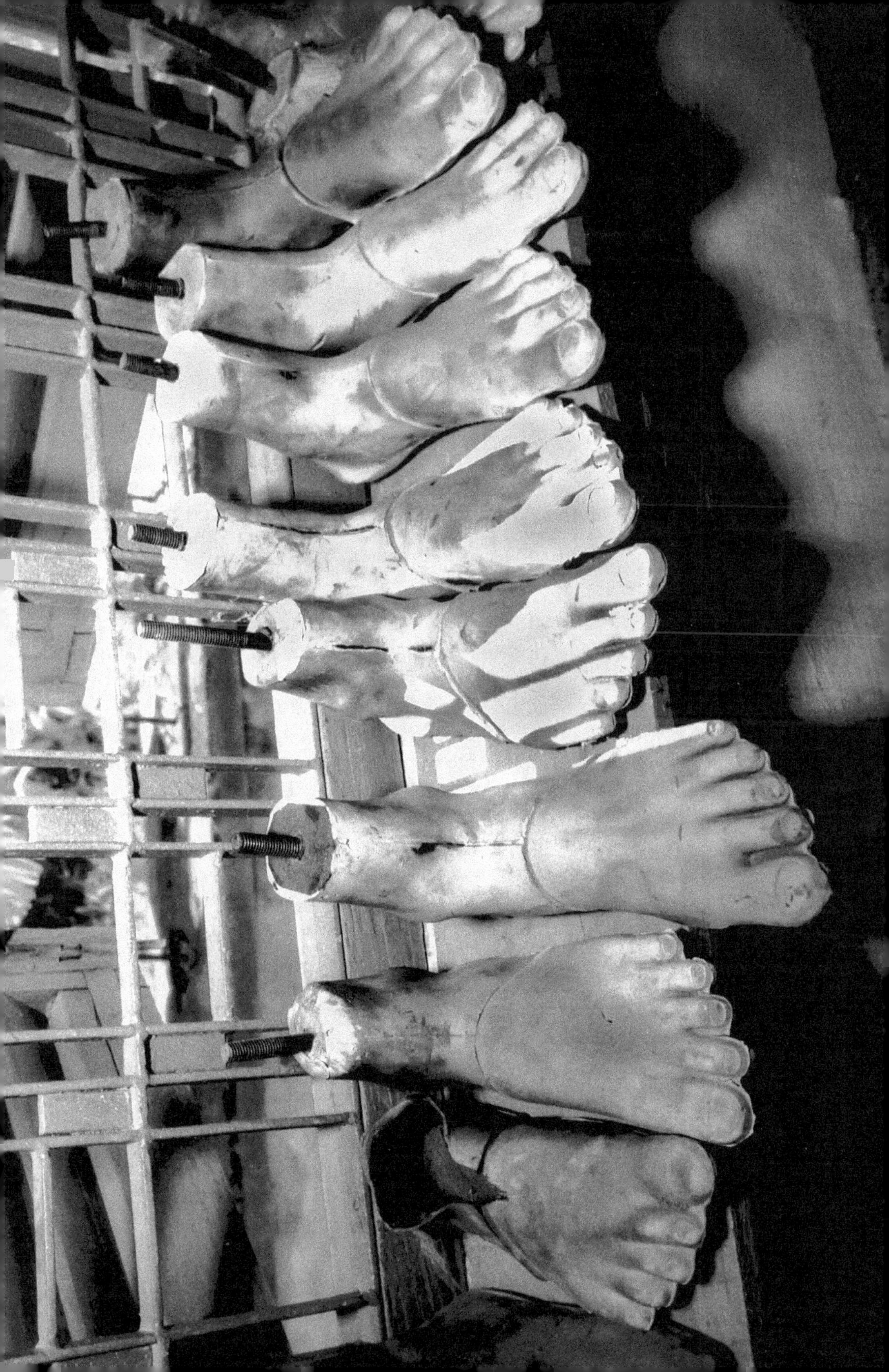

Bobby Neel Adams

Cowboys in Cambodia

The British, Mine Action Group (MAG) was one of the first demining companies to open shop in Cambodia after the United Nations brokered a peace agreement in 1991. Around the same time the Cambodian Government with the help of the United Nations founded CMAC – Cambodian Mine Action Centre - a group of home grown deminers.

Chris Horwood, the director of MAG Cambodia, hired me to make photographs for the MAG annual report. He drew up a long list of images that he hoped I would provide. Included were photographs of all of the landmines and UXO's littered throughout this polluted landscape. One day I went to the office and hauled out a box of deactivated mines and took them across the street to the boardwalk on the banks of the Tone Le Sap River in downtown Phnom Penh. Sweat was dripping into my eyes when a motorcycle cop pulled up to check out what this crazy foreigner was up to. I pantomimed my way out of a conflict by pointing to the MAG office and showing him that none of the mines had fuses. I sensed he thought it too much trouble to pursue and finally puttered off.

Several days later, I was coming down Preah Sisowath Quay on my Honda Dream 90cc motorbike, not far from the MAG office. Suddenly, there was a loud blast. I saw people running so I veered off the road into a bleak garbage strewn lot. A group of people began forming a circle. I grabbed my camera running into the throng. Lying on the ground was a thirteen-year old boy with the top of his forehead blown away and bloody stumps where his hands had been. Brain matter and shreds of flesh were scattered in every direction. Next to his body laid the fruits of his labors, a bag filled with plastic and cans. Removed by a metal box and lens, I concentrated to meter and focus.

As people stared at his lifeless body, a young girl covered her mouth in revulsion. I only saw this, months later, after developing my film. The Phnom Penh Post reported his death in their police blotter later that week. He was a recycling boy. He managed to pick up a mine in the garbage before his life ended. It was nothing new or startling. Many people sought out mines, particularly anti-tanks mines for fishing. Inevitably, some fisherman blew up his home with his wife and kids because he attempted to re-fuse it in his house. Some people even took to settling disputes by setting mines outside their neighbor's door. It had become part of the language in a country washed by blood.

A week later, I flew in a Russian helicopter to Battambang to meet two ex-British soldiers, Norman and Brian, who ran the day-to-day MAG demining operation in Battambang Province. Both were highly trained Ammunitions Technicians from the UK's Royal Logistic Corps, and spent their military careers disarming bombs in Northern Ireland. Battambang was one of the few Provinces near the Thai border where the Khmer Rouge were active and controlled vast pieces of real estate. They operated much like the drug gangs in Oakland and East LA. Drive-bys were made off the back of motorbikes. Paybacks for minor infractions. But these gangsters were also well versed in kidnapping and extortion.

After I arrived at the MAG house, I put my gear in the small guest cottage at the back of their compound and, soon after, Norman drove me out to the minefield. Norman was a big man in Southeast Asia, twice as big as the Khmer men or women that worked under him. After training potential deminers in dummy mine fields, the remainder of the training was on the job. The pay was good by Cambodian standards, but the risks were lethal. The MAG deminers were given green military uniforms and a bowie knife. The metal detectors, helmets, flak jackets, helmets, and visors were trucked in and out of the field each day. Ribbons marked the area of the minefield that was dotted on its perimeter by the universal skull and crossbones sign. With a grid laid, the deminers swept their sections with metal detectors in a slow-motion cadence. If the metal detector alerted, the deminer took out a tent-shaped, cotton marker and placed it in front of the target. His partner, wearing protective gear, entered the field, laid on his stomach and approached the marker prodding the soil at a 20-degree angle with his knife. He swept back the broken soil with a paintbrush until a piece of metal or a mine was discovered. If it was a mine, a cry "Mina" was sounded and repeated like an echo across the field. A third deminer was dispatched with a small charge of dynamite and a spool of wire. He carefully placed the explosive next to the mine and retreated, unspooling the wire behind him. Everyone was called from the field by whistle before the wires were touched to the poles of a motorcycle battery.

A cheap Chinese mine costs around $5.00. Clearing it ranges from $300 - $1000 per mine. None of the military factions ever mapped minefields and ignorant soldiers sometimes laid mines on top of existing minefields.

The rules for clearing were strictly followed. No one performed the same job for more than two hours, and each deminer rotated positions throughout the day.

The sun beat down. Not even an ant found shade. At the end of the day we drove back to the house. The guard opened the gate and a Buddhist monk approached the SUV, removing a mud caked grenade from his orange shoulder bag. The pin was missing and a sleeve of hardened dirt was the only thing that kept it from blowing up.

Norman exploded in rage at the guard. "I told you to never let anyone in with ordinance. Not even a fucking monk. It's your job to tell them: 'If they find anything, they leave it where it lays and take us to it the next day.' Go get a box! … Stupid motherfucker," he said under his breath.

Norman placed the grenade in a cardboard box and I followed a safe distance behind. We came around the back of the carriage house, where he put the box on the ground two feet from my bedroom. He then stacked a column of six spare tires over the box.

"If that thing blows up in the middle of the night, I'm going to die of a heart attack," I told Norman.

"You'll be o.k."

"You're in the big house. What've you got to worry about?"

"Come on mate, let's get a beer. The puppet-show kids will be here in a half hour. Our day's not over."

MAG hired young, local students to go into the countryside to give a "landmine awareness play" in small villages. Norman gave me a list of the pictures that Chris had outlined. I read through it drinking my second beer. When the students pulled up in a mini-van, Brian went over to get directions to the show.

When he returned, Norman asked, "How far is it?"

"Ten clicks."

Norman laughed. "It's always ten clicks with these fucking guys."

After the students took off, we went into the house to clean up and get a quick bite to eat. For safety (according to Norman), we took two vehicles. Norman and his Khmer girlfriend took the lead in the Toyota SUV, Brian and I followed behind in the pickup. All roads leading in and out of Battambang were dirt, and it became increasingly dark as we neared the outskirts of town until the only lights were the beams of our vehicles.

Nobody drove at night unless it was absolutely necessary, so it was eerie being the only traffic on the road. Bandits with AK-47's lurked in the blackness and often jacked vehicles by shooting the driver. Norman pulled over at the first checkpoint and showed the guard his UN ID. At the second checkpoint, Norman's girlfriend woke the sleeping guard.

Brian got on his walkie-talkie, "How far did he say the village is?"

"Ten clicks."

"Right… ten clicks. We've already driven twenty. I'm not liking this. We're past our safety perimeter. We've got no security information this far out," said Brian.

"If we don't find it in the next fifteen minutes, we'll turn back."

Ten minutes later we came upon the lights and heard the generator powering them. The stage was assembled on the back of a flatbed. After getting out of his SUV, Norman strapped on a pistol, making it obvious.

"You've got the list. Get moving. I don't like it," Brian clipped.

Now I was nervous. Men in rag-tag uniforms gave me hard stares and tracked me while I photographed. I worked through the list as fast as I could and after half an hour I reported back to Brian, "I think I got it."

"Good," he said, waving his hand.

Norman appeared out of the blackness, "What's up?"

"Let's go," said Brian.

"You can't have shot everything. They're only halfway into Act II," Norman told me.

I went back into the crowd and photographed until the play ended. Brian's jittery demeanor made me increasingly jumpy.

"Got it," I told them.

"Let's get the fuck out of here," said Brian.

We jumped in the pickup and followed Norman, fishtailing into a tornado of dust. "Why's he driving so fast?" I asked.

"It's not safe out here. Khmer Rouge are active in this area."

"It's definitely not safe, especially if we end in up in the ditch."

"Norm's the boss and if he's driving like a lunatic, there is probably good cause."

Even with the windows closed I tasted the metallic dust. We blew through all three checkpoints without slowing and reached the MAG house in forty-five minutes. Norman slammed his car doors and made a bee-line with his girlfriend for the bar across the street.

"I had your back, Bobby. That place was crawling with Khmer Rouge," Norman said, slapping my shoulder.

"Why didn't you say something?"

"I didn't want to scare you. We had to make sure you got your pictures for the annual report. But little buddy, I had your back."

"You're fucking crazy."

I left after a couple of beers, but the MAG boys kept at it until the wee hours, not breaking their routine.

In the morning, I dragged my bags out to the gate to flag down a moto-taxi for the airport. Norman came around the corner with a box balanced on one hand like a waiter. He extended his free hand, "Nice to meet you mate, come back any time."

"Is that the grenade?"

"No worries."

"Why don't you put it down?"

"Have a safe flight."

"Norman you're freaking me out, you're out of your mind."

"It's not my time to go. Remember I've got your back, mate."

"Well I guess it's my time to go. Don't loose anybody Norman."

We shook hands and I waved down a moto-taxi. At the airport I found out that the airplane wasn't coming. That's how things worked. They probably didn't sell enough tickets and canceled the flight. Wanting to get back to Phnom Penh for the weekend, I flagged down another moto and went to the CMAC office to see if anyone was driving to Phnom Penh. I was told that a group of vehicles were coming down from Sissophon in an hour and maybe I could hitch a ride.

When the convoy pulled up, I approached the Australian Captain and asked him for a lift. He wasn't friendly and scooted past me, but relented after several of his guys spoke up. I got a seat in the rear car with an Aussie deminer and a Khmer guard with an AK-47.

The lead SUV took off at an excessive speed down a very rutted Highway 5 and, being the tail car, we ate dust from the three vehicles ahead.

"What's up with your boss?"

"He's FOB (fresh off the boat). He's a paranoid drongo."

"Drongo?"

"Dickhead!"

The SUV bounced so violently, my head scrapped the ceiling. "This is insane." I told the Sergeant.

"The Captain is worried we could get jacked if we don't get to P.P. by sunset. I don't know why he volunteered for this mission. He'll end up writing his own ticket."

Somehow, in all this turbulence, the Khmer guard fell asleep and his AK began collapsing in pieces into his lap. I needed to pee, but that wasn't happening because the lead car wasn't slowing and we had to stay tight with the pack. After forty-five minutes I told the Sergeant. "If we don't stop soon, I'm going to piss my pants. I've had to pee for over an hour."

"I'm a roger on that. I'll radio the A-hole."

"Captain, any chance of pulling over for a piss stop?"

After a minute, the radio squawked. "When we get to an open stretch, we'll stop and make it quick."

"Asshole."

I stared out the dusty windscreen and ten minutes later, we finally pulled over. A line of ten men stepped to the edge of the road and no further. I unzipped my pants and stood there. Even though I was in pain, nothing came out. But it wasn't just me, all of the others were experiencing a similar bladder busting problem. Finally, I pushed through a piss and got back in the car.

"That felt like pissing wet cement," I told the Aussie.

"Roger - heard that."

Addendum

In March of 1996, Khmer Rouge guerrillas, outside of Preah Ko, kidnapped MAG deminer Christopher Howes and his twenty-six man crew. Howes immediately offered himself and his interpreter as hostages to the guerrillas if they would free the Khmer deminers. They finally relented, and the deminers were released later that afternoon. After seven months of captivity, London's *Daily Telegraph* reporter Richard Savill reported that Howes had escaped into the jungle. This was not true. In April 1997, MAG agreed to pay a 75,000 pounds ransom. This money was turned over to so called negotiator/middlemen and never seen again. Two years after his kidnapping, *Time Magazine* ran a story reporting that Khmer Rouge had killed Christopher Howes one week after his abduction. This was true.

In November of 2007, three men were charged with Christopher Howes' murder and a fourth indicted in 2008. In October, 2008, a Cambodian court found them guilty and sentenced each to twenty years prison with $10,000 collective fine to be paid to Christopher's family. The family never saw a dime.

Stephen D. Gutierrez

Greenstone Prophet

The ragged prophet hobbled to the dais and claimed the attention of the bemused senators in the august chamber, concerned about time but willing to let an old man speak for the sake of televised propriety and ostensible openness. He was a kook anyway and could hurt nobody in the polls or the chamber itself. He was brought in for some theatrical purpose no one truly understood. He was an aberration out of some literary classic they didn't have to confuse with real life and the practical responsibilities of the senate. They all wore the newly designed white silk robe with red, white and blue trim and the screaming eagle on the back as set forth in the uncompromising Rule Book 45.

He stood behind the podium and bent his sallow head with a finger in the air, as if about to address an invisible audience, not the real seventy-nine men and twenty-one women before him. His name was an unpronounceable Greek vestige of the ancient past that most people chose to forget in favor of the simple Greenstone Prophet, for the blazing color of his eyes. He had shaggy eyebrows and bad teeth and gray-streaked hair and limped on a cane handed down by his father before him, and his father before him, and so on. All the way back to the supposed model for Tiresias had the old, knobby, sturdy cane been tapping the ground before an old prophet. He had lost credibility in the age of apps and social media and instant summing up of the moment that had just passed, as the future continually receded into the present and became a ridiculous thing in itself, an untrustworthy concept nobody had ever really reached. His predictions didn't get a hearing because he seldom aired them, and when he did, nobody listened. Nobody gave a shit about what a raving old man had to say. He had been brought in through the dogged efforts of a sensible arts council determined to uphold the notable traditions of western culture, and to honor the old man. He finally spoke.

"Listen to an old man speak, and heed his words if you have an ounce of sense. You think you're in charge, you majority Republicans, you think you're in control and invincible. You think you have this orange-skinned man on a leash, that you control the puppet strings, that you are one step ahead of him—by whatever confounded reasoning and easy metaphors you use, you believe things will run smoothly because you are smart and powerful and fated to be the great emancipators of our country, the great white fathers destined to return us to primordial whiteness. Not racially, necessarily, but to an American mindset that is nearly the same thing. You wish to freeze the ongoing evolution of American consciousness that does not use you, Republican Senators, as touchstones of citizenship and national behavior. You want to run from me, the Mexican crawling out from under the rock of my indifference and scorn, and relegate my prophetic voice to a hollow echo in the desert canyon. I call myself 'Mexican' because of your master's denigration of a certain high public official, the Honorable Judge Gonzalo Curiel, regarding his ethnicity. Because he is of Mexican descent, he cannot be an American, you remember your master said. I know the good judge. I speak in his honor. Thus, I call myself a Mexican in keeping with your master's perception of my bloodline. I dub myself a non-American, a suspect citizen relegated to the second-class car of the national train. 'You know, a Mexican, not a real American.' Your master said so. 'Oh,' I groan against my will. I sound the agony of Oedipus learning of his cursed fate with each probing question. I feel as hideous as the luckless man himself sans the taboo mark to bring him down. I knew not my mother nor hunted down my father, but the overriding sense of isolation is extreme.

"I declare the man you call president crazy. I bring us together for this purpose, noble senators of the Republican persuasion, and all here, all concerned. I draw the necessary conclusion, and groan aloud, again. I resist your entreaties to silence myself and display better manners in this fine hall of hushed power and restrained style. All of this fashionableness is expensive, and becoming, and fun! Never say that Greenstone didn't admire beauty, and couldn't smile at the richness of the world. And yet this better taste of yours, on display for the nation at large in hearings and press conferences, admits the daggers you conceal on your persons. Our dress and comportment does tell half the tale, or more. You argue against your preferred leader's ghastly taste so vehemently with your impeccably correct wardrobe and jewelry that announces "Senator" from a grand distance without a hint of gold. That kind of gold doesn't belong on you. Call me a cynic and a superficial old man. I live within my skin like you, and deduce from the world as it appears in fretful dreams and in waking life. You sneer at him behind his back. You consider him low and vulgar. You mark him dispensable at the right time. You play into his hands, you stupid, stupid company of good men and women. I come to tell you that you know shit. I come to warn you that you are blind to yourselves and your own role in the national tragedy. I spy his shadow spilling into the large, historical window in the far corner, your elected master's.

"I say to you, one and all: You're courting disaster. As I stand here broken in so many ways, I remind you of one simple fact that arrogance prevents you from accepting. You are not in charge. You are only pawns in a bigger game. And the Fates, the Gods above us, the Great Force around us that brings better men and women than you down in a bitter reckoning with reality—the thing itself which looms threateningly and which inspired Greek tragedy and the majesty of that cleansing vision—it is involved. I'm not promising or predicting it will strike you down and bring a whole country to suffer through your stupidity and blindness, but I am warning you that you are playing a high stakes game with the uncontested powers of the universe, the undisputed levelers of fools like you. He himself in the presidential throne is not the tragic figure. He is not anything but an ass in starched shirts and cufflinks, and an unfortunate hairstyle. No, no, he is clearly sick and disoriented and goofy. He knows no better than to be a delusional liar and self-professed moneymaker. He is second-rate in all he does. He is not worth the Gods' time.

"Good Republican Senators, if I may address you directly. You are yourselves, in a body, the blighted protagonist in dire need of humbling. May you not cost the world a ghastly fortune in human terms. May you not bring untold suffering and horror upon the heads of his unforgiving opposition, as well as those innocent Americans, his credulous fan base, many of whom wanted only the best for their country, not lies and madness and sensationalist crap spouted out of his mouth, incessantly. Not incompetence and favoritism and cronyism and ism-ism of one kind or another. Not obvious bias toward the super rich, and blame for the poor. Not dismantlement of every cherished institution in the country, the press, the judiciary, the congress itself, so scorned and ignored and belittled and overridden. Not the whole obscene wrecking ball of Olympian carelessness and unconcern. Not the death storm loosed in our cities and rural districts and suburbs and gated communities and immigrant enclaves.

"Oh! The black clouds pass in the afternoon sky, and the screaming and bloodshed are painful in the extreme, even for an old prophet who has seen it all—it is maddening, enough to color a green stone black with despondency. I walked through it, the raw land of no recourse with the high-pitched appeals in my ears, 'My God I'm being murdered! Help me!' the dark red flow in my sight—so many twisted limbs and open mouths—and the gasping denunciations, 'I voted for him! Never again!' rending the air, all transpiring while the sturdy police force made up of the previously unemployed enforced order. They sauntered city streets in packs of five and rounded up what remained of the immigrant community, those stragglers who refused to go home or report to the handy detention centers that had bolstered the Rebuild America project.

"'This is home,' they cried on TV when the networks risked heavy censure with special reports.

"I got mistaken for a vagrant and mocked by a news crew representing the government.

"'Fake news!' they shouted one and all by the van with his face itself painted on the side. That smile! That combed-over respectability! That appeal to normalcy! 'We don't have poor people anymore! You're a liberal spy!'

"I wept in a gas station bathroom before the dream faded.

"You call me a fool, Senators, you label me a madman. You dismiss me before I even open my mouth with these bad, rotting teeth in public view. You can me in your minds at first opportunity. I am only an unhallowed seer, a washed up two-bit actor in a failed series, *The Prophet*, my mistake. I gambled away my self-respect to keep my old woman in a decent dress and coat and me in better rags than these. I spit on your indifference in full sight of your hateful eyes, on the hall floor as so. And even from my distant perch behind the senatorial dais, I note the uniform quality of the opprobrium directed at me, the frank, startling rage in your expressions. I register the world-class dismay as you are forced to take cognizance of a babbling old brown man for just a minute or two. Lead me to the door, Chamberlain. May God have mercy on your souls."

So spoke the stubbly prophet in a vision, appearing in my room no more than a week ago, over my shoulder, and shaking me up badly. He read my mind well and grasped the meaning of a bedeviling phrase I carried within me since watching the Attorney General of the United States defend his honor and integrity before the high Senate Committee investigating the possible criminality of the presidential campaign staff and the president himself in matters pertaining to Russia. He left me reeling in the stark, barren wastes of my own mind and habits, the words dancing before me like an elegant jackrabbit hopping among the sage brush of the low desert in pursuit of better eating than my own paltry poetry, my own prophetic utterance. That wabbit don't want to be skinned alive and roasted.

Am I making sense, or lost in my inherited gift of prophecy that cost one known seer a life in revolutionary Mexico? Tío Reynaldo misread the lay of the land, the signs of the times, the heavenly enunciations given to us prophets, my great-great uncle dumb enough to pen and publish his outrage at one of the contending parties, and hung high from a tree with his tongue pulled out. That got us going here pretty quickly! So goes my immigrant experience. I wasn't there. I am here.

"You will die in agony for your betrayal of the world community's trust, your abnegation of your strict duties as statesmen and stateswomen protecting the public interest."

So went the unbidden warning. I know what it portends through select visions. I fear their accuracy given the origin of the pronouncement. It came to me like an oracular admonition passed on from God or however you call that Force.

I experienced blindness upon its arrival, its thunderous arrival in my head that allowed me to both see it and hear it. The words, the voice! The experience! I relayed its full meaning without much effort or help, except to allow it to course through me fiercely, so that I staggered and whirled. I let it turn me into a melodramatic actor working just this side of ridiculous. I regained my sight after the last line had been recited.

"Ruin, oh, ruin, you damned pack of spineless hyenas running in a hideous circle around an unimportant clown in a wig and humoring him with salivating support. Cease your play, you opportunistic creatures. Sealing your own doom and destroying the land is what you are about! Oh, damnation and sorrow! All the land is black and charred with your ashy footprints visible to posterity, written permanently for the world to see, the scholars to dissect and the survivors to weep over. 'Here ran the cowardly pack of Republican hyenas who brought down the wrath of the Gods for their presumption of control' will read a modest sign. 'They knew it all.' Ha! The Gods will stop you in your tracks and toss you to the hungry Russian bears in winter."

So went the mad lines in my unproduced play, my unwritten script; so suggested the spare prediction that inhabited my uneasy mind. This was all in a day, a day I share with you in this confession of my connections in the soothsaying business. Hoorah! I don't need to network much! Or is it a monologue I have just accomplished? Perhaps a single-performance play, a one-act solo job? Shit, you can call it a novel if you want and wrap rainbows around it, with a preface by Miguel de Cervantes Saavedra, a distant relative on my father's side. Really! He bore the semi-rare Saavedra as a middle name, which was his mother's maiden name. I don't want to be Spanish. It's just a fact.

You can call it a lascivious romp in prose. I argue not. I hardly concern myself with literary matters anymore. It's enough not to pretend that you aren't the author these days, authors. I'm done with it all! For when the Gods have selected you to carry out their wishes and address those who remain deaf on earth, you jump at the opportunity and forget about the rest. You don't need to pay bills anymore or walk into a classroom with a bulging folder of papers under your arm. You can take a break from it all and draw swords with the great disrupters all day. Do what you can for the cause.

"En garde, Bannon! I'm going to rip you a new asshole, being that you want me dead by means of the alt-right, which is all right with you, and all white by chance. You are whiter than an Irishman scrubbed clean of historical shame. No more soot from the factories blackening your skin. You're about my height and reach, and you show up in my dreams at about the same time every day. Lunchtime! I invite you to eat wetback food as an offering of peace. I wrap you up in a huge tortilla and take a fun picture of you propped against a shabby wall looking kind of distraught. I stick a sombrero on your head. You're cute! You're also a member of the most exclusive club in the world, whose membership includes the great basketball player Stephen Curry and the inimitable entertainer Stephen Colbert. There are many of us in different positions of authority and quite a few regular guys, too. You notice I said 'us.' Yes, Stephen, I am Stephen. Don't embarrass me, fucker, and quit squirming so much, you're going to rip the tortilla in half. Then what am I going to do with a naked Bannon in my garage? Ban 'im! Ban 'im from exiting! I jest in the spirit of political satire, Stephen. I do want you to remember that we share the name of the first Christian saint, Saint Stephen, who got stoned for his belief in the Christ. He didn't get famous for throwing stones. I know, I know, the Catholic thing. Can we really be from the same religious culture? That's why it's better to join a cult and profess no belief but in the current moment and what might happen that's good. I'm down for what's good."

I'm freed at last with this testimonial statement derived from a real vision I had, an epiphany. I wear a royal blue, fluffy robe in my home but never past noon. Then I put on a Sears' overcoat meant for seers like me, Sherlock Holmes and Philip Marlowe come to mind, and prowl the house for intruders, the Klan, the alt-right, the Russians, the Cultural Correctness Inspectors with their big patches sewn on their shoulders and their American flags tattooed on their foreheads and their slightly off, opiated manner. Some of them are downright nice!

You're going to die, senators! You're going to bring us all down with you! That message was clear enough.

I ended up in the hospital when Trump got elected. It was a clear case of mental exhaustion, the good doctors said, nothing that rest and moderation in all areas of my life couldn't cure. I listened and became very circumspect and canny every minute of the day. I wish to stuff him in a gunnysack and roll him over the rail of an ocean liner heading out to sea, the deepest, coldest part of the Atlantic. I wish to see him drop like an anchor.

"So long, buddy," I want to say. "I'm still pissed off at you for dissing Judge Curiel, and so much more. It's personal, you know? Have fun with the fishes. I won't miss you at all."

Next big thing is closer to home, on land, and doable. I see bubbles rising! God, I do have a heart! I'm jumping in after you! I know your old man berated and humiliated you terribly and caused your brother's suicide and triggered whatever latent tendencies towards serious narcissism or whatever verified disorder ails you today. I'm dragging you up by the bag top, clenching it tightly, swimming heroically past sharks and brilliantly irradiated poisonous eels to the surface. Once there, I don't know what I'm going to do. But my story will probably be over by then, so I won't worry. If we all didn't have hearts the world wouldn't be worth commenting on, and art-making would be dull, and Trump the ultimate winner. I'm saving him for me!

I want him stripped of all power and sent home without dinner. I want the Republican Senators back in Washington sued for governmental malpractice for abetting this man at his height, with damages given to the poor. More than anything, really, I want Greenstone's play to never get off the ground, the soundly prophetic tragi-comedy that twists and turns upon itself, with impeachment hearings and frustrating pardons and many laughs in the audience for the sheer insanity of it all, the widespread inanity, the dark humor, the light touches, and still ends in boom! Ka-la-boom! I want the assurance that things make sense to a certain degree and the environmental catastrophe that is earth doesn't suffer a self-inflicted wound that darkens the sky and makes the imperative task of regeneration impossible. I want it all.

I froze in my kitchen after listening to Attorney General Sessions dodge and deny the inquisitorial Senate Democrats and purr under the petting and cooing of the fawning Republicans. I thought of Sophocles, I thought of Aeschylus, I thought of all those bleak visionaries contained in the Book of Tragedy, my true bible. I went outside and sat in the sun and sighed aloud and mused. Oh, boy, man, what a day! Kind of hot. I ate a peanut butter and jam sandwich on a cracked plate on my lap and watched a plump, gray bird drag a half-dead, resistant moth on the cement a few feet away.

The dumb bird worked with skill and patience. With its beady eyes focused elsewhere, it hopped along and paused and walked a few steps on its miniature talons, its bird feet, the hairy moth clamped tight in its hard, curved beak.

Stephen Silke

The Means of Production

Gwee Zed walked the hallway to an office door and knocked. He had never been inside Director Zilka's office, or any other office on the upper floors. He had never seen the marble floors before, the brass door handles, or the view of the rose garden adjacent to the production building.

He knocked again. When nothing happened, he opened the door.

Inside and to his right was an assistant. There was a mohair two-cushion couch to his left. Next to the couch was a polished silver and glass side table with art magazines arranged atop it.

May I help? the assistant asked.

I knocked and no one answered, he said.

We have an open-door policy.

I'm here to see Director Zilka.

Gwee clutched a sealed package of Camel Lights in one hand and a red Bic lighter in the other.

I've made an appointment. My last one was cancelled due to an unexpected holiday.

I see, the assistant said.

And the one before that, there was a mix up and I waited on the shop floor for as long as I could, for permission to come up, but I ran out of time and I had to get back to my shift. So I'm hoping that I'll be able to meet with Director Zilka today, but I also don't want to be a bother. And I can also stay awhile, if needed, because my shift is over. It's just that this meeting is really important to me.

One moment, the assistant said, depressing a button.

An unlabeled frosted glass door next to a second unlabeled frosted glass door opened and Zilka stepped out. The assistant quickly stood up and walked behind Gwee as he approached Zilka's door. Gwee was ushered in. A different assistant shut the frosted glass door behind Zilka and Gwee.

Come in. How are things on the floor?

Fine, Gwee said. Thank you.

What can I do? Zilka loosened his tie and fell into a leather desk chair.

I'm here because of my current situation.

Yes?

Gwee placed the pack of cigarettes, still wrapped in its plastic packaging on the shiny dark wood of the desktop. He placed the plastic lighter next to it. May I call you Sven?

No one calls me Sven.

Gwee paused for a heavy breath. Well, you can call me Gwee.

What else would I call you?

Okay, well—please hear me out.

Okay.

See, I frequently watch TV. And I also watch commercials. This last week a certain commercial has been playing nonstop. It's a "*truth" commercial. Have you ever seen a "*truth" commercial?

No. I've never seen a "*truth" commercial.

Well, in a "*truth" commercial there are a lot of edgy graphic animations and progressive video editing and some mind-entrancing music, and there is a voiceover by a narrator who is cool, but also honest and down-to-earth. Gwee fidgeted with the lighter in his lap. That narrator lays down a riverbed of truth about whatever social issue is really important at the moment for those of us who don't already have a riverbed of truth undergirding us.

I see.

And "*truth" is spelled lowercase and includes an asterisk in front of the word—I think to appeal in a hep way to a younger audience. Gwee leaned in. Anyways, there's this one "*truth" commercial that significantly impacted me. It featured some statistics that really opened me up to question my current situation.

Zilka rocked in his chair. What situation are you referring to?

The fact is, people who don't smoke make 12% more than people who do.

Zilka looked down to straighten his tie.

I'll get to the point here, Gwee said.

Please.

I'm here to give you my pack of cigarettes and my lighter in exchange for only a 10% raise.

Zilka still fiddled with his tie.

I've decided to concede the extra 2%—12% less 2% is 10%. This is just a request, but the request includes a 2% reduction—a compromise as a gesture of goodwill.

Zilka looked up at Gwee quizzically.

I'm also conceding the extra 2% because there probably still might be quite a bit of smoke in my—inside me. In my bronchials.

Zilka gave up on his tie. I see. Gwee, smoking is not really an issue, I mean, here at the factory. We don't mind if you are a quote-unquote smoker. Sure, you can't smoke on the executive floors, and sure, as an aggregate, it—smoking—makes our insurance rates go up slightly, but other than that, there are really no negative consequences, professionally, for you as a smoker, in the big scheme of things.

I understand.

Understand that you're being paid more than fairly with respect to the market zeitgeist. Am I using that word correctly, zeitgeist? In fact, you make more than the fair-market going-rate for what you do.

I don't know what zeitgeist is, said Gwee, but I kind of expected you'd say all that. And I've thought long and hard about this. You need to know that I'm aware that it's in your best interest, as an employer, to pay me less. I read an article this week about lawyers, and a few weeks ago I read an article on economics. These were published in respectable periodicals. So, anyway, if you think about it, the way this is structured, you, as an employer have to get the most work out of us workers for the least amount of money. So, then, it follows that you're going to try to pay me as little as possible.

Zilka scratched his neck. Well, in that case—

—Also, there's something called a job market—

—I know what The Market is, Gwee. But since there are a lot of people with jobs and a lot of employers, we have to offer the going pay rate for all of our workers. This is to compete for the best workers.

Fine. Right. So then, here I am raising my value as a worker. My cigarettes are on the table. Take them. I'm giving them up for a raise. And because I'm giving up smoking I have an advantage over others. Now you can pay me more.

Well then, we can't afford you.

It was apparent in the indirect lighting from the table lamps and the subtle shadows from the brutalist wall sconces that the flushed color of Gwee's face was deepening.

So quitting smoking makes me too expensive to hire? He shifted to a more upright position in the leather chair. So, what? I shouldn't quit?

Not at all, Gwee. Quitting smoking is, on the whole, good for you. You'll probably live longer if you quit. You *should* quit smoking, if that is what you want to do. That's one way you'll earn more money. You'll be able to live longer. Probably.

Fine then, Sven. Gwee reached his hand toward the cigarettes. I was hoping I wouldn't have to do this, but here we go. He focused his stare on Zilka. He picked up the pack and slowly pulled the red band that tore the cellophane across the paper box. Then he opened the top of the box, unfolded the metallic-coated paper wrapper, and pinched out a cigarette. He held the cigarette out at Zilka.

If I don't get a raise, I will smoke this.

Zilka shook his head and folded his hands in his lap. Is this some sort of blackmail situation?

I guess it is, said Gwee. He readied his thumb on the lighter's metal wheel. Now, give me my raise.

Hold on a second. Hold on. I'll tell you what. How about this. If you don't smoke that, I'll reduce your pay.

Gwee stammered.

How would you like that?

But I'm quitting. You're gonna help me by paying me to quit.

Zilka swung around back on his chair and while sitting, rolled on its wheels out to the side past the edge of his desk. He picked up a remote-control wand and pressing on it with his thumb, caused an automated window to open slowly. He got up from his chair and slid a polished-silver side table on wheels over in front of the window and placed his desk fan on top of the side table. He turned the fan's switch to *ON* and directed it so that it was blowing out the window. He walked back behind his desk and took another fan from the credenza. He set it up on the far corner of his desk, pointing it across his desk toward the other fan, which itself was directed toward the open window.

He sat on the edge of the table. Light it.

Are you saying I can't quit?

Zilka rolled open a side drawer and pulled out a thin, silver case and popped it open. What do you think of Nat Shermans? *I* think they're, on the whole, really good. He lit the cigarette with a bronze-filigreed blowtorch and stuck it filter-end into Gwee's mouth. What you don't know is that you actually make more money than anyone else at your level.

Zilka lit a second Nat Sherman and took a drag himself, blowing the smoke from his nose in twin jets.

Gwee took the cigarette out of his mouth.

Now put that back in your mouth and smoke it.

Gwee put the cigarette back in his mouth and with great effort inhaled deeply.

Nice.

Nice.

And Gwee, another thing you don't know is that I juice.

How would I know that?

Zilka folded-up his sleeves to expose his forearms. He opened his desk drawer and took out a mahogany ashtray. After placing his cigarette carefully on its crenelated ledge, he removed a Vitamix from his credenza, set it on his desk, and slid a silver-netted basket of fruit from the edge of his desk. Smoothie?

Gwee paused behind his cigarette.

No? Well, *I'll* have one.

Zilka threw a pear with its stem, three unhulled strawberries, and a whole lime into the blender. He fell into his chair with theatrical force and rolled back away from his desk with his hands reaching toward his credenza. From his personal freezer he removed a plastic package of frozen mangoes and a handful of ice cubes, dropping these into the blender, then pulsing the mixture.

The blender's dissonance mixed with the smoke in the room and Gwee settled uncomfortably into his seat.

I'll have you know, Zilka said into the noise of the blender, we have to let you go.

What?

We must let you go.

What? I can't quite make out what you just said.

You're fired!

I'm sorry, I can't quite hear you clearly.

It's over. You can't work here anymore. Zilka stopped the blender and poured himself a smoothie in a crystal highball glass. Are you sure you don't want one? I have another glass.

He took another drag of his Nat Sherman.

I'll say it again. You're fired.

What? Why?

Workers may not smoke in the building. You should have quit when you had the chance.

You made me smoke. You're smoking. What?

Did I call this meeting? Did I walk you up here to my office and set you down here in front of me clutching a cigarette and a lighter? Did I play your lungs like an accordion to get that smoke into them?

No.

Zilka threw back his glass and gave himself a fruit mustache, which he wiped with a pink silk handkerchief from the back pocket of his trousers. But don't worry, I will quit with you, in solidarity.

Gwee stood up and took a swing at Zilka from across the desk, punching him in the jaw.

Zilka hit his intercom button. Security, he called out, grabbing hold of Gwee to wrestle him to the ground on the far end of the desk. You'll have to wait for me to quit, Zilka said in a halting voice, stilted by the jostling. In two weeks, my 401(k) will be vested. At that point, I'll quit. And I'll make a big show of it.

Gwee was pinned.

Maybe we could take our story to a journalist, or we could jointly write a book about our unjust treatment?

What are you talking about? Gwee said, pushing away Zilka's arm so he could get another shot at his face.

Or, you know what? I have a better idea. Let's take it to the "*truth" people. We'll be one more horrific story in their horrendous case against big tobacco. Because we're helpless. We couldn't even quit if we wanted to. Our story, presented as fact, will make everyone want to quit. Maybe we could even get a movie deal?

Gwee hit Zilka in the ear and threw him off.

Guards flung open the door and took hold of Gwee Zed. They dragged him out of the office and down the marble-floored hallway toward a bronze elevator.

Zilka closed his door, rubbed the side of his head, and dropped into his chair. He took up a silver-plated pen and some crème-colored paper to draft his resignation, but he couldn't. He had no such 401(k). And the more he thought about it, the more he understood that he had done Gwee Zed a favor.

J.A. Sinclitico

The Eulogy

When he thought about Grace, all he could remember was her coffin. It was miniaturized, of course. Maybe four feet head to toe. His wife, Merriam, picked it out. She asked him what he thought, wanted to show him pictures on Amazon but he couldn't look. So Merriam picked it.

It was an "art" casket, made of eighteen-gauge steel with an inner bed that Merriam called a half couch. Pink crepe interior, zinc handles, cost $4995. Merriam said all this to him wanting his input. That's what she said, "I want your input."

"Sure," he said, "Sounds good."

But she didn't tell him about Monet. The outside of his daughter's coffin was covered, tattooed, with Monet's Water Lilies. "A perfect solution for the individual who has left a beautiful Impression on you," is what the warranty card said. The rendering of Water Lilies [workmanship and materials] was guaranteed for life the card said. The warranty card was dangling from one of the zinc handles when UPS delivered the coffin to the house. Now when he thought of their daughter four years old and a year dead, he thought of Water Lilies. And the warranty card.

He didn't blame Merriam for the Monet coffin. It was actually rather typical. Merriam was an off-key person. She was like the child in the first row of the fourth grade choir, the one who sings the loudest, can't hear the other singers and can't be made to tone down her out of sync warbling with diplomatic suggestion. This child believes that the choir's sweet sound is her sound, its voice her voice.

Merriam was a lawyer—a litigator. This meant that she rarely went to trial. Instead she spent her days bedeviling her opponents with interrogatories, depositions and requests for production of documents. She dealt with her opponent's tit-for-tat with ferocity and 80-hour weeks. When asked about what she did Merriam sometimes said, "I'm in the snack business. I pick the peanuts out of the elephant shit."

Her clients were polluters, insurance companies and real estate developers who wanted to continue to poison, cheat and blight for as long as possible. They lusted for the status quo. Merriam was the champion of the now. The past was definitely an inconvenience-but in her crafty hands a malleable, manageable inconvenience.

Merriam told the same stories to the same people. She knew five jokes. She told everyone she knew, everyone he knew these jokes. Several times. He asked her to stop telling the jokes to the other psychologists from his clinic but she just changed the joke about three chimps and a rabbi in a bar to one about three gorillas and explained, "The chimps grew up."

Merriam felt that good story telling was like playing a violin. Playing the same pieces time after time, over and over again was a means to proficiency, to mastery, and everyone always laughed so why not? She was the same way with Grace. She bought 4 copies each of seven outfits. She rotated the outfits according to a plan she kept in the calendar section of her phone. If you came to their house on the 6th, 12th, 18th, 24th, and the 30th of any month you would see Grace in a red jumper, French blue blouse with white swans, pink ruffled socks and infant Nike's with blinking lights on the heels.

Obsessive-Compulsive Personality Disorder, category 301.4 of the Diagnostic and Statistical Manual of Mental Disorders (DSM)—if the DSM had pictures, Merriam's face would be on Pg. 725 with her Frida Kahlo unibrow bunched like a large caterpillar struck by a drop of gasoline. "[A] preoccupation with orderliness, perfectionism and mental and interpersonal control..." is how the description of the disease begins in the DSM. What follows is a description, in bland, of their married life. Preoccupation with lists, details, rules and on and on. He had it all memorized, categorized and attached to vignettes of their twenty year marriage. The family escutcheon was a yellow field of Post Its.

In college, when he met Merriam, she seemed efficient and organized rather than compelled. He like this about her. His own family were drunks. When his father died in a single car accident, running his Altima into a gray freeway abutment, he thought the bedlam was over. But his mother seemed to catch his father's disease from the germs of her grief.

He was 12 when his father was killed. His mother never drew a sober evening breath from then on. She was an emotional whirl-a-gig when drunk. She extracted pledges of love with the pliers of her widowhood. "I'm trash. Since your father died I'm trash," she'd whine.

"You hate me. You must," she'd continue until he gave the programmed response.

"No you're not. I love you Mom," were his lines.

"Are you sure?"

"Yes. Mom," his reply.

Then the inevitable promise of reform and golden days to follow, "I love you so. You'll see...I'll be good," she'd say.

But in the morning with an eye-bleed, tongue-lolling hangover she'd say, "I think I've got to get better to die," and last night's sodden love fest was forgotten.

Merriam never forgot. She always kept her promises. If she said, "I'll be at the clinic to pick you up at 8," she was there—at 8 not 7:59 not 8:01. He believed her timeliness and reliability were signs of love until they became obsession.

Merriam treated his infrequent rebellions of spontaneity and mess as clowns' noses. He bought a motorcycle. She called the incident a force majeure – a legal term for some unknown, unpredictable, catastrophic event like a tornado or a terrorist attack that required planning for, "drafting to" is how she put it. Something that needed to be included in the contract of their life for the sake of completeness. She didn't seem to worry that howling down the freeway at 75 miles an hour might put him in one of the cemetery plots Merriam had purchased for the three of them at Long Horizons a few months after Grace was born. By buying the "Millennium Pre-Need Package" she had, or so he screamed at her on one bad drunk night, drafted to death.

Grace loved her mother. She and Merriam played blocks every night. The blocks were discovery blocks with small, red animals nested inside their clear plastic sides. After a few months of observing his wife and daughter's ritual, he became convinced that Grace played blocks not because she liked the game but because she thought Merriam liked blocks. When Merriam said, as she did every night, "A 'G'. What lives in G?" Grace would clap her hands and say "Goose. The goose, the goose lives in G."

His own play with Grace was only play, not disguised learning. He told her stories using a brown and white sock monkey with a red heel grin as a prop. They also played the story game. He'd begin, "Once upon a time there was a lovely, smart and fierce warrior princess whose name was Merriam. She worked very hard to rule the realm of Tulip. All of her subjects adored her and her gorgeous daughter Princess Grace. Then one day and evil prince came riding into the Tulip town square on a red elephant. The evil prince shouted at Queen Merriam's throne room window..."

Grace supplied the evil prince's demand or changed the story by saying on behalf of the prince, "Help me! I'm a bear in a prince body."

Grace's favorite twist was to insert an animal in the story—a bear or a gorilla or a duck and call it Daddy. He would kiss her hand and say, "Sweetheart, your animal needs a real name like Bob or Tom or Harold." Reluctantly she would change the name but only after she kissed his hand as an apology for writing him out of the story.

****

Gwen Boite, the box, Grace's nanny. He should have known. Gwen was 20. She had rust hair and acne. She was English. One of the reasons that Merriam was so fond of Gwen was Gwen's blind support. Gwen never questioned. Never smirked or rolled her eyes. Never complained. She just opened the carefully labeled [#6] drawer and took out one of the red jumpers, French blue blouses etc. and put the clothes on Grace. The tossel. The tossel of Grace's corn silk hair appeared first. Then her eyes with a hint of a squint. Then her mouth. Grace had her mother's only carnal feature. A full pout lower lip. It was the last thing that appeared on the 6th, the 12th, the 18th, the 24th and the 30th as the French blue blouse was tugged over her head.

Gwen followed Merriam's clothes plan without deviation. When Merriam came home from work Grace was always wearing the expected outfit. Always, without fail. So Merriam assumed that Gwen was also unwavering in her dedication to the activity agenda that Merriam created each week for Grace. Merriam used an Excel spread sheet program, printed out the week's plan and taped it to the refrigerator, Gwen's bedroom door and the horn of the SUV.

Wednesdays' at three Grace should always be at Tune Your Tyke playing with the other children and receiving instruction in physical culture. Physical culture not P.E. which was a blue-collar notion—a time of embarrassment and self-consciousness for low class girls whose bodies were sub-standard. Grace and her little girl friends would never face this humiliation. Not if Merriam had anything to say about it and she had everything to say about it. Grace had play dates, Baby Einstein consulting, youth massage and Musicale and physical culture not P.E. All under the aegis of experts. All at specific times. The child picked up and delivered like just-in-time raw materials in a well run manufacturing plant. Developmental activities, then private schools and head start for rich kids camps—all part of a plan, a program. Gwen's job was the program. Except that Gwen thought she should have "an ever so small" life separate from Grace and Merriam's regime for the girl.

So on Wednesdays when Gwen should have been sitting in the multicolored, dolphin wall appliquéd, well magazined waiting room of Tune Your Tyke, Gwen was in Starbucks at the other end of the mall, talking to the boy who took the orders for grandes, and fat ass soon mochas and lattes with cinnamon.

No one was quite sure how it happened. It was just, his therapist, colleague and officious asshole friend, said, "a confluence of outrageous bad luck and weird circumstance."

Tune Your Tyke was right next to the main entrance to the mall. The doors opened and shut electronically. Grace weighed 1½ lbs. more than the 26 lbs. necessary to trigger the "door open" feature. Apparently Grace walked out of Tune Your Tyke, out these doors, onto the exit lane of the parking lot and into the path of the black Mercedes

Martha Welt, the driver of the Mercedes S500, was slowed in her reactions because of the 2 margaritas and 4 glasses of pinot noir she had consumed at lunch while listening to her friend discuss her next day hysterectomy. The paramedics got to the mall pavement a few minutes late because of the Fiesta del Sol parade and the "Long in the Tooth Longboard" drill team's confusion about which way to turn at the corner of 6th and Lomas. And alignment of the stars and the phases of the moon and karma and on and on, the details and bullshit were endless but Grace was dead. Murdered by a drunk driver because her nanny was flirting with a zitdripped moron. Huge sopping pimples. "Grace dead," he keened.

****

He tried to recreate the exact sequence of events, to make a coherent story out of the dreck of bits and pieces. He always believed that there was an order to the collage of the world—cause and effect. Shrinking taught him that order is often disguised by the mentally ill with the cosmetics of fear and desire. Before, he believed that this lip-gloss of irrationality was a distortion, a dent in the psyche of the deranged to be repaired on the couch by mechanics of the mind such as himself. Now, now after Grace he believed that control is an illusion; cause and effect, a delusion hiding the utter randomness of events. Except for one thing. The Box, the nasty careless twat. Gwen.

He seemed OK through all the vicious, vacuous platitudes like "I know how you feel", "call me if you need anything" and even the vomitus "she's an angel now." And through all the babblings. Confronted with the guilty pleasure of other's grief, people babble. But then came his fellow shrinks. When they weren't betraying patient confidences by telling anecdotes of other child deaths and parental griefs, they were telling him what he should do, what he should feel, when it was healthy for him to go back to work and even some half remembered religious dross. " Fuck God" was his standard response. It was effective. They fled.

The other group that was intolerable was Merriam's female law partners. They were aware of the difficulty that Merriam had in conceiving Grace. Infertility wasn't a private thing for Merriam. It was a merely a matter of conscientious application of her analytical and advocacy skills, as if her uterine follicles were a panel of appellate court justices to be briefed then shucked and jived. These women seemed determined to comfort Merriam and him with comments about how it wasn't too late to have another and descriptions of the latest ARTs {assisted reproductive technologies}." Fuck you," was his standard response. It did no good with these women. It even seemed to encourage some of them.

The death festival was over after five or six days. No funeral of course. Too ethnic for Merriam. "A Festival of Life" with the art coffin lid closed, then a private burial with a popular Yoga master presiding. Then nothing but the house.

****

Merriam immediately began to empty and clean Grace's room. It was all gone soon. The toys, the shoes, the bed. She vacuumed. Then she opened the vacuum trap, removed several strands of Grace's gold hair and strung them inside the cover of a worn copy of Goodnight Moon.

After a day or two, all that was left was a room painted eggshell white and the outline of Grace's miniature chest of drawers on the rug. Merriam tried to get these marks out of the rug. She sat there with a sponge and vinegar and wiped and cried.

The thing that finally got Merriam to stop cleaning the rug was the criminal proceedings against Martha Welt, the driver, the killer. The District attorney charged Ms. Welt with negligent homicide because of the drinking. Possible sentences ranged from two years' probation to 6 years in jail.

There was no doubt about the drinking. Welt's blood alcohol level was 1.5, far above the legal limit. The only question was punishment.

Merriam followed every cul-de-sac and nuance of the case against Martha Welt with the intensity of a hunting hawk. She appeared at every hearing. She used her firm's influence and history of lavish campaign donation to encourage the judge to see the case in the correct light and select the high end of the sentencing range.

The report of the probation department was helpful. Ms. Welt, it said, had a "wet reckless"—a prior arrest for drunk driving that had plea bargained down to reckless driving.

The day of the sentencing he knew Martha Welt was going to get the minimum. He knew this the minute he saw Merriam. She was dressed in one of her lawyer costumes—three-piece dark blue gabardine suit, starched white blouse with frilled collar and a black string tie like the ones worn by Wyatt Earp and Doc Holliday in the post-OK Corral photos. She carried a deep blue Paloma Picasso handbag with a gold X clasp and a shiny metal briefcase the color of burnished copper.

The judge was confused when Merriam stood up to make her Victim's Impact Statement. He said, "Counsel who's your client?"

Merriam replied, "I'm my own client, your honor. My daughter was the person that Ms. Welt murdered." This was the tone of her statement. She cited statistics about drunk driver recidivism and about the average sentences for drunk drivers who killed someone. She derided Welt's remorse by citing the woman's statement to the probation officer that Grace was neglected. Welt's lawyer objected, a long, animated side bar conversation followed. Merriam won the argument. She looked pleased. Until the sentencing. Two years probation. Merriam keened. Her ululation could be heard in every courtroom in the court house. The bailiff restrained her. She smashed at the steering wheel all the way home. It broke 3 blocks from home.

****

She drove. She always drove. The anniversary memorial service was Merriam's idea. She said she needed closure. Her friends said she needed closure. He didn't understand closure. A life a baby's life wasn't a cheap novel or a bathroom door—push, turn page, shut, over. He understood wailing. He understood gagging and vomiting until all that was left of your guts was a string of food-spackled drool. He didn't want closure. He wanted Gwen Boite dead. Tortured. He wanted to beat her pig face with the forked end of a claw hammer. He wanted her to scream like a house cat being chewed by a coyote. Merriam wanted closure. He wanted murder. He said nothing. Merriam drove.

When they came to a four-way stop at Mountain and Frost, Merriam gestured, "halt" to a man in a yellow Hummer who arrived at the intersection at about the same time as they did. This man started his lumbering truck despite Merriam's open-handed traffic cop demand to stop. Sometimes when she came to a stop sign, Merriam waved cars through with a flap of her fingers as if she were miming the twitching tail of a caught trout. She controlled traffic. No number of flipped fingers or horn blares made any difference to her. This morning he said, "Please" but it was too late. The Hummer driver stopped in the middle of the intersection and shouted, "Fuck yourself bitch." Merriam blew the horn and made a half armed Italian "fuck you" gesture. For a moment it looked as if the driver was going to open his door and get out but instead he inched out of the intersection.

"Dickhead," Merriam said "On this of all mornings. What an asshole."

He turned his head and touched his forehead on the window and said, "Yes, of all mornings."

Merriam said, "What? What did you say?" He didn't reply. He was exhausted.

He hadn't slept much the night before or much any night for the last year. Hating was a stimulant. He was a helpless, bereft, tweeker of loathing. Finally, most nights he'd give up

They passed the golden minarets of the Self-Realization Fellowship, turned left and parked on the shrub-shaded street. The Self-Realization fellowship was known as Swami's to everyone but its few monks and nuns. Surfers first used the name to locate the world-class break that twined at the bottom of the cliffs. Now everyone including the local politicians and Episcopalians called the bluff top retreat Swami's.

Except for the gardens. As an exercise of religious devotion, the monks created luscious gardens. Despite their purpose as a prompt for ascetic exercise, the gardens were a harem of color. The artificial rill, instead of dripping and lapping promises of synchronicity, was a lewd chuckle. The pond was scum free and filled with enormous, gulping red Koi. Instead of connection to the peace and harmony of natural world, these whip whiskered things suggested gluttony and genetic fracture.

The gardens looked good, elegant, he thought, just as long as you don't look too close. It is an elegant place. The bluffs were inverted with the lip of the garden jutting out over a shear wall of decaying brown sandstone. Over the years the bluff had eroded and the Swami's swimming pool had crumpled so that the boulders at the base of the bluff were mixed with huge blue tiled concrete chunks.

He and Merriam walked up the long patched stone steps, passed the fishpond and arrived at a small clearing at edge of the cliff. They didn't touch. In the near distance, the heirs to the surfing namers of the place rode the sliding sea hanging from black winged kites.

There was a redwood meditation bench parallel to the cliffs. They were a little late. People were milling about. What do we call ourselves, he thought? Celebrants, mourners, closers what? But as soon as they stopped walking Merriam's personal trainer and spiritual guide stepped up on the bench. He wore a white Nehru jacket, loose white hemp pantaloons and a baby blue sash. The eulogy was brief. That's right, he thought, keep it short. She lived so little. Then the speaker recited Frost's poem about the snowy fucking wood and miles to go and everyone it seemed wept but him.

In a moment, all of Merriam's friends put away their Kleenex, lifted their heads and put their sunglasses back on. He had no glasses so he had to shield his eyes from the lancing sunlight. He was blinded for a moment. Then he saw her. Gwen. Next to Merriam. Merriam was holding her hand. The trainer was holding one of Merriam's hand and one of Gwen's. A circle. Merriam said in her courtroom contralto, "I forgive you Gwen. I know you loved her."

He covered the 3 yards between them in two steps and tackled Merriam at the waist. His feet didn't touch the ground. Neither did her's. They sprawled together into the air beyond the edge. Then they separated. Came apart. Before she hit the blue tile boulders, he saw Merriam gesture. She held up her hand like a traffic cop halting a flow.

Gerald J. Butler

She's Dead

She, she is dead; she's dead; when thou know'st this,
Thou know'st how ugly a monster this world is....

Donne, *An Anatomy of the World*

Much is known and can be explained, even more than twenty years ago when on moonless nights the Galaxy made shadows on these hills of California. Light from new houses dims the stars now. But the names and stories of the stars were already lost—the princess in the sky, the giant man, the scorpion with the brilliant ruddy heart. No, if data is what counts, stars convey that best to instruments in outer space resolving suns to atoms of hot gas.

And much can be explained as atoms of hot gas.

On the fourth floor, where felony is arraigned, we join the crowd whose loved ones must appear; we're like some hot gas of atoms all pressing against the courtroom door that opens when it does. Then in the hot gas flows, the prisoners are led in, another crowd of atoms settling now to rest, hands chained before them in that courthouse in that California county where one bright night police shot one young woman thirty-seven times when she woke up in her car. Atoms are made of even smaller things that are themselves composed of vibrating tiny strings that make the universe a perfect symphony, so perfect and so beautiful.

Then does it matter that the harmless insects that used to appear in the vacant lot in spring have disappeared, that small frogs that made their chirping sounds at night are gone, that there was a little pond here once where houses glow now? Does it matter that no one knows that woman's story or her name?

Grace Patricia Kelly, Princess Grace, was another who perished in her car. It rolled off a Riviera cliff. Academy Award for *Country Girl*, she's famous for many films. So *her* name is known—or once was known.

In one of her films she only narrates: a video documentary about how children were discovered then trained for the Leningrad-Maryinski stage, "The Children of Theater Street." Those children would cry *the poor Odette* when the White Swan Princess folded herself in sadness. But they didn't cry from hunger though they lacked calories enough. For their duty was to another world—so claimed Baryshnikov—to a fairy tale land where the love of Siegfried and the White Swan triumphs in the end in spite of whatever Odile can try with all her tricks and thirty-two *fouettés* of self-display. Grace Patricia Kelly, Princess Grace of Monaco, narrator of the film about the nameless, hungry children dancers doesn't say the costume of Odile, rival to the White Swan Princess, was dawn-like, pink and green and gold but never black until they made it black in America.

And one night here in California the terrified police, caught up in fairy tales they believe, killed a woman waking in her car.

The constellation of the Swan was high that summer night when she fell asleep inside the car she'd locked to keep her safe there. Her worried parents called Emergency, police came and thought she had a gun. The hot wind kicks up out of the darkness, raises dust, it gets in the eyes and throat, a wind hard on the nerves, irritating, making it easy to pull a trigger.

The Swan stands for Orpheus, his lyre of stars is by him in the sky. Music is divine, celestial, but the cellist's wrist hurts her from so many repeated movements. Lots of pain since childhood makes an orchestra and that is music, delight that people will pay for and demand. Their houses glow in California darkness. Yes, but here's another death. Early March up Interstate 5 the tops of fruit trees are frost-burned, and the whole Central Valley is in blossom, peach trees and plum trees—*le ballet blanc*, if they were all white. And included in the stories about frost that hurt the citrus industry of California is a *fait divers*, small newspaper item: woman frozen to death in Bakersfield. "From a weekend cold-snap, said authorities, the fifty-one-year-old was found dead in a downtown alley in her sleeping bag."

And so Orpheus, who descended into Hell just to find a woman, is also dead, though Jean Cocteau in his movie version opium-dreamed up a modern Orpheus—one inspired by voices from the radio who lives happily ever after with his wife. For the Princess of Death, eyes filled with tears, violating every law, surrenders him to his Eurydice. No wonder the Muse, old drunkard in a sleeping bag, freezes to death in Bakersfield, and all the stories she ever told us turn bitter and praise nothingness.

Well, here's a palliative. Does it help?

If a will carves a universe from darkness, maybe that will could change, become less terrified and even let the dead come back to us some early winter morning. A spray of sweet alyssum, lavender or pink, leans from its container by the door in January sunshine. So maybe winter isn't always real in California. Seasons follow no calendar of ancient saints. They never walked here or dreamed their holy dreams in such a place as this, where winter means a blue and empty sky, cactus, oaks that never shed their leaves, where this spray of tiny flowers softer than stars can lean in early morning sunlight just like the tutu of a bending dancer, and even dances in the wind without her.

Margaret Hermes

Dust

Tonight I am bringing Rainbow home to meet my parents.

You are trying to imagine what this Rainbow might be. My striped cat maybe. An exotic bird, you congratulate yourself. Something with a pot of gold at its end? I will stop teasing. Rainbow is my girlfriend.

She is not, as you might speculate, a homosexual. Or a child of mixed race. Her parents were, in the words of my mother, both round eyes.

Rainbow is not a nickname. It is the name her parents gave her—cursed her with, she says—ten days after she was born. I told her that a delay of ten days is nothing to the Vietnamese. Some parents wait as long as ten years before conferring a name upon their child. Namelessness is a protection. It makes it harder for evil spirits to find the child.

Her parents had been waiting for inspiration. They got it when their colicky newborn finally took to the breast. The storm of those first days of parenthood was over—the rain of tears had ended, emotional skies cleared, all the colors of joy arced before them, and so on. I am paraphrasing Rainbow's mother, the only hippie I have ever known.

I could not add Rainbow's father to my list of hippies as I have never met him and am not likely to. He drifted out of their lives when Rainbow was six years old. She claims she has no memories of him and, while I cannot dispute this, I cannot believe it.

"Why don't you change your name?" I asked her, being no stranger to name changes myself.

"You think I haven't?"

When she was seven she told everyone her name was Barbie. At twelve she answered only to Kate. "But those were other people's names—well, another person's and a doll's—anyway they didn't belong to me." In college she went by her last name: McAuley. But she said that came to feel like a statement of its own. "I don't know if I just gave up or I matured, but McAuley is back to being my last name and only my last name and I'm answering to the ridiculous

Rainbow again."

"Why don't you use your middle name?" I asked. Everyone born in this country has a middle name.

"Brilliant!" she said, "Why didn't I think of that?" She smacked her forehead and then smiled insincerely. "My middle name is Bliss."

Rather than two impossible names preceding my last name, I have one very serviceable name twice. And even the way my last name, Le, is pronounced could pass for a first name in this country. As a surname, Le is the Smith of Vietnam, the Park of Korea, more common than rice at an Asian table.

My two American names are both Daniel. Our sponsor to come to the United States was a Lutheran church here in St. Louis. So when my parents had to choose an American name for me, they selected a saint's name to honor the religion that had proved to be our salvation, at least here on earth. My father announced that my saint would be the prophet Daniel and I would be called Dan in the American tradition. He did not mention to our Lutheran brethren that Danh is also a boy's name in Vietnamese. Like all Vietnamese names, it has a meaning. The qualities of Danh are fame and prestige. So every time they said my American name, my parents would also be invoking the traditions of another land to bring me honor. "Double dipping" my father titled it with delight when the expression was explained to him. My mother liked the story of Daniel in the lion's den. She felt that if the American god were too busy to intercede on my behalf, he had shown he would send an angel to protect a Daniel in times of trouble. In any language this was a good strong name.

But at home my parents call me Hien which means kind and gentle. This was the name that accompanied me from Vietnam.

When I told my parents I was bringing a girl named Rainbow home to meet them, they weren't at all put off by her name. They are more apt to be dismayed by typical American names. "What is the point of a name that has no meaning?" my father would shrug. My mother would just cluck her tongue.

She seldom speaks her disapproval. But that tongue loudly taps her exasperation against the roof of her mouth. My mother does not believe in wasting breath. She thinks we each have a specific number of inhalations allotted to us and she doesn't often use hers up in scolding or complaining. Besides, she knows it is more effective if the listener imagines her chastisement while she clucks away. Then she is not just releasing words into the air, they are growing, expanding in his—usually in my—head.

Rainbow was taken with this image of my clucking mother. Her own mother never conserves words. I have been in the company of Janelle McAuley on several occasions and have not yet found a subject on which she doesn't have plenty to say.

"Did I tell you there's an FBI file on me?" was Janelle's announcement, unrelated to anything that preceded it, as she handed me a bottle of beer. "From my days as a draft evasion counselor and demonstrations and stuff. I was very much against the war in Vietnam," she says, pausing for my approval, perhaps for my gratitude, failing to appreciate that my father was a soldier whose family in the South came to regard her kind as the enemy as much as they had the Viet Cong. "I even met Jane Fonda when she came to St. Louis to speak. Well, sort of. She was staying at my friend Ellen's house and we had this fabulous potluck—everybody went all out—but Jane was up in the bathroom putting on makeup until it was time to go, so she never did eat with us."

I know if I don't interrupt she will go on to describe the movies that Jane Fonda appeared in. And the people she saw those movies with. And another tangent, and another, on into infinity. So I ask if she has read Rainbow's dissertation, knowing that she hasn't and thinking this will stem the flow. But instead she starts talking about her first lover who wore his lucky underpants the whole time he was writing his dissertation. Wore them on his head like a turban to keep his long hair from falling into his face as he sat before his typewriter.

That is the way Janelle talks. She does not make conversation but rather a light, jangly noise, like wind chimes in an inconsequential breeze.

It is no wonder Rainbow looks forward to meeting my quiet, clucking mother.

She will be the first round eyes I have brought home. Oh, there were a few stray boys who ventured into the front room of our South St. Louis bungalow, but never any girls.

When it comes to coupling, only Vietnamese girls—I say "girls" because my parents regard all unwed females as girls—are eligible for consideration. Not girls of Asian origin—my people are not racists—but exclusively Vietnamese. And if we were back in Vietnam my prospects would still be restricted. I was born in the Year of the Tiger. Of the twelve lunar years, there are many with which I am incompatible. For example, for me to marry a woman born in the Year of the Horse is unthinkable in Vietnam where the first question asked of a prospective bride and her family would be the year of her birth. Here I think my parents would prefer not to know so as not to have to rule out any of the limited Vietnamese prospects.

My parents know that Rainbow is Caucasian, but I have emphasized to all three the things they have in common. Rainbow grew up eating only with chopsticks. Her mother believes that metal should never be placed inside the human mouth. Janelle follows a macrobiotic diet, so I assume that metal is considered too yin or too yang. My mother was very surprised to learn of a round eyes who ate without a fork. "Is this Rainbow very thin?" she asked, thinking of the Americans who amuse her with their fumblings when we go to Pho Grand or Lemongrass or Mekong or one of the other Vietnamese restaurants on South Grand. "She is proficient with chopsticks and she loves me," I tell my mother. "What more can you ask?" I can see my mother thinking that perhaps this girl's mother will be an ally of sorts. If she permits only chopsticks, perhaps she too has definite ideas about whom her child should marry.

Janelle repeatedly asks me to invite my parents to her house for dinner, but I hope to keep these mothers apart for as long as possible. Chopsticks aside, their differences would be most obvious at mealtime. At home my mother doesn't eat when we eat. She serves my father and me and then hovers in case we forget and get too boisterous. She then cautions us to calm ourselves, to speak sparingly, and to move about as little as possible. Agitation stirs up dust and then the dust settles on the food and is ingested. This is to be avoided. I can only imagine what conclusions my mother would draw from Janelle's sweeping gestures and nonstop chatter. She would probably deduce that Rainbow is filled with dust.

When I was growing up, my parents didn't object to my best friend being a Caucasian. They wanted me to be successful in this new life that had cost them so much. I think they even liked him, found him funny. His name also was Dan and he attended the same Lutheran church and lived just two blocks away. When it came time for me to take a confirmation name, I chose the name of my best friend. So I became Daniel Daniel Le. Or Dan Dan as my friends teasingly called me. I remember that he tried to choose the name Hien as his confirmation name, but his parents vetoed it.

Besides Dan, my other close friend from childhood is Kim who is one year older. Also the child of boat people, she is the only one of her siblings to be born in Vietnam. Her father talks about their experiences—the pirates they survived on the South China Sea, wading ashore on the coast of Malaysia carrying his sick wife and his sick daughter both, the three different refugee camps, the first year in St. Louis. My parents do not enter those conversations.

Kim's name at home is Qui which means sacred turtle, but elsewhere she is called by a sturdy American name that too has its counterpart in Vietnamese. Kim means golden, and golden she is. By the standards of both cultures, my friend is beautiful and very smart. I can easily imagine her in someone's arms, but sadly not in mine.

Both families have made known their hopes that we would marry. And we are sorry to disappoint them.

Kim has entered into her fourth official betrothal. Official as far as the man is concerned. But unheard of by her parents. At some point in each engagement, she initiates an argument out of all proportion to the trifle that seemingly provoked it. She breaks off the engagement with her bewildered fiancé, spends a month or so in mourning, then eases her heartache with a new romance. Typically the end is precipitated by his unwitting suggestion that he begin to get to know her family. This, of course, will never happen. Turtle will never take one of these hapless, tanned young men home, influenced neither by the size of their income or the size of her feelings for them.

She has managed this sleight of hand by rising to a level of management in a large company that demands considerable travel. Kim simply tells everyone except her employers and me that her business trips last longer than they really do. So she stays with her parents while her fiancés think she is negotiating in China and she stays with her fiancés when her parents think she is at meetings in Los Angeles. And in St. Louis it is surprisingly easy to keep her two worlds from overlapping.

Kim is torn between envy and disapproval of my plan to bring my two worlds crashing together tonight. She says to do this to my parents is unpardonable. And I tell her that many would say that what she does to the men she promises to marry is unpardonable. She says the difference is that they will recover.

Dan has gone to a microbrewery and to a Cardinals' game with Rainbow and me. He approves my choice wholeheartedly. Thus far, Kim has neatly avoided meeting Rainbow, claiming travel as her transparent excuse.

To tell the truth, I was of two minds about taking this step. Part of me thought that Rainbow and I could drift indefinitely, pleasing each other, upsetting no one. Marriage seems to be less necessary in this culture in this new century. Certainly Rainbow was not pressing me to make our union legal or even to reveal it to my parents.

The visit from my Auntie Nhung ended my indecision. Auntie is my mother's younger sister. They had not seen each other since Auntie Nhung stood on a dock in Vietnam waving goodbye as we huddled in a packed wooden boat. Auntie had wanted to flee with my parents but there was not room for one more body on the crowded boat. That much I had been told, but my parents never spoke of the anguished moment of separation. And now, after twenty-nine years, they would have their reunion.

Auntie Nhung had never left Vietnam. Some hard years followed for her but, as she pointed out, some hard years must have followed for my parents too—first came our long voyage, then the refugee camp, and then a new language, a new culture, new kinds of mistreatment in the U.S. In Vietnam things improved politically and economically. "Slow. It was slow. And not an economy like you have here," she conceded. "But while I had the pain of missing all of you, I did not have the pain of missing my country." When Auntie said this, my mother cried and my father followed her out of the room.

This seemed like a good time to take Auntie Nhung, whose name means velvet, for a walk to acquaint her with the neighborhood. I had expected my aunt to be like my mother, only more provincial. Instead, she was like my mother, only more worldly. She enjoyed looking into the shops along South Grand. She said they were not as intimidating as she expected American stores to be and she was amused that all the nail salons appeared to be staffed by Vietnamese women. "Perhaps I was sleeping on the airplane when the class in applying nail polish was taught," she said.

We walked into Tower Grove Park and sat on a bench where we could admire one of the intricately painted pavilions. After a few minutes I said, "Auntie, I could not help noticing you were upset when my mother said, 'Look at the fine man Hien has grown into. He is his father's son.'"

Auntie Nhung frowned and turned her face away.

"I am sorry if I am troubling you, but I feel there is something everyone avoids telling me. Something no one will ever tell me unless you do. Is it about my father and the war?" I was afraid to learn that he had done something terrible, or many terrible things, but if I knew then at least my fear of knowing would be gone.

Auntie Nhung shook her head and held her face away from me. "Please, Auntie Nhung," I said. When she turned back to me, I could see she was crying.

"I am sorry," I said again.

"It is a day for tears," she said, shaking her head gently. "It is a day for remembering." She lifted my hand from the bench and took it between her own small ones. "You are not Hien," she said softly. "Hien was your twin brother."

I stared at this woman, this stranger speaking these preposterous words in an alien tongue. I tried to withdraw my hand but she would not release me.

"It was the hardest day," she said. "The other hard days did not compare. We had been walking all night to reach the coast. Your father carried the bundle of our most prized belongings. Your mother held you and I had Hien in my arms. When we came to the sea, there were too many people and only two boats. One of the boats was already so full that people were hanging onto the sides from the water. Others in the boat were pleading with them to let go for fear the boat would sink. How foolish we had been to carry our precious bundle with us when there was no room even for people.

"Your father pushed his way onto the second boat and then ordered your mother to throw you to him. At first I didn't think that she would do this. She held you tighter, but your father yelled again. She did as he said. He caught you and then screamed at her to jump. This time she did not hesitate, even though the boat had begun to move away. She jumped right on top of other people in the boat. I was afraid they would push her out, but they didn't.

"Then your father shouted at me to hurry and throw Hien. I threw him as far as I could. Your father reached as far as he could. So many arms in that boat reached out for Hien, but he sank like a stone. We all stared at the place in the water. Your parents from the boat. Me from the dock. Your father could not leave your mother and you – the boat would not wait for him. And I could not swim. A man from the dock dove into the seaweed, but he came up with empty hands. I could hear a wailing, but I cannot say if it was your mother's voice or mine. There was nothing to do but look at that place in the water as the distance between us grew."

I was crying then. But not because I had lost my twin on the same day I found him. And not because I had lost the kind and gentle Hien part of myself. But because I began to understand my parents. Auntie Nhung was right: it was a day for tears.

I didn't tell my mother or my father that I finally learned the story of our flight, the unspeakable story of their loss. And I am sure Auntie Nhung did not mention our talk. Yet somehow they know I know, and still we will never speak of it.

The day Auntie Nhung left, I drove her to the airport. My parents had made their goodbyes at our front door, promising to consider a trip to Vietnam for their next reunion. A promise politely urged and politely made. None of the parties expect it to be fulfilled.

At the airport Auntie Nhung hugged me and said my parents were very clever, protecting me as they did by calling me by the name of my dead brother. That had surely thwarted any evil spirit seeking me.

It was not until Auntie was well beyond the security gates that I realized that in all the weeks of her visit I had never asked what my real name was. I felt a moment of sheer panic. Who was I? I couldn't ask my parents. I would never know!

But then I saw that any name will do. My best friend Dan's grandfather liked to say when introduced, "Call me anything you like, only don't call me late for dinner." We would roll our eyes, but there was something to what he said. It's not what a person is called, but how. It is the feeling that goes into the speaking of the name—not the pronunciation or even the meaning. It is my respect for Rainbow that makes her name respectable to my ears. It is how Rainbow makes me feel when she speaks my name. It is how tenderly my parents say Hien.

Kendall Klym

Come Dance with Me

Winter 1919
Grace accepts the job, says goodbye to her family, and sets sail on the Leviathan, bound for war-torn Turkey. On her first day at sea she starts a diary, in which she makes a vow to uphold her duties as a nurse for the American Committee for Relief in the Near East. For two years Grace has thwarted the affections of a surgeon attempting to shame her into a romance, claiming she would turn into an old maid, if she didn't settle soon. I will not be forced into something I do not want, Grace has said to the doctor many a time. She dips pen into ink. The health and welfare of the Armenians in Turkey come first. If anyone ever gets his hands on this diary, let it be known that I am taking this position to help the unfortunate, not to find a husband. Grace is 25, the surgeon, 42.

The exclamation point in the sentence fragment Learning to speak Turkish! contains a smudge caused by the movement of Grace's right hand, as the Leviathan pulls to starboard, somewhere in the Sargasso Sea. Her second diary entry is short, written in weak and wavy print, for Grace has discovered an innate inclination for seasickness: I have fully decided never to take an ocean voyage just for pleasure, and to advise all family and friends to see America first. Grace falls in and out of consciousness as the ship makes its way through precipitous swells and troughs. Dr. Bellson, easy to spot with his thick black handlebar mustache, cares for Grace. When the sea and her stomach return to a state of tranquility, Grace waltzes with Dr. Bellson during one of the ship's dances. If ever I need an appendectomy, I trust the hands of Dr. Bellson, writes Grace in the margins of her diary. He moves me across the crowded dance floor as if he were slicing into flesh, cognizant of every layer of skin he penetrates, every organ he avoids.

Fall 2014
Peter breaks up with Stephen, gets a checkup, and starts a diary. In the first entry, he makes a vow: I decide how I spend my free time. Nobody else. He signs the first letter of his first name in HIV negative blood and the rest in red ink. A professional actor, Stephen had called Peter boring in bed, just before the two broke up. I need a change of pace, writes Peter, before closing his diary and locking it in the secret drawer of his desk. Scrolling though the apps on his phone, he finds a meetup with the following description: Travel the world without leaving town. Learn folk dances from six continents. Sounds possible, says Peter, who loved to dance around the house when he was little. Unlike his father, a retired war correspondent for a major newspaper, Peter has no intention of ever leaving the country. Last month he turned 42. Stephen is 39. Both are in excellent shape.

The first *d* in the phrase *I did it!* contains a smudge caused by the sweat of Peter's brow, deposited in his diary during a break at the International Folk Dancers weekly meetup. His handwriting is a bit wavy, the steps of the last dance still reverberating through his body. Judging by looks, I'm the youngest one in the group. We dance in a big room in the basement of the Unitarian Church. A heavy-set man with thin white suspenders taught the steps of an Armenian dance called the Kochari. We stand in a line interlinking pinkies. Then we swivel and jump and tip our bodies forward. The dance makes me feel different, like I'm learning to be someone else, but that person is also me. The teacher says the Kochari was designed to imitate the movement of sparring rams. Peter switches from printing to cursive, red pen digging deeply into the beige lined page, as he imagines Stephen's disapproval of what he writes. Nobody remotely attractive. Don't care. Last thing I need is sex. No condoms, no worries. Now I have dance.

Winter 1972
Grace is finally well enough to spend time with the baby, her grandchild. He's very particular, warns Susan, Grace's daughter. In an attempt to bounce Peter very lightly on her knee, Grace experiences the shrillness of the baby's screams. At 78, her hearing is still in fine condition. Doctor's report? asks Grace. Clean bill of health, says Susan. Grace stands up, still holding the crying baby. Let me try something, she says. Twisting with a slight bow, Grace imitates the movement of an Armenian mother trying to calm her baby during a siege of gunshot during a long-forgotten war. We're dancing, she sings. Yes, we're dancing. Peter stops crying and grabs his grandmother's pinkie.

Spring 1919
Grace and her colleagues arrive in Smyrna, Turkey. They move into abandoned boxcars in the freight yard, where they will remain until they can find a suitable home. Grace marvels at the stony landscape with hills and gorges. A native gave us large bunches of lilacs. A pious Turk orders that a place be made on his tomb to catch water for birds. I saw a woman feeding an infant by first masticating the food and then putting it in the baby's mouth. There were donkeys leading camel chains. Men ride while women walk. These people need education, Christianity, and health centers with district nursing. I know I am here for a purpose.

Winter 2014
Peter becomes a regular at the International Folk Dancers' weekly meetups. For the first half hour, a volunteer teaches new dances, and after that, the group moves from dance to dance without instruction. Peter works hard to commit some of the dances to memory. In addition to taking notes during class, he takes great care to record his impressions in his diary. I couldn't believe it. Joe—got to be at least sixty and a fantastic dancer—gave me a red handkerchief this evening. This means I was given the privilege of leading the Halay, Turkey's national dance. I love waving the hanky, stepping and bouncing, listening to the zurnas—so reedy, the music tickles a part of me I never knew existed. (Can just imagine the cracks Stephen would make, if he saw this entry.) Fran, Joe's wife, says I'm a natural folk dancer. Feel like I'm somewhere in Turkey—desert, rocks, camels. Dancing almost makes me want to go abroad.

Spring 1993
A 60-year-old American journalist is killed during heavy gunfire between Muslim-led forces and Bosnian Croat soldiers in the city of Mostar. When the news comes across the TV, the journalist is not identified. Peter thinks his father is dead, until a phone call proves him wrong. Waiting with his mother at the airport, he runs his fingers across the embossed 21 on the birthday card his father had sent him from Europe. At the celebration dinner for his father's return, Peter orders a glass of wine, showing his identification to the waitress before she has a chance to ask. When the drink arrives, he hands it to his father, who asks him why he ordered it, if he didn't want it. Just to see what it feels like to be 21, he says. You know I don't drink. Sometimes I wish you would, says his mother. Then you might learn to socialize, that is, with people your own age. Peter's father praises his son for his individuality. His mother tells him that individuals sometimes end up alone. Peter's best friend

is a 65-year-old woman, a docent at a local historic house open to the public during the warmer months. When they get together, they talk about antiques.

Spring 1919
I prepared breakfast for our family of 14 and made hot biscuits. Then to the warehouse to help unload supplies. One of our hamals, a laborer trained from childhood to carry heavy loads on his back, tore the skin off his finger today, and to my surprise, he powdered it all over with tobacco from a cigarette and tied it up with a black rag. This to him was much better treatment than we would have given him.

We borrowed the Victrola and had a little dance this evening. Dr. Bellson was in rare form. During the waltz, he counted one-two-three in English, Turkish, and Armenian. I started laughing as he spoke Armenian. When he uttered the word for *two*, his moustache bunched below his nose in such an odd yet adorable fashion that I couldn't help myself. Dr. Bellson is only 30.

Winter 2014
Read on the Internet about how the Turks oppressed and then annihilated the Armenians back in the early 1900s. Couldn't fall asleep. Thought about dancing the Turkish Halay. Joe's description of how to perform the steps made my arm hair stand on end. Give a little kick in the direction you're going, then a little kick in the direction you came from. Makes me think of an army invasion, death and destruction. Trying not to think negatively about Turks.

Zoned out at work. Imagined I was dodging Turkish shrapnel. Strange thought: I wonder if folk dancing can keep people from warring. Act out frustrations through dance and avoid violence. Read somewhere that the Army prohibits soldiers from getting close to the culture of the people they're fighting. Went to dinner with Joe and Fran. He asked if I had a girlfriend, and she told him to mind his own business. Told them I'm gay. Seemed to go over well. Got a text from Stephen. Can't find his leather harness and wanted to know if I'd seen it. I said no.

Fall 1990
Two days after Peter's eighteenth birthday, his father accompanies him to the post office. Peter drives. On the way, Peter confesses that he hasn't the capacity to kill another human. His father says every American has the right to make such a decision. At the post office, Peter registers with Selective Service.

On his way out, he looks into his father's hazel-green eyes and asks him if he would miss his job, if, suddenly, all wars ceased to exist. His father says no, definitely not. On the way home, Peter's father asks him if he's sexually attracted to other young men. Peter stops the car on the side of the road. He says he's attracted to no one; he will never get AIDS, nor will he get a woman pregnant. His father assures him that he and his mother would support having a gay son. Peter says nothing.

Spring 1919
News came at noon that Smyrna was given to the Greeks. So now we are living in Greece! What rejoicing among the Greeks and what heartaches among the Turks and Armenians. At 1 p.m. word came that Dr. Bellson had taken over the whole Turkish hospital and wished me to come up. As we drove along, the people all cheered us, shouting, Americano. As our carriage came in view, both Greeks and Turks who were still shooting at each other across the street, held their fire to let us pass, and then resumed their shooting. Armenians who had worn the Turkish fez for protection against discrimination were now going bare-headed.

A ship loaded with Armenian refugees stopped here today for six hours, and oh, the suffering I saw made me thank God for my blessings. Most of the people were in utter rags and so very dirty. Several of the girls had branded faces, done by the Arabs, and, in some cases, the marks were not yet healed. And the characteristic Arab indelible ink mark was to be found on many. Most of these women had husbands at one time, but the Turks had taken and killed them. Things are very tense and peace is to be signed in Paris tomorrow. What is to become of Smyrna no one knows.

Winter 2014
Received a text from Joe. Told me folk dancing is canceled tonight. Unitarian Church on same street as a fundamentalist Christian church. Christians planning a protest against proposed mosque a block away. Fundamentalists going to burn a page from the Koran on church grounds. Got a leaf-burning permit—means they can start fires with paper. Wish religions didn't exist. Text from Stephen. Invited me to a protest against the church and mosque. Texted Stephen and Joe with same message: got a stomachache, staying in.

Don't know what's going on, but can hear gunshot, sirens, people shouting. Wish this room were soundproof. Vacuuming to drown out the noise. Stomach's gotten worse. Can't eat. Going to bed. Heard a huge bang and then felt like throwing up. Tried to but couldn't. Dry heaves. Just need to get through the night. Wish Stephen were here. Too busy dressing up in macho gay attire to worry about me. As if protesting in a leather harness is going to accomplish something amongst the fundamentalists and Muslims.

Winter 1973
At 79, Grace dies at home, a few hours after having an argument with her only daughter. Grace leaves her house to Susan and an annuity to Peter, to cover his college tuition. When her mother's house sells, Susan finds Grace's diary, chronicling her time in Turkey. Susan throws the diary in the trash, but then picks it up and puts it in a box, which ends up in her attic. Her husband finds the russet-colored volume with gold-leaf pages and places it on a bookshelf. No one reads the diary, and Susan eventually forgets about it.

Spring 1919
We had a very bad case today. At 5 a.m., the night watchman woke me up to say there was a man at the back gate who needed help immediately. He was a Turk, the watchman said, but the Turks wouldn't take him in. I dressed quickly and sent the watchman to awaken Dr. Bellson. When I approached the man, he was holding his face in his hands. It had been partly torn off by a jackal, according to the watchman. With each hand, the man was holding a cheek in its rightful place. Blood was streaming down below his fingers. With everyone working together, we prepared him for the operation in less than 10 minutes. The man is comfortable in bed now. His face is swathed in bandages with two catheters sticking up like tiny periscopes so he can breathe. Another tube goes down his throat for feeding. When I go to him and speak, he reaches out to take my hand.

Winter 2014
Broken sleep. Sirens and smoke at 2. Dreamed Stephen asked me to stand in for him in a play that featured an elaborate set with Middle Eastern pointed archways. He handed me a three-pointed sword and told me to joust. Some guy in a 1970s leisure suit demanded I atone for my sins. The sword flew out of my hands and entered my stomach. Luckily, I woke up. Took my temperature: 101. Stomach's a lot better. Stephen said he would have never felt the need to cheat, if I weren't so straight-laced and predictable. Wasn't so predictable when I shouted the word *AIDS*, after he told me I was boring in bed. He's right, though. Sex is no good, when all you can think about is disease, especially when it's not there. Slept another hour. Dreamed of fundamentalist Christians protesting at the funeral of an American soldier killed in action.

These people really exist—those who blame gay men for the loss of soldiers' lives. Read about them in the paper. Fever up to 103. Joe and Fran here. Taking me to the hospital.

Spring 1994
Peter graduates from college with a degree in professional writing and no debt, thanks to his grandmother's annuity, alongside his job selling vacuum cleaners. At his graduation party, his parents give him a framed picture of his grandmother at age 25. Sitting atop Chochuk, a horse she used to ride around the streets of Smyrna, the young nurse with close-cropped bangs looks down into the camera, her eyes wide, spine erect. I wish I could have known her, says Peter. She really loved you, says his mother. Peter claims no recollection of his grandmother. His mother shakes her head and says she wishes that love wasn't something that had to be recollected.

His father offers to take him on a pleasure trip to Europe, just the three of us, he says. Peter declines, says he wants to focus on finding a full time job as a professional writer. His mother and father go on the trip without him. Peter gets a well-paying position writing operation manuals for vacuum cleaners.

Spring 1919
Danced with Dr. Bellson during a grand affair and loved every minute, especially when he lowered me into the most elegant dip. Helped him with a difficult case of appendicitis, and he took me for a walk to the top of Mount Pagus. From there we viewed the ruins of the Greek and Roman Theater and Polycarp's tomb. Dr. Bellson and I talked and talked. He loves eating strawberry ice cream, playing whist, and riding his motorcycle on Cape Cod. I called him Son of Alexander Graham, and he laughed. We both miss home.

I felt a slight chill in the air, and the good doctor gave me his jacket. Then he told me to make sure to dress properly when I ride Chochuk. Said people might start calling me Lady Godiva if I didn't. I couldn't stop blushing. Not sure how I feel about the comment. If I were back home, I would have slapped his face. Here, where ladies do not need a chaperone to walk with a gentleman, I am not sure how to react.

There is a rumor going around about Dr. Bellson and me. After last night's shift, he told me about it. Said the others didn't understand our platonic friendship. I agreed. We both decided to spend less time together aside from work. Cried myself to sleep.

Winter 2014
Burst appendix. Sepsis. IV drip, tons of medication. Nurses with needles won't leave me alone. Machine bleeps when my blood pressure gets too low.

A bit better. Mom brought the newspaper. Dad stayed home because he has bronchitis. Front-page picture of Stephen—mouth open, spittle on his lip. Definitely shouting. Love to know what he's saying. Article says protest got out of hand, people arrested.

Fall 1993
In order to fulfill requirements for his undergraduate writing major, Peter takes a journalism course, for which he must choose a local business, interview an employee, and write a feature article about the business. He chooses a housecleaning company, where he meets Stephen, who says, Come shadow me for the afternoon. When Stephen's vacuum cleaner breaks down, Peter fixes it by bending, twisting, and jiggling a set of poorly designed parts. Not bad for a college kid, says Stephen, who then invites Peter to dinner. They agree to meet again, next time at a dance club. Peter makes an A on his assignment.

Winter 1920
Planned trip to Proti to meet a ship full of refugees. Heavy snow and blizzard. Admiral Bristol said he would send his yacht up the Bosporus for me. So, in the middle of the storm I started down the long hill to the quay. Couldn't make it. Came back and phoned headquarters and was told the ship could not make it either! Was told car would come for me the following morning, but I would have to meet it at the bottom of the hill. Met the car but not without freezing my feet. Never have I felt so cold, not even at home in New Hampshire.

Headed to Proti. Found out that the ship with refugees was still floundering on the Black Sea. We shoved off, and then a few yards from the quay, couldn't see more than a few feet off the boat. Soon the captain didn't know where he was. The trip should have taken an hour, but instead took six. We had to drop anchor quite a way offshore and had to ride in a rowboat to the dock in a furious storm. I fell in, and a sailor rescued me.

Slept in our coats last night but still nearly froze. Refugees arrived. A destroyer arrived with beds and other supplies. Refugees in bad shape. Women sick with either pneumonia or typhus. We all helped with moving them off the ship, and I stood and dished up mugs of soup until my arm hurt senseless. Work is nonstop, but so necessary. Got to bed at 12:30, and couldn't fall asleep thinking about those so unfortunate. My foot hurting something terrible. Thinking about the refugees, I found the pain superfluous. So many in such awful condition. Wounds alive with maggots, heads full of lice. Malnourished and mentally broken by unbelievable horrors.

Winter 2014
Doctor finally put me on soft food. Happiness short-lived. Diarrhea: just writing the word makes me never want to eat again. No one can come into my room now without putting on gloves and a gown. Precaution so that any infection I have doesn't spread. Feel like a leper. A young nurse named Brie was horrified when she had to take the bedpan. Who names their kid after cheese? Wonder what happened to the lady I used to be friends with at the historic house. Forgot her name.

Last night Mom sat on the edge of the bed and told me about her mother working in a hospital in Turkey. At twenty-five, my grandmother assisted an appendectomy in a city under siege. Whole building was shaking during the operation. Every movement she and the doctor made required intense concentration and precision. When Mom left, I turned out the light and imagined my grandmother holding ether over my mouth while a doctor dug out my burst appendix, bed jolting and bouncing, as mortar shells shook the hospital walls.

Bad day. Potassium drip. Pain so sharp, bit through tongue. Couldn't help it. Nurse stopped drip. Arm and stomach a little better. Going over dance steps in head to get mind off pain and break up monotony.

Winter 1979
To break the monotony of being snowbound for a week, Peter's mother and father decide to clean the house. At 7, Peter is allowed to use the little vacuum cleaner, which has a wedge-shaped piece to clean corners. Peter turns the switch on and off twice without plugging in the vacuum. His father tells him the appliance will not work without electricity. Peter tells his father he knows all about electricity, that he turned the switch on and off on purpose to warn the little people that he was going to clean the floors. Then they can get out of the way, he says. His father asks who the little people are. Peter tells him they are invisible miniature humans, one assigned to every average-sized human to make sure the person lives a happy life. His mother asks where he first

heard about the little people, a cartoon or a book? Peter says he made them up on his own, after falling asleep on the living room carpet during the news. He dreamed the little people ended the Vietnam War by making normal and big-sized humans too happy to fight. The little people jumped around and wiggled their hips so the big people couldn't help but laugh. Peter's father assures his son that little people do not exist. Peter asks his mother to tell a story, the one about how she gave up her job in order to have a baby. Come dance with me, says Peter's mother. Peter's father puts disco music on the stereo, and mother and son make indentations in the carpet, as they skitter across the floor, jumping, laughing, and wiggling.

Winter 1920
A little after 2 in the morning, I screamed. The girls got Dr. Bellson, and he said I had frozen my foot and had neglected it. He dressed it with icthyol ointment and then gave me a sedative. Assured me I would be fine. I wish he liked me as much as I like him.

Winter 2014
Nurse and someone else came to take out drains. Eternity of pain—two tubes sliced through my guts. Nearly made the nurse deaf. Back on morphine. Mom came by with a book: Grandmother's diary. Too weak to read.

Winter 1973
Grace has an argument with her daughter about dressing the baby to go outside. His feet must be kept warm, she says, even if he's out for just a few minutes. He's not trudging through a snowstorm on his way to help refugees, says Susan. We all know your story. You've told it a thousand times. Don't you think it's time to let it go? Not everyone who goes out on a winter day is going to get frostbite. Grace gives the baby a kiss on the forehead and mutters something about his sensitive nature. She says nothing to her daughter as she leaves. This is the final interaction between mother and daughter, before mother dies.

Winter 2014
Still hooked to an IV, Peter starts his grandmother's diary, which begins with her boat trip to Turkey. He tries to imagine what it was like for a single woman to break conventions and travel so far, live such an exciting and dangerous life nearly a hundred years ago. He cries when he gets to the parts that deal with poverty and war.

Joe and Fran come for a visit. Instead of bringing flowers, they present Peter with a DVD of a folk dance festival in Riga, Latvia. The three watch Ukrainian men dressed in red boots and white shirts with colorful brocade drop to their knees and kick their legs with great speed and scissor-like precision. My Ukrainian ancestors settled in Latvia after Ukraine was decimated by the Russians, says Joe, who then tells Peter about the Holodomor, Joseph Stalin's starvation of nearly 7 million Ukrainians in the early thirties. Joe's face becomes red when he utters the name Stalin. Peter mentions the Armenian Genocide. Joe and Fran leave a few minutes later, and Peter reads the rest of his grandmother's diary.

When his mother visits, Peter thanks her for the diary. She says she's only read parts because the book brings up memories she doesn't want to deal with. Like what? asks Peter. His mother says that she and her brother had winter and summer sets of shoes when they were growing up. Two different sizes, the winter shoes big enough to house their feet, along with three pairs of heavy socks. The silver fillings in Peter's mother's teeth sparkle, as she utters the word socks. I always resented my mother, she says, for forcing us to wear so many pairs of socks. I resented her as long as she lived. Peter asks his mother if the resentment is gone. She says she's not sure, yet she feels guilty for her anger. Peter tells his mother that Stephen feels the same sort of anger toward him, for growing up privileged, for being so particular. Before his mother can respond, he asks her if she wishes she had gone back to work after he was born. She says no.

He then asks if she knows what happened to Dr. Bellson. She tells him the doctor went to Marash with 2,000 Turkish gold lira to help supply food to nearly 10,000 Armenian refugees and orphans. Makes me feel foolish for worrying about little things, says Peter. This was the last correspondence between Grace and Dr. Bellson, says his mother. Your grandmother remembered exactly what the good doctor told her about those times. Used to repeat it, when she was angry with Father. What did he say? asks Peter. Even if you didn't know where you were going, you could easily find your way between Islahiyé and Marash by following the line of skeletons along the path. Peter calls Dr. Bellson a hero.

Peter's mother tells him that her brother has a theory that the doctor was gay. Peter asks her if she agrees, and she says it makes sense, but doesn't really know. Your grandmother and I gradually grew apart. She stopped confiding in me. Once, not long after you were born, there was a TV news segment on homosexuality. My mother quickly turned it off.

Peter's mother continues to talk, but he loses concentration. The painkillers have begun to wear off, and he doesn't want to think of his grandmother as a homophobe. His abdomen reacts with a sudden jolt, and Peter remembers a story from Grace's diary, about the man whose face had been ripped off by a jackal—the Turk who was turned away from the Turkish hospital. As Peter's mother continues to speak, he thinks of the day he asked Stephen, his only boyfriend, to move in with him. It was right after Stephen had told him the story of two men picking him up at a bar and inviting him to their place. When Stephen got into their car, they told him they were straight. Then they beat him up. They might have killed Stephen, if he hadn't escaped, face, arms, and legs bleeding, clothes torn off. The police refused to take him seriously, not in his blue bikini underwear. They called him a prostitute, even though it wasn't true. Nobody's safe anywhere, mutters Peter. His mother asks what he said, and he says it's nothing. She follows up with a question about his plans for a future without Stephen. Peter says he has no plans, and then pushes the button to call the nurse, who comes quickly and replenishes his painkillers. The nurse leaves, and Peter's mother tells him she has a better remedy for his pain. What would that be? asks Peter. The little people, she says. Peter laughs. As the medicine takes effect, he begins to feel sleepy. Come to folk dancing, he says, when I'm better. Come dance with me.

E. Kelly

Harbor Lights

On a May evening Clara stands at the window of her dark office feeling the civil service building getting progressively empty. Her feet hurt, back aches, chest feels tight, and a band of pain circles her head above the eyes—not unusual these days.

Her top floor window overlooks the port. It's getting foggy and the street lights are on. She thinks of a day fifty years ago when her father's ship came in, followed by an immense fog bank. His ship seemed to loom up against a swirl of mist. Looking up from the dock, then twelve-year-old Clara saw her father with other officers in white uniforms high on one of the top decks. She recognized him right away, square shouldered and imposing. She wanted to be like him.

Even then she knew she didn't resemble her mother, a frail brunette with the air of a princess in exile. She has a vague memory of three Irish aunts surrounding her as a little girl, talking about how Clara was going to be like their side of the family—tall and sturdy with fair hair and blue eyes. Their brother, Clara's father, had been the local hero, a boxer and swimmer and finally an officer in the Navy. Her family moved away from those aunts when Clara was small and all three ladies have passed away by now, so Clara has no way of knowing if her memory is imagined. But she feels that her childhood was hard. At any rate, she has tried to be like her father—strong and dependable. In his wartime absence, she felt protective of her pretty mother and little sister; she worried that someday she might have to support the family if her father died. In school she studied hard.

But her mother shrank into herself, worrying only about all the things she had no control over. And Clara's sister Madalyn, bright and darling, occupied center stage in their house; she could make the mother smile and forget sometimes. Clara had no memories of anyone fussing over her, no little hugs or special dresses. Did no one care?

The older she grew, the more Clara wanted to be considered, and the more her mother treated her like a nuisance. By high school she was bigger and stronger than her mother, and they would have distressing fights. Once when both (separately) had been drinking, the mother tried to strike out at Clara, who grabbed the woman's wrists in self-protection; the next day there were blood-red marks on her mother's arms. Clara was the one attacked, yet she felt ashamed and guilty. Because of scenes like this the father requested shore duty, came home, and introduced peace and stability into the household.

Then for her own sake Clara could work to excel in every class; she would come home talking about current issues in Civics, or how difficult chemistry and Latin classes were, and sometimes at dinner her father came out of his shell and complimented her on good grades or discussed the news with her. At least he took her seriously. It must be that only men cared about serious issues. If so, Clara resolved to fight for respect in the world of men. In spite of this she knew that little Madalyn, who resembled their mother, was his favorite. But Clara could try to be a man's equal. She dreamed of becoming a surgeon, traveling in Mexico and South America, succeeding in law and politics, earning fame as a journalist. By her senior year in high school she was editor of the school paper and would canvass downtown businesses to advertise in it, arriving home late, ravenous, her feet throbbing.

After the student newspaper was set up at night, she and her friends would sometimes go out for a few beers; because of her size and the way she carried herself, no one asked for proof of age. Later they'd catch the ferry—there was no bridge then—they would ride across the bay and back, singing "Harbor Lights" together. It felt so sophisticated! Clara was a senior at the age of sixteen; most of her pals were older. She thrilled to see the stars in the night sky from a boat, but even better was when the fog came in; they'd huddle together and keep each other warm. The island itself meant nothing to her; they never once got off the ferry. Only that boat ride, and the closeness of friends, made life seem urgent and precious.

Afternoons when she pounded the pavements looking for advertisers, Clara felt part of real life and wrote editorials about social conditions she observed. She thought her stores of energy were endless, that the future held out infinite possibilities.

Tonight, she looks outside across the bay at massive shadows of cruise ships and military vessels, but her glance falls to a cluster of fragile sailboats moored like sleeping ducks below. Her top floor office is some proof of success achieved through hard work and persistence, but it is hardly what she had aspired to in high school; economic realities ended those dreams.

When it came time to apply for college, Clara was summoned by the old woman who served as Scholarship Adviser. She asked what Clara's plans were; the girl answered she'd thought of applying to Harvard, Stanford and the University of California, hoping for a scholarship, and maybe going on to study medicine. Her face a mass of wrinkles. This woman calmly disabused her of such notions. To go to any of the big schools, she said, your parents will be expected to match any funds provided by a scholarship, and beyond that, there are living expenses which are rarely included. Unless her parents were able and willing to pay quite a lot of money, she had better confine her applications to the local State College; that was her advice.

For a moment Clara stared at her. Why did this woman even bother to call her down there? She herself thought she could make it by working, but if the Scholarship Adviser was against her, how could she hope to be accepted? She stood up so suddenly that the woman cringed as if fearing for her safety, but Clara just excused herself and left the room.

Only years later did she think she understood. That old bag was protecting the interests of more wealthy students and their parents from having to compete with a high achiever. Clara was only a problem in that adviser's agenda. Clara doesn't like it, but understanding helps her overcome the pain. At the time, she refrained from telling her parents what had been said, and after a period of anger and confusion, resolved to be undaunted. Her own father had never gone beyond eighth grade, but through hard work and heroism in battle rose from the ranks to become a naval officer. She too would fight to find her way. Kennedy's recent presidential acceptance speech confirmed her decision: "Ask what you can do for your country!" And she did go to the local college, majored in Journalism and Political Science, minored in English and Spanish, and wrote for its newspaper. She made friends with a few Mexican poets and several young veterans of the Korean War who were back in school on the G.I. Bill. She read *Lady Chatterley's Lover* and had a brief affair with a Portuguese fisherman, who beat her. Her heart speeds up remembering him, though she could never put up with physical abuse.

Now, the building acquires that total quiet characteristic of Friday night. When she thinks everyone has gone, Clara turns on her desk light and gets to work. How rarely she makes a secret of any project, professional or otherwise; nevertheless, she swears to herself to keep everyone ignorant of these actions and motives. That small part of her which can still be hurt—which was hurt when her husband Sam deserted her thirty-five years ago—no one must see.

Sam joined her crowd in college, at a time when all the men she knew wanted to go to bed with her. That power to attract had thrilled Clara! She'd slept with Sam but not because he attracted her—rather because he was so healthy and naïve she thought he would be good for her. A Korean War veteran in school on VA benefits, Sam lived alone on a sailboat and was hoping to sail back to Japan to marry his girlfriend there. Everyone she knew had dreams back then. When Clara got pregnant he asked her to move onto the boat with him. Her father would not have approved, but he died the year before of a heart attack—on an exercycle at the YMCA.

Staying on Sam's little boat was the only time in her life when her weight went down and she looked tan and glamorous. She grew her blonde hair long and told her friends she must be made to have many children, she felt so healthy. When Julie was born Clara and Sam married and moved into student housing. Clara graduated first, got a job as a social worker, and supported him through college. But he resented being "kept" and they had terrible fights which always followed a pattern. Clara, expounding on some idea or cause, would provoke him into an argument, which he could never win verbally. Gradually he became so angry he'd find a way to hurt her; she would cry like a little girl; they would make up, and were good together until the next time. As soon as he graduated, Sam accepted a job in Oregon and deserted her and Julie for good.

It was about this time that the American President was assassinated. Whatever pain Clara suffered from Sam's desertion was submerged in that greater tragedy. After a period of depression, lightened only by her little girl, Julie, Clara decided that the only sane thing to do was to fight for better leaders, for justice and a better world. Julie, her job, and her political work kept her going—until the second Kennedy was assassinated. To her it meant that the system itself was infiltrated with criminals you couldn't fight—then what could anyone do? What would her father have done? She recalled him as tough, unsentimental, silent but kindly. He had endured two wars and, harder still, enforced retirement and inactivity. She would be like him and endure. That was years ago, and Clara has worked in this building ever since. Perhaps she has done some good for a few people; after awhile, you can't be sure.

* * * * * * * * *

Now her problem is to deal with what she hopes is an irrational fear of cancer. She's nearing the age when her mother died of lung cancer, and last summer the doctor admonished her to stop smoking and lose weight. She hasn't done either. At the time Clara simply didn't believe she was vulnerable, and the bad habits she has are dear to her. But lately she just hasn't felt right: a lack of energy, headaches, chest pains. Probably it can all be blamed on stress and too much drinking.

During childhood Clara was often called strong as a horse, and she came to see herself as a workhorse. Intelligent, yes—passionate too—but above all someone who could be counted on to get the job done, any job however hard. All her friends would say so now. They certainly wouldn't understand why she doesn't want them to know about her pains. Clara acknowledges she should face her fears, see the doctor early and get checked. But it would be too humiliating to admit she couldn't follow his instructions—she who is known for her strong will power. Rather she's decided to follow them *strictly* now. How satisfying it would be if she could heal herself! And why not? She'll tackle this problem the way she would any other, efficiently and thoroughly. Before her is a list of things to do: 1) Strictly limit calories, including from alcohol. 2) Absolutely cut down on cigarettes, and quit soon. 3) Take strenuous walks on the beach every night. 4) Take a class in aerobic exercise at a swimming pool where no one knows her.

On a map she's drawn a ten mile circle that includes pools she knows about; but most have been crossed off because friends and acquaintances go there. Searching the computer she finds one a bit farther north, up the coast, a YMCA, and decides to try it. Some well-known fish restaurants in that area add to its attraction, but at first it'll be strict rations prepared at home. Mentally she plans her regime: hard boiled eggs and grapefruit alternating with berries and yogurt for breakfast, with plenty of black coffee; cottage cheese or salad for lunch; fish or chicken for dinner, with another salad and only one glass of wine. By late August she hopes to lose thirty pounds and be back in shape. No weakening!

The next day she visits that YMCA up the coast. Clara hasn't been in a bathing suit for thirty years; polyester pants and power jacket have been her uniform at work, sweat suit at home. She's not obese, just overweight, but that doesn't make her any less self-conscious. When she grew up the images of sexy big blonde movie stars of the fifties, like Jayne Mansfield and Anita Ekberg, haunted Clara's self-image. So on this first Saturday at the pool she emerges from the dressing area cringing to think all eyes might be on her heavy white thighs and protruding stomach revealed by the new black suit, purchased at Target. But she holds her chin high and strides out.

In fact though nobody occupies the water yet. When the instructor arrives, Clara is already submerged. She introduces herself and explains about her intensive diet and exercise program.

This woman is just as overweight as Clara, only younger. "I'm Carolyn," the instructor says. "I'm not paid to teach this class—I trained to teach aerobics after a car accident hurt my back and I volunteered to teach here Saturdays, so there are certain exercises even I can't do...."

The way Carolyn puts it, Clara understands there won't be unstated competitions or cattiness in the class. Cheered, she paddles out to the deep end, hanging on to rubber bar bells. By this time several others enter the pool and they begin. It isn't so hard. Though she has been hurting in her chest and stomach for a long time now, Clara's muscles are in good condition—in spite of sitting at a desk for fifteen years. In fact, the warm water soothes her joints even as she exercises. Lovely, these smooth exertions in the liquid element. It's like nothing else! She finds herself performing motions she thought only a gymnast could do, and afterwards she proceeds to the nearby beach.

Parking on the road, she walks south along the sand. Maybe she'll make this a three mile walk all the way to the end of a secluded stretch where nudists go; a few naked men sunbathing there won't bother her, and perhaps it'll make their day to think they've titillated her. Up ahead she sees an elderly couple strolling along; they must be ten or fifteen years older than she, but are small and trim, dressed elegantly in beach attire. As she passes, she overhears their conversation, spoken with a pronounced French accent. They are talking about how much they like it here in Southern California.

Clara passes them quickly on her power walk, amused. It's odd to hear that woman praise this sleepy place where she grew up, and in touristy, clichéd terms. For years she's thought of Europe, especially France, as the center of intellectualism and glamour. How many vacations she spent in Paris, St. Tropez, Rome, London. She took her daughter on a tour of Europe's major cities when Julie was ten, partly to give Julie a sense of the elegance that exists in the cosmopolitan world, partly to visit all the legislative centers wherever they went—in hopes of inspiring Julie to become a lawyer and politician. Well, that was thirty years ago and, for all Clara's pains to educate her, Julie is now just a modern dance instructor in Seattle.

The sun is full in Clara's face. In spite of her determination, she tires. Up ahead is that rocky point which separates the sand she's on from the nudist beach. She stops and drinks deeply from her twelve ounce water bottle, her chest hurting. She wishes she had a cigarette. This diet has required a herculean effort. She hurts all over, her head aches, she's dying to call a happy hour pal and go out for pizza. Instead she decides to turn back; it'll take more than an hour to get to the car as it is.

In white clothes and wide beige hats, that French couple approaches from a distance. When they meet up with Clara, the woman stops and asks her about the trails that seem to go up the cliff. Can anyone go up? Clara advises them against climbing the cliff. There is only one official trail she knows of, she says, and it's very steep. People often get stuck and have to be rescued by lifeguards. Sometimes parts of the cliff collapse. Much better to stay close to the water! They thank her profusely, treating this meeting as if it were a delightful experience. Clara wishes them a pleasant vacation, feeling inexplicably grateful.

With renewed energy, she continues back. That French couple makes her think about foreign films she loved in the 1950s, she and her friends: *The 400 Blows, Jules and Jim, Breathless, La Dolce Vita, Wild Strawberries, Two Women*—there were so many. From those movies Clara acquired the notion that sophistication meant being sexually experienced, seeing through the social lies of morality and convention, and meeting life with courage and honesty: being "existential." Were those just idealistic clichés? Clara believes she has been a sophisticated woman in her own sense; but, she thinks now, the trouble is that the movies glamorized a way of life by means of those actresses who actually were so beautiful and rich. She pauses, looking out at the ocean, so chaotic and grey-green-blue. Don't people only consider a woman sophisticated if she is slender and glamorous-looking? Or if she is rich—and preferably married to a rich man? Isn't it really money that provides the glamour? The line of the horizon she's looking at seems a dreary grey, merging into mist.

Shaking her head, Clara starts walking again; she'll stick to the diet, but will indulge in a crab and shrimp salad—with wine but no bread—at a nearby restaurant overlooking the sea. Then, sitting on a balcony at that restaurant, she sees the ocean in a new light, evening sunlight turning it silver. Far out, silhouetted against the horizon, a Navy ship passes, patrolling the coast perhaps, or headed to parts north. She decides her depression is only a "surfed out" feeling caused by the exercise. To counteract that, she has several cups of black coffee and almost feels her old self.

At home there's a phone message from her daughter Julie, wishing her happy birthday. Disturbed, Clara realizes she's forgotten her own birthday; well, there's no one to celebrate with. Last year she and her ex-boyfriend Welton went to Puerto Vallarta for the weekend. Welton is a lawyer and can afford such things; but he's just one more in a long line of disappointments. Oh well, tonight she'll clean the kitchen thoroughly, then call Julie.

* * * * * * * * * *

After two weeks of self-imposed punishment, she has lost ten pounds. At night she still hurts all over and her cough persists, but she just takes cough drops and aspirin. Friends leave messages on her answering machine, wondering where she's gone. Her work pal Maureen must think Clara is back with Welton, since she pointedly avoids asking Clara to Happy Hour. Well, later when her weight loss becomes more obvious, Clara will explain.

One grey June afternoon after two late interviews have been cancelled, she finds herself staring out the window at the bay again, trying to remember the words to that song.

I saw those harbor lights,
They only told me we were parting

—she hums the rest, forgetting what was so familiar years ago, caught up in feelings she can't describe. "Now I know lonely nights...." At sixteen these words seemed poignant, glamorizing the pain of love. At sixteen she believed that everything good, sexy, adult just waited to be experienced. It irritates her to admit now that those were illusions created by movies. Now Clara believes that growing up is a process of fighting, then shedding, your illusions.

Meanwhile it's no joke working in the public sector. No wonder she once wanted to be in politics; politicians are actors, outside it all; someone in her position of responsibility services everyone, politicos, victims, at times even criminals. You are there to clean up the mess. It's exhausting. Nevertheless, Clara maintains her schedule as if her life depends on it, and by late June she sees the difference twenty pounds less can make, calling for new outfits and even another bathing suit, which she's no longer embarrassed to be seen in. By July she admits to friends what she's been up to, though now these friends seem to believe it's all been for Welton's sake—and Clara is silent about his betrayal and her health fears.

But when by August Clara has surpassed her goal and lost forty pounds, she's not sure this is a good sign. The energy she hoped to recover hasn't come back; her chest, back and arms still hurt, and she can't overcome that depression, though an occasional valium helps.

To buck herself up, on the Friday before her physical exam, she takes the morning off to get her hair cut and colored, with streaks bleached in to set off the blonde, and as she returns to work several people remark how young she looks. That's a shot in the arm she needs, for two hours in a hairdresser's chair have almost undermined all ambition. Plans for a nap later at home barely keep her going till five o clock, when there's a knock on her office door.

Opening, she sees Welton, who has never come to her office before. She just looks at him.

"I can tell you're still angry at me," he says. "I don't blame you. But I've been going crazy missing you."

"Try being nicer to your wife and she'll make you feel better."

"Clara, I never mentioned her because we don't live together, I feel like I'm divorced. She says her religion is against it, but she just wants me to be unhappy."

"Welton, I'm too old for soap operas, and tonight I'm very tired. Please go away."

"Come over to the Pelican Café and have coffee with me; just once? I have something to tell you."

She feels too tired to argue; and when he sits there in their old booth that looks out across the bay, his whole large proud body exuding sadness, and explains that his "ex-wife" does everything she can to persecute him, Clara finds it hard not to sympathize.

"Remember the story you told me about your first husband—"

"—my only husband—"

"—and living on his sailboat? I thought maybe a boat was what we needed to get close again, so I went out and bought one."

"You bought a boat?"

"Yes, I'm too old to learn to sail, so I got a trawler yacht, but it's a sweet little thing just the same. I hoped you would come out in it with me."

Clara stares at him, speechless.

He's already up, his eyes gleaming, and she can't resist.

Twenty years fall away and she lets herself be caught up in the evening boat ride, salt air, sparkling lights, the warmth of his extra sweater and cap, dinner he makes while moored at the marina, red wine shared, the bunk just wide enough, making love as if she were still twenty-five or thirty, and the world of promise were still within them both.

What is the truth? she wonders while falling asleep. But she wakes up, coughing, with her neck feeling wrenched; it's dark, but the light from street lamps shows she is still at her desk at work. Just another deceptive dream. Fog horns groan. When is she going to learn? She makes her way home and falls into a deep sleep seemingly without dreams, as if she were dead.

Next morning is sunny but she doesn't want to get up. Why go to the pool? She's achieved her goal of losing weight. Next week she'll see the doctor—maybe he'll take a lot of tests. What good is one more day's exercise? But from habit she gets up, drinks coffee, eats yogurt, dresses, and starts driving to aerobics, mocking herself all the way. Isn't it ironic that she should have chosen this particular place to whip herself into line, when so many years ago her own father died of a heart attack at a YMCA?

At the pool a couple of women praise her new hairdo. Clara pretends to respond; she never felt less like putting up with small talk, not to mention compliments. She escapes to be alone at the deep end, though farther along the wall a young woman is working out. Clara has seen her before—in fact, dislikes her. The girl has an uncanny resemblance to her younger sister Madalyn. Yes, her sister grew up to have many of the things Clara was denied in life. Delicate and pretty, her mother's pet and her father's favorite, she became a quiet, well behaved student who won the highest grades. Though she began in the local state college just like Clara, Madalyn went on to finish her B.S. in biology at the University of California, supported by their widowed mother. She married a fellow student who became a doctor and has three beautiful children that seem to love her. Madalyn lives far away, but Clara suffers every time they meet.

Lunging back and forth along the side of the wall, Clara stretches her thighs, deaf to any instructions going on in the class. That persistent pain fills her whole head now. What a series of disasters her life has been! With energy, intelligence and talent, Clara was still unable to accomplish even one of her greatest goals or dreams. When she gave herself to politics, nothing but disappointing things happened; approaching the world with honesty and what she thought was fearless determination, all she seemed to do was alienate people or invite them to take advantage of her. She'd attracted many men, but never was able to keep even one she wanted. Even her own daughter, to whom she'd dedicated herself, lives far away. Why does nobody care?

"Are you all right?" A voice breaks in on her. It's that young woman from down the wall. Clara closes her eyes and tries to get some kind of control over despair.

"It's funny you should ask that," she answers in what she thinks is a joking tone. "I'm going in for a yearly physical next week, and I've just been imagining what terrible things could be wrong with me."

"What are you afraid of?" the other asks, with a look on her face as if to say she knows Clara fears the worst.

Clara shifts onto her stomach and begins kicking behind her. *None of your business* she wants to say. *Who are you to me?* She turns and scrutinizes the other. Yes, she's a little like Madalyn, and you could call her pretty—anyway, pleasant looking, with brown frizzy hair bundled up in a high ponytail, her small arms muscular and solid. The look in her eyes is serious and friendly.

Clara's feet churn up the water, but inside she's even more chaotic. Has she fallen so low that she'll tell her fears and problems to the first person that shows a little sympathy? But really, when you think about it, a stranger you might never see again could be the perfect one to talk with. "My name's Clara."

"Hi, I'm Jinny. I'm not usually so nosy, but I've seen you before and you always seemed strong and confident. Today I happened to glance over and you looked like you had a dark cloud hanging over you. But I didn't mean to intrude."

She sighs. "To be honest, my mother died at seventy of lung cancer; I'm nearing that age and have smoked since I was sixteen. Lately I quit, but I wonder if it's too late."

Jinny turns out to be a nurse who works in intensive care. She asks Clara a few questions, but instead of lecturing or giving some standard professional opinion, she comments, "I've just quit smoking again, myself. It seems every time I get divorced, I get back on them."

Clara looks more closely at Jinny. You'd never know to look at her that she has any problems. Like Madalyn, she's small and well-proportioned, pretty, friendly with everyone. Quick to laugh, she seemed to take things superficially—and yet there Jinny is, working where the awareness of life and death is always present and you definitely feel needed.

"Every time? You can't have had very many."

"Three," the young woman says, but her voice is wistful. "I think I'm cured of that, anyway. Obviously marriage is not for me. Recently my son insisted it was way time to quit smoking again, and I agreed. I certainly don't want him to start."

"How old is your son?" she asks, feeling jealous about this too.

"Jason's in his last year of high school and his father is dying of pancreatic cancer. It's been tough. Jason can't stand to watch his father melting away."

A wave of compassion for a boy she's never seen wipes out that pack of furies which were tormenting Clara. "The poor kid. How is he taking it?"

"Jason is confused and hurt. The sicker his father gets, the meaner he gets; it's as if he doesn't even want to see his son now. I feel terrible for Jason. Oh, we're dealing with it, though I might have to send him to a therapist when it's over. In fact, right now I ought to get going to watch him at baseball practice. Anyway, I hope your exam turns out okay. Maybe I'll see you next week."

Clara just waves and continues kicking the water. Looked at objectively, Clara tells herself, social work is as worthwhile as medicine. Over the past thirty-eight years, how many women might have seen their babies go hungry if Clara hadn't helped them? Is the self-worth that comes from both of these professions paid for by the suffering you share, trying to alleviate it? And though Clara has often felt a victim for being a single mom, now she's met a girl three times single, so to speak. What could that be like?

What the hell! Whether the news from her doctor is bad or not, she'll go on one of those cruises from Seattle to Alaska—sail pass the glaciers, eat fresh wild salmon, see the harbor lights in some far-off fishing village. It's something she's always wanted to do. She's tired of tame cities, however glamorous; and maybe on the way she could drop in on Julie, for once. And then, if necessary, she'll have an operation—fight for her life.

Gregg Williard

Backroads

When she considered where she had been, a map of blood and stiches that presented one surface, laid out as a small table cloth, her stroking hands flattening the folds. So unlike the maps from a single, fixed location that bear the YOU ARE HERE assurance. No such orientation for her, the map being the territory of her own skin. YOU ARE EVERYWHERE, all landmarks, signposts, geographic features, each spot, like every word of Gertrude Stein's, a vanishing point. Directly in front of her position was THE BATTLE OF FORT TYLENOL. And to her left, northwest, was NIGHT OF THE FLYING SKELETONS. Just beyond NIGHT was a red river flowing down from SARGASSO SEA in the north named CAMEL LIGHTS. She pulled a flask of memory: cigarettes inhaled in a fever, inhaled and then ground out into angry ash white as milk or milk-based glue, and an ashtray of a heart. All back to the top bunk-mate Meg Pall, dropping the live butt onto Bridey's sheets, watching it burn a little brown hole that grew into crisp red actions with smoke. Fire and smoke piled higher, still no sign of her, why doesn't she get up and get out? Circling back, there was a recurrence with what she had started with. There it was. And she suddenly was wearing something that fit her like a glove. The skin of her own hand. And having your own private tailor, and letting them take in the material, take out the hem, to out the hem of the pants. I don't suppose at that point that there was any real question that she would end up in a uniform, at

THE SCHOOL FOR WAYWARD GIRLS.

SHE READ THE MAP OF HER OWN BODY AND CHOSE ONLY BACK-ROADS TO HER HEART

Bipin Aurora

The Medicine Shop

The Medicine Shop. Have you seen it? Some people are sitting on the chairs in the lobby. Some are sitting on the ledge outside the building. Some are standing against the wall. And are the people idle? No, they are not. Some are eating *kak* (for this ailment or for that), some are eating the leaf of the *tulsi* plant (for malaria). Some are taking cardamom (is it for boils?).

The leaves of the lemon tree sway outside in the breeze.

Some people are waiting for the doctor. But just who is the doctor on duty today? Dr. Sachdev? Dr. Jaswant Kapoor? Brigadier General (and also noted surgeon) Mahendra D. Singh?

Suddenly there is some commotion. People shuffle here and there. Have they seen someone coming? Is it the doctor himself that they have seen?

No, it is not the doctor. It is a girl, perhaps six years old, perhaps seven. The girl walks with a tin box and she also carries a cardboard sign. The sign reads:

One Candle Lights Another
Donate Eyes After Death

An old woman sees the girl and smiles. "I am not yet dead," says the old woman. "When death comes" . . . but she does not finish the sentence. A lower-class man squats on the floor wearing an old brown shirt and striped pajamas, a green cloth of some kind draped over his left shoulder. He speaks to the girl: "Where will you keep the eyes? In the tin box?" Another man, better dressed in a white shirt and black pants, speaks up as well: "Whose girl is she? Six years old, no more than seven. And who is she to speak to us thus?"

Yes, for a few moments the attention shifts from the doctor on duty—who he is, who he isn't—to the girl and her tin box.

"This girl, who is she?"

"Eyes, does she really want our eyes?"

"A candle I will give her, even a whole box of candles. But eyes?"

The girl herself does not speak. She seems poor but is dressed in a dark-blue school uniform. Her hair is braided in two long pony tails. She carries the tin box in her left hand—carries it by the small handle. A picture of a cow can be seen on the box. (Is the box a children's lunch or Tiffin box?) She carries the cardboard sign in her right hand. The cardboard is old and worn but the sign, written in bold black ink, is quite clear:

One Candle Lights Another
Donate Eyes After Death

A few minutes pass. A man comes running in from the glass doors. He seems to be laughing happily. His laughter is almost uncontrollable—once or twice he hiccups.

The people in the lobby look at him. Some of them smile, some of them laugh. Others look at the floor. Others return their gaze to the girl with the tin box and the cardboard sign.

The man is of medium height with pitch-black hair and his name is Ved Prakash. He is dressed in a khaki uniform and he seems to be a clerk of some kind. He walks up to the front of the lobby and then stops. He clears his throat—and then he clears it again. (The people grow silent.) Several sheets of long, thin paper are in his hand. His voice is flat but loud and clear. He reads about the incidents—the "events," he calls them—of the day.

Assad, a resident of Jaffabad, was stabbed to death by his brother Arshad. The latter, in Standard X, did not study or do his homework. Arshad was scolded by his father and he beat his father. He was scolded by his mother and he beat his mother. He was scolded by his brother Assad and he killed him.

"With a knife?" someone in the audience asks.

"Yes, with a knife," says Ved Prakash. "True, all true."

Ved Prakash continues to read:

Ghanshyam, the sixty-year-old resident of Mangolpuri, was shot. Two men approached from the alley, took Rs. 325, and shot him. The men escaped on a motorcycle.

Sateh Singh fell from a running bus. He died on Hoshiar Singh Marg.

Sunita Tiwari, a resident of Lajpat Nagar, had her purse snatched by a miscreant. Then she was beaten until the blood came from her face and also her eyes.

"A lot of blood?" someone says.

"Yes," says Ved Prakash. "A lot of blood."

"Was there weeping and wailing?"

"Yes, that as well."

The people in the audience nod their heads. Again they nod. Ved Prakash is talking and the people listen to him with interest. Many of them listen with the deepest interest. He goes on:

Pankaj Chopra, of West Patel Nagar, hanged himself. What did he use? A ceiling fan. The ceiling in his house is low and it can be reached by standing on the bed. The reason for the hanging: a love affair.

Hawa Singh, 45 years old and of Rohtak, also hanged himself. The method: a nylon rope attached to a tree. The reason: an unsuccessful love affair.

Raj Kumar, 28, and Reshma, 25, also died. They were married five months ago without the consent of their parents. There was increasing harassment from the latter. The lovers locked themselves in a room and then hanged themselves from the ceiling fan.

Again the people in the audience nod their heads. Some of them are moved and shed a few tears. "Hanging, hanging," says one person in the audience, "it is quite popular in our time." "Death is popular," says another. "It is all around." A few chuckles are heard from the audience.

Ved Prakash ignores the chuckles and goes on. So some people want to make light of his important words, let them do it. He has a job to do—to read, to read. He clears his throat, again he clears it. And then he continues:

Ram Avtar burned himself to death. He tried to bring back his wife from his in-laws. He did not succeed and so he burned himself to death.

Shanti, wife of Constable Manipal of Mangolpuri, also killed herself. The method: burning. She locked herself, her one-year-old son, and her brother-in-law, and set the room on fire. The other two were rescued by neighbors. She herself died.

Several women were burned, allegedly while cooking: Munni, 30, of Shastri Bagh jhuggies, Jaitun of Jafrabad Seelampur (a pregnant woman), and Kalawati, of Jehangiripuri. The first two women are expected to survive; the last is not.

Again, the people in the audience nod their heads. Some of them are moved and shed a few tears. One person speaks out loudly: "Hanging is popular, I say, but do not forget fire and burning. They are popular as well."

"This is our India, modern India. What are we to do?"

"Modern India, you say. This is not 'modern' India, it is India, period. It has always been this way."

Some people claim that hanging is more popular, some people claim that fire and burning are more popular. The discussion is heated and some voices are raised. Ved Prakash clears his throat and asks for silence. "Both are popular," he says. "There is no need to argue. I have studied the evidence—studied it for some time. Stabbing is also popular in India, and so is falling from a running bus. This is modern India. We are a free country and everything is allowed."

"Everything is allowed? Is it really?"

"It is, it is. Stay with me, follow the facts. Everything is allowed."

Yes, this is the pattern every day. This is the Medicine Shop and at 10 o'clock every morning, a man comes running in through the glass doors. Sometimes, as today, the man comes in laughing uncontrollably. Sometimes he is more serious. He stands in front of the people in the lobby. And then he reads.

Why he reads, that is a different question. What it all means is a different question. Yes, there are these incidents and incidents, but to what do they add up? There is a stabbing here, a hanging there. A burning here, a fall from the bus (or from the roof). Are they just curiosities, nothing more? Do they say something about India, a *cultural* thing? Do they say something about God's creation? And just what is that they say?

"They say that India is a bad and inferior country," someone in the crowd offers.

"They say that God has created an odd and crazy world," says another.

"You have it all wrong. The incidents say nothing big about India and nothing big about God. They just say that the world is what it is: nothing more."

Nothing more. The people in the audience are not philosophers. Many of them—perhaps most of them—do not get into these big questions. No, they just see these things—the stabbings, the hangings, the burnings—as bad things, just that. And perhaps even as bad things that should be investigated.

"The bad things *are* being investigated," says Ved Prakash.

"Are you sure?"

"I am sure, I am sure. They are bad things and they *are* being investigated."

"So I can rest easy? Have a good night's sleep?"

Ved Prakash is not certain if the other is serious or just mocking him. But he has a job to do, an important job. He takes a deep breath, and then another. And then he goes on:

The police investigated the case of Ghanshyam, the sixty-year-old resident of Mangolpuri who was shot, Rs. 325 taken. They also investigated the case of Sunita Tiwari, whose purse was snatched and who was then badly beaten. Two days later three burglars were found: Shankar, Kalu, and Har Gobind. They were said to have taken Rs. 25,000 of building material from the DDA self-financing scheme flats in Ashok Vihar. All kinds of building materials—door frames, wooden shutters, cement bags, grills, and manhole covers—were found to be in their possession.

Yes, the burglars were found. But could they have taken the Rs. 325 from Ghanshyam and the purse from Sunita Tiwari? Could they be at all the same villains? The police interrogated them at some length. "Are you the villains?" they said. No answer. "Are you the villains?" they said again. No answer. "The building materials, of that we can be sure. But the purse and the wallet, can we be sure of that?"

Ved Prakash speaks and the people listen with interest. Some stroke their chins and others nod their heads in approval. Others, however, are not so convinced.

"The investigation was not thorough."

"A better investigation should be done."

"Building materials on the one hand and wallets and purses on the other hand, what do they have in common? Our police are who they are: small, limited. Are they even capable of a good investigation?"

Ved Prakash hears these words of the listeners and is quite pained. "Rest assured," he says, "rest assured. Our police are slow but not incompetent. Give them some credit for the work they do."

Some skepticism is voiced. Even some guffaws are heard. "'Not incompetent,' you say. 'Give them some credit,' you say. You are a funny man, sir, you are quite funny.'"

Yes, some people are convinced about the thoroughness of the investigation but others are not. New points—additional points—are raised as well.

"Investigation is important, yes. But even if you do investigate, what do you accomplish?"

"The person who is the victim is already scarred for life."

"Scars, scars, we are *all* human. We all carry them."

At the last words in particular, a few are impressed. Some cluck their tongues, some shake their heads. Two people—an old man and a young village woman in a bold-colored orange sari—are even seen to shed a few tears.

Ved Prakash notices the reactions—how can he not?—and is quite pleased. He is even encouraged that people are impressed by the goings-on and feels his confidence returning about the words that he speaks. But he still has a job to do. He clears his throat, again he clears it. And he continues:

The hanging of Pankaj Chopra, of West Patel Nagar, was investigated by the police. They spoke to his parents, they spoke to his alleged lover. They spoke to the parents of his alleged lover. They found the lover resting under the shade of a tree on Najafgarh Road. Her head was in her hands and a bicycle stood nearby, leaning against the tree. They asked the lover questions, but to no avail. They offered her a drink in a small paper cup and she pushed it away. "My throat is fine," she said, "in no need of water. But my soul is parched. Can you take care of that?"

The police were at a loss. "A parched soul," said one of them at last. "No, Madam, we cannot take care of that."

The people in the audience hear these last words of Ved Prakash and seem quite intrigued.

"A nice investigation," they say.

"They found the culprit or they did not, who after all can say? But 'a parched soul,' yes, that is nice. The police found poetry on Najafgarh Road—a humble road in Delhi at that. Yes, yes, at least they did find some poetry there!"

Ved Prakash hears the words of the audience and is not pleased. "Do not mock the police," he says simply. "They do the best they can."

"Well, maybe they should do better."

"A parched soul in Najafgarh Road, a parched soul indeed! I am sure that discovery will help to solve the case."

Again Ved Prakash is irritated by the words of the people in the audience. Do they not realize how important these incidents are? Do they not realize the importance of the work the police do? Do they not realize the importance of his own work?

He takes a deep breath. He takes another deep breath. And he goes on:

The burning to death of Ram Avtar was investigated as well. The police were intrigued by the victim's name: "Ram" as in the Lord Rama, "avtar" as in incarnation: the incarnation of the Lord Rama. So Ram Avtar burned himself. Was it because he missed his wife? Was it the shame that her absence from home brought him from his relatives and from his neighbors? Was it the desire to sacrifice—"to make sacred"? But what was he making sacred: His wife? Himself? The Lord Rama? All of the above?

It was a serious question, even a question of philosophy. And are the police seriously trained in these matters? They are trained in breaking down doors and in baton-charges against unruly crowds. But questions of philosophy, are they trained in that?

The people in the audience listen with interest, even with great interest. And how do they react? A few are silent. A few stroke their chins. "The work of the police is not easy," someone calls out at last.

"We need to give them a pay raise," says a second person.

"A pay raise?" says a third person. "They are minting money, as it is. They are swimming in bribes, *drowning* in bribes. *Pay raise*, you say. How innocent you are, how innocent indeed!"

Ved Prakash listens to the reactions and is again troubled. These are important events and these are important investigations about them. Why must the people be so skeptical? Why cannot the people take them for what they are? And why must they be skeptical of his own words—yes, yes, even of them?

Yes, this is the pattern in the Medicine Shop—the pattern every day. The people gather wherever they can in the lobby. Some sit on the few wooden benches along the walls. Some sit on the floor, some stand. But all the people crane their ears and listen. The man in front of them, the important Ved Prakash in his khaki uniform, is speaking important words. And they do not want to miss these words.

The guards move around in the area as well. They patrol the hallways and the front door. The sweepers move around and also do their jobs.

One of the employees, a receptionist of some kind, breaks out into song. "Mere Mehboob," she sings out loud in Hindi. It is a pretty song, quite upbeat. The title means "My Love." Why she sings, or sings this song in particular, is not clear.

Ved Prakash speaks about the events of the day—about the bad world out there. Some people speak about the medicines that should be taken to make things better. Some people, like the little girl, walk around with the sign:

One Candle Lights Another
Donate Eyes After Death

With the sign, the girl seems to speak about the *good* deeds that should be performed.

"The world is a complicated place," someone calls out loud. "It is what it is."

"The world is a mystery. It is too deep for us to fathom."

"But some people try. Is that not all that we can do?"

Ved Prakash hears the words but tries not to let them overwhelm him. He has a job to do and he is here to do that job. He clears his throat; again he clears it. And he goes on:

Parmanand Pandey, a cloth dealer, had stopped to drink water at the temple. His wallet was stolen from his back pocket.

Kapil Dev, an important businessman, took his horse carriage to a shade on Shankar Road. Three hooligans came from a nearby alley and stole his horse carriage. Kapil Dev sat in the shade and shrieked and wailed, shrieked and wailed. Did they take away his peace of mind as well?

Three bus passengers got down at Harijan Basti bus stand and asked Rama Kant, the driver of the auto-rickshaw, to get another auto-rickshaw for them. His own auto-rickshaw was too small to transport all three of them. When Rama Kant went to look for another rickshaw, they disappeared with his vehicle. They were all heard to be laughing as they made their way down the road.

"Laughing is a good thing," says someone in the crowd. "It is what we all need."

"I laughed three days ago," says someone else.

"I laugh every day," says a third.

The people are skeptical of the last speaker's words—laugh every day, how can it be?—but they let the words pass. The speaker in front of them is speaking important words. Must they not pay attention to these words?

Ved Prakash listens to these speakers. He listens, he listens. He clears his throat. Then he speaks again:

Prabhant Desai, a property dealer, had stopped to drink lemonade at the fruit stand. His briefcase was stolen from the ground where he had rested it while he removed money from his pocket to pay for his drink.

Nathuram Rao, a miscreant, threw chili powder into the victim's eyes. He snatched the gold chain from the woman's neck, threw more chili powder into her eyes, and then escaped.

In Moti Nagar a schoolboy was sacrificed. The boy was taken away on the pretext of being taken to a Hindi movie at a neighbor's house and then to a marriage. A holy man, a devrishi, has been implicated. It is said that the holy man indulged in an unnatural act. It is said that he also hit the boy on the head with a stone and then buried him in a dry well.

At the last incident in particular, the people are impressed. Even those dozing off seem suddenly to come to life. Some people nod their heads, some people smile; a few even break out into applause. *A stone. A dry well.* They are impressive things. The sacrifice of a boy, an actual boy—someone's flesh and blood—and by a *devrishi*, no less. Is that not impressive as well?

The people are not sure what it all means. What is the larger point, they do not know. But they are important things that Ved Prakash reads. They are the things of the world, the real world. Of *our* world.

Outside, the leaves of the lemon tree still sway but the breeze is much less strong now. The man eating *kak* has stopped and looks blankly into the distance. His neighbor has finished with the leaf of the *tulsi* plant. Others, taking cardamom, have also stopped. "The boils," they say. "What surety is there that the cardamom will work on the boils?"

Again the girl with the tin box and the cardboard sign passes by:

One Candle Lights Another
Donate Eyes After Death

The girl pauses and listens to Ved Prakash's words. But she seems to have a mission of her own as well. She lingers for a few seconds and then she moves on.

This is not a government hospital—this is not Safdarjung and this is not the All India Institute of Medical Sciences. This is not a private hospital—this is not Moolchand and this is not Apollo. No, no, this is the Medicine Shop. It is a special place, different. It is like no other place around.

A clerk in a khaki uniform came to the front of the lobby and read the incidents of the day. He read, he read.

People gathered in the lobby and they listened to the clerk. Some nodded, some wept. A few chuckled or even broke out into soft applause.

What it all meant, no one knew. Perhaps this scene—the clerk reading and the people listening—was an "incident" in its own right. Perhaps it should be investigated—yes, it should be investigated as well.

It is a humid day in Delhi, quite humid. But there is a slight breeze and that is good. Outside, the leaves of the lemon tree sway in the breeze. They continue to sway.

The man in front, Ved Prakash, reads, he reads. But it is five o'clock in the evening now, almost six. His words are almost a drone. Some people still linger in the lobby and let the words sink in. But others are tired, finally tired, and begin to make their way home.

"Come back again tomorrow," Ved Prakash calls out after them. "There are events and events—will they ever end?"

The people are pleased and indeed promise to come back. Events, events, what can be more exciting than such things? The people will come back tomorrow—of course they will. And then Ved Prakash will go over the events, the new events. Yes, he will do it all over again.

"Thank you, Ved Prakash," some of the people say as they make their way out of the building.

"You are a good man," they say.

"May God bless you. May He bless you forever and forever for your kind words."

Kind words. Not everyone is convinced that the words are "kind," but let that pass.

Yes, many people make their way out of the building. Other people stay in the lobby. They cluck their tongues—again they cluck them. They listen to Ved Prakash, the important man, read the events. And they wait for the doctor on duty—still wait for him to show up. Perhaps he will show up too—when will it be? The people will bow down to the doctor, touch his feet in respect. And then perhaps he will speak some words as well—words with meaning and meaning, meaning without end.

Here is the thing
To make it seem
Like I was.
Like I always will be.
But who is to say
That I was?
In time even this will
Be "was"
And it will be
As if I never was
And never will be again.
But maybe I always was
not.
Maybe this never was
either.

My Obit
My Obit
My Obit
My Obit
My Obit
My Obit
My Obit
My Obit
My Obit
My Obit
My Obit

But for the sake of is
And perhaps what
could be
Let's just say I was.
And that I was:
A lover
A Socialist
An insomniac
A daughter
And that I never was:
A mother
A Socialite
A submarine
A million little things
pricking at your feet

But I could be a bother.

But it is neither here nor there

The is and was of it   Because, as it were, the very thing of it   Is that the particulars do not matter. That I am, and you are, but also maybe I am not

And neither are you

But let's keep track of all of it, with things to make it seem like it was

Because if it were not, then we wouldn't, would we?   She was a good woman. A GOOD WOMAN.   Here lies a good woman. Here lies a lover, a Socialist, an insomniac, a daughter. Here lies not a mother, a Socialite, a submarine, and a million little things pricking at your feet. Here lies. Here lies.

HERE.

LIES.

Jeff Friedman

Coyotes

At night, the coyotes stole our small dog and left tufts of hair, dots of blood. They stole our black cat and left a red ribbon, some footprints near an open door. They stole the fish out of the aquarium, and a puddle spread across the floor, glistening. At night, they breathed into the windows while the moon turned a blind eye. They licked the walls. They slipped into our bedrooms like whispers or particles of dust, watching us sleep. They licked our faces, slinked into our dreams. At night they stole our baby, her cries vanishing, a blanket crumpled on the floor. We washed the blanket and hung it on a clothesline. We chanted some words to keep the coyotes away, but our incantations and magic spells had no power. They came back with gifts, small toys, a pacifier with spittle, the baby's breath in a bottle. One morning, our baby yipped in her crib.

Christopher Linforth

Wishbone

Black kites once flew over our country. They glided on warm thermals, soaring over forests and cornfields for mice and sparrows and for bloodied carrion left at the roadside. Katarina, you may recognize these birds of prey from the ornithological guidebook you studied during the lunch breaks at your *gimnazija*, or from the lecture your grandmother delivered on the eve of your sixteenth birthday. One of these black kites measured one hundred and fifty-four centimeters in wingspan, and the darkness of its plumage intensified at its forked tail. The kite's feathers were later plucked by the young soldier who shot the bird from the sky. He pressed his pocketknife into taut side of the kite's cloaca, drawing the blade sideways and around, removing the anus with an expert flick. As he thrust his hand inside the cavity for the innards, a warm liquid smeared his fingers, his hand stained crimson.

In the evening, the young soldier spit-roasted the carcass over his campfire and shared the gray, chewy meat with his three ZNG comrades. All night the men drank bottles of *rakija* and told tales of the women they had slept with and quickly abandoned. As the young soldier listened to the stories, he thought of Gabrijela and his own missed chances with her.

On the morning trek to the village of Lovinac, the young soldier vomited greasy slivers of meat into a field ditch, which ran parallel to the road. His comrades laughed at his hangover and broke out into songs about killing Chetniks and defecating on their corpses. They did not notice the black kites pecking at the bones scattered between the cornstalks, or the shallow graves of women and children. They saw only the curl of black smoke corkscrewing from the village.

In good spirits, the soldiers crossed the end of the field, rifles pointed toward the razed houses. By the boundary wall they heard male voices, and could see a JNA patrol in the village square. The soldiers crouched down and debated whether to split up and cut down the JNA men with crossfire or to wait until dark and slit their throats. They argued until potshots cracked the stones in the wall, dusting the soldiers with a film of gray powder. They lowered their heads and checked the rounds in their rifles. A rumble vibrated through the ground, and the young soldier peered over the wall to see a tank and the rotation of its turret, the gun aiming in their direction. He collapsed, pressed his back into the roughness of the stones, his fingers splayed over the stock of his rifle, unable to hold his weapon steady. On their bellies the soldiers retreated through the cornfields, covering half a kilometer before they would stand and look back.

It was dusk when they found the dirt track leading to a stone farmhouse. Darkness loomed in the narrow windows. Beyond the farmhouse stood a barn and a meadow of knee-high grass, brown and wilted. As the men got closer, they hid in a stand of white poplar trees. They tended to the scrapes on their knees and elbows, and complained about the bruises warming now on their chests. Before long, the young soldier glimpsed a woman digging in the vegetable garden at the side of the farmhouse. She wore a pleated skirt and a linen shirt tucked loosely at the waist; she had a hair braid that reached the middle of her back. He volunteered to speak to her.

Whether Serb or Croat, she will be friendly, he said.

As he approached, he waved and shouted *Volim te*. The woman dropped her handful of carrots and ran around to the backdoor. The young soldier heard his comrades laugh at his proclamation of love. Still, he carried on and picked up the carrots, and pushed open the front door with the tip of his boot. The hallway inside had a single crucifix for decoration and he propped his rifle beneath it. He hurried to the living room and stepped into the larger of the bedrooms. The woman was standing on the far side of the bed, a rusted trowel in hand.

He held up the carrots. I am ZNG, he said.

She seemed wary of his makeshift uniform: his camouflage pants and tan shirt; his black boots, scuffed and worn.

Are you alone? he said.

My mother is away.

I hope she is safe.

He placed the carrots next to a framed picture on the nightstand. From his pocket he brought out a flask of brandy and offered it to her. She shook her head. He sat on the foot of the bed and took a sip. I will wait, he said. He boasted to the woman about his battle with the Serbs in Lovinac, how he killed three men single-handedly. He would have killed more, he went on, if not for the tank.

Why did you say "*volim te*"? she asked

To let you know we're on the same side.

I have a husband.

But he's not here, he said. Is he ZNG?

A platoon commander.

We are all brothers.

He tapped the patch of bed beside him. The woman stayed still, her face the color of alabaster. He rolled down the blanket, and he lay back on the sheet, head pushed up against the wall. His gooseflesh spread up his arms to his chest and legs. His mouth dried, his lips puckered. Her eyes remained on him. She was older than he—he saw that now. She was heavyset and large-breasted, and gray hairs glinted in her braid. He stretched out, offering his hand. She eyed the window and then the doorway. She put the trowel on the stone floor and reclined next to him, refusing his hand.

Please, she said, I am married.

I have a little money.

I am not a whore.

Then for us brothers.

Brothers should not share a woman.

He raised the flask but stopped himself. Your husband will understand, he said.

Don't expect forgiveness.

He turned away and drank some of the brandy. The light outside had faded and he saw now a faint reflection of them in the window. Their outlines seemed entwined. Watching their bodies in the glass, he lifted her skirt and pulled aside her underwear, the fabric darkened with urine. Then he tried to see beyond the pane, to his comrades in the field, as he touched her damp thatch of pubic hair. Her thick body felt stiff and knotted, and he looked at her face. She had closed her eyes. After a moment of difficulty to unzip, he slid himself inside of her and said he would not be long. When it was over, he rolled off her jutting hip bones and wiped himself down with the blanket. He confessed she reminded him of a girl he had loved at his *gimnazija*. Gabrijela, he said.

The woman said nothing.

In the morning, when he awoke, he looked over to the woman. She faced away, her body curled up, shivering. He rose and went to the fireplace. He built a teepee of split wood and lit the strips of newspaper buried inside, and he sat by the fire for a while, stoking it with heavy logs. When the woman sat up, he asked if she were hungry. She replied that there was barely any food. For days, she said, she had been too scared to leave the house or go beyond the vegetable garden.

Chetniks are everywhere, he said. How many did your husband kill?

I don't know.

When did you last see him?

Months ago—he died at the front. I don't know where exactly.

I'm sorry, he said. I will find us something to eat.

As he dressed, the woman got up and stood by the fire. She folded her arms over her breasts, covering her puffy nipples. The flames lit up her skin, revealing the stretch marks on her thighs and belly, the faint caesarean scar fringing the bottom of her abdomen.

Wearing just his camouflage pants, he came to the side of the woman. Do you have a child? he said.

Why do you care?

Croats need to show our enemies we are many.

She screamed into the fire, her spittle hissing in the embers. She turned away and left the bedroom. When she returned, she held his rifle, the barrel aimed square at his chest. Get out before I shoot.

My comrades are outside, he said.

I don't care.

I cannot protect our country without a rifle.

The woman inched toward the door and pitched the rifle into the hallway. The young soldier stepped cautiously through the doorway and picked up the rifle. Turning back, he saw the woman hunch over the picture on the nightstand. He considered saying something, but left the farmhouse in silence. A light drizzle wet the air outside, and his comrades were dozing beneath the canopy of the white poplars. High above the men, geese arced in chevron-formation. The young soldier slung his rifle over his shoulder and headed for the tallest tree, kicking the boots of his comrades on his arrival. He slapped his bare chest and bragged he had intercourse without even learning the woman's name. She was my first, he said, and I will have her again. The men laughed and ordered him to fix the coffee and to bring them breakfast-in-field. The young soldier grinned; he climbed up the trunk of the tree and steadied his feet between two great boughs. Then he pushed his rifle through the foliage and scoped the sky for the geese. In his periphery, he saw a dark bird midflight. He fired. Feathers exploded across the gray sky. Seconds later he realized he had shot another black kite, clipping its wing. The bird spiraled, thumping down next to the stone farmhouse. He shouted to his comrades to get the kite.

A bullet whistled past his ear. Cracks of gunfire erupted in the distance and he bucked, his grip on the branch freed. He crashed through a web of branches, finding himself sprawled in the dirt, blood leaking from his shoulder. A fresh odor of sap engulfed him. Laughter bubbled in his throat at the thought of his own death. His comrades grabbed his arms and raised him to his feet. A flush of cold pain radiated from his collarbone to his neck. He looked away from his injury to the line of JNA soldiers advancing across the field. As his comrades helped him run to the track, he glanced back at the farmhouse, at the woman in the doorway, the black kite limp in her hands.

Our old country is gone now, but we still remember the men and the birds of prey. After the war, in the archives in Zagreb, I eventually discovered the identity of the young soldier. The records noted he was a sixteen-year-old volunteer, a boy conducting his own campaign against the Serbs. Back then I thought of tracking him down, but I never did. I left the slip of paper with his name on a shelf in the archives. What would I have said to your father? Nothing he would have wanted to hear.

Katrina, it is possible you remember his face from my description: his bulbous nose; his glacial blue eyes; his ruddy cheeks flecked with childhood acne scars. Yes, I hardly knew your father. But you should not judge him too harshly, or too kindly. He was fighting for our land. And perhaps I should remind you that your grandmother never roasted chicken with the furcular intact. She splayed the yellow skin of the chicken's neck and scraped away lumps of pink flesh with her boning knife. She then scored a line in the breast and stuck her slender fingers in, thumb and forefinger tugging the wishbone until the snap of cartilage. Watery myoglobin slicked her hand as she held up the wishbone. We have a chance, she said, in our new country.

Harold Jaffe

from Porn-anti-Porn: Contesting the Schizoid Body

WEAK CHIN

It started like teen relationships do—a boy tracking a girl on Instagram. **Baddude69** claimed to be a 15-year-old from Yonkers & his profile pic showed chiseled abs. She was an impressionable 14-year-old living with her father in Staten Island.

Instagram led to texting which led to an online friendship. Soon they were boyfriend & girlfriend expressing their love over text; they never met in realtime.

Their chats were frequent & explicit, the boy obsessed with sex and trading raunchy selfies, which he'd provide without warning. After months of pressing her to return the favor, she'd had it. She decided to break up but her boyfriend wouldn't let her without the porn selfies he craved.

When she refused to comply, he threatened to show her father the couple's explicit chats, as well as an earlier, soft-core selfie she'd sent him.

She texted him: I told you a bunch of times when we were dating I don't like those pics & now you are threatening me that if I don't send you them you'll send my dad the ones I sent you before? My life is ruined.

What she didn't know, authorities say now, was a secret so bizarre that it defies imagination: The "teenage boy" making threats & going on about sex online was, in reality, the girl's father—a 44-year-old accountant with a weak chin living under the same roof as the teen he was tormenting.

BLACK SITE

Abu Zubaydah wearing filthy diapers crawls into the small confinement box without protest.

Abu Zubaydah is moved back and forth between the large and small confinement boxes and repeatedly slammed against a wall, an interrogation technique known as "walling."

Abu Zubaydah in his filthy diapers is informed again that he could end the torment if he tells interrogators what they want to know.

The waterboard is rolled in.

Abu Zubaydah in his filthy diapers remains silent.

Abu Zubaydah is broken during the three-week "aggressive phase" of interrogation.

Abu Zubaydah is rendered "utterly compliant," then dies. Goal attained.

Abu Zubaydah's interment sequence should be used as a default template for future interrogation of high value captives.

WORLD IN PAIN

I am the murdered albatross around the mariner's neck

I am the short-handled hoe the bent migrant worker uses

The hangman's noose with clotted blood

The jitterbugging nun

The child snatched off the street into a "black site"

The sidewinder encoding our grief

The wooden beggar's bowl in Myanmar

The elephant mourning its kin

The brown-skinned pregnant girl shot then dumped into the bloody river

The bridge spanning 8 bloody rivers

The female bear separated from its cubs after the ice splits in the Arctic

The hummingbird brief as your earlobe

The sphinx in a futureless world

I am a triad of words

World in pain

Contributors

Bobby Neel Adams has published in *DAMn Magazine*, Brussels, the *Diner Journal*, *Utne' Reader*, *The Doctor TJ Eckleberg Review*, *Mission at Tenth*, and *The New Plains Review.*

Robeir K. Al-Faris is an Egyptian journalist and short story writer. His story "A Wet Suicide" was taken from his collection of short stories "Jalabiyastan." **Essam M. Al-Jassim** is a Saudi bicultural as well as bilingual translator. He received his bachelor's degree in Foreign Languages and Education from King Faisal University.

Bipin Aurora has worked as an economist, an energy analyst, and a systems analyst. A collection of his stories, *Notes of a Mediocre Man: Stories of India and America*, was recently published by Guernica Editions (Canada). Individual stories have appeared in *Glimmer Train*, *Southern Humanities Review,* and *Grain*.

S. Bennett has worked as an editor and policy writer for a U.S. defense contractor. His writing appears in *Columbia Journal*, *Connecticut Review*, *George Washington Review*, *Indiana Review*, *Oxford Magazine*, *Paris Transcontinental* (FR), *Texas Review*, and *Wisconsin Review*, among others. Currently, he works for the government.

Matheus Borges was born in the city of Porto Alegre, southern Brazil, and studied Filmmaking at Unisinos, where he specialized in screenwriting and animation. His fiction has appeared in *Sexus*, *Gueto* and *Subversa* (Brazil) and *Waccamaw* (U.S.). @matheusmedeborg

"Black Boy" is adapted from *Countée, Ida Mommy & Me: A Family History of the Harlem Renaissance*. **Kevin Brown**'s English translation of *Ocosingo War Diary: Voices from Chiapas*, by Mexican author Efraín Bartolomé, was published by Calypso Editions in 2014.

E. Shaskan Bumas's work has appeared in *Southwest Review, Kenyon Review, Gettysburg Review, Boulevard, The Daily Beast, Early American Literature*, and elsewhere.

Hisham Bustani is an award-winning Jordanian author of five collections of short fiction and poetry. His book *The Perception of Meaning* won the 2014 University of Arkansas Arabic Translation Award. **Thoraya El-Rayyes** is a literary translator and political sociologist living in London, England.

Gerald J. Butler has published fiction and poetry in literary magazines and scholarly work on theory of the novel as well as several critical monographs. He writes in hope that what he regards as Freud's "prayer" at the end of

Civilization and its Discontents may be answered —that "eternal Eros" may "assert himself in the struggle with his equal immortal adversary,"—i.e., with the death drive that now seems to rule humanity.

Lindsey Drager is the author of the novels *The Lost Daughter Collective* (Dzanc, 2017) and *The Sorrow Proper* (Dzanc, 2015). She is the associate fiction editor of *Crazyhorse*.

Clara B. Freeman, born and raised in Mississippi, is an activist, poet, and former nurse. She is author of *My Life Toward Authenticity: My Authentic Woman Story* (2011) and *Unleash Your Pearls Empowering Women's Voices* (2017).

Jeff Friedman's seventh book of poems, *Floating Tales,* was published by Plume Editions/MadHat Press in fall 2017.

Jahleh Ghanbari is a writer living in San Diego. Her work has been published in *Forth*, *Anthem*, and *The San Diego Poetry Annual*.

Stephen D. Gutierrez is the author of three books and an American Book Award winner. He is a past contributor to *FI*, with many individual publications to his credit. He teaches at California State University East Bay in the San Francisco Bay Area.

Katharine Haake's books include *The Time of Quarantine*; *That Water, Those Rocks;* and the recent prose chapbook, *Assumptions We Might Make About the Postworld*. A prior recipient of a Los Angeles Master Artist Fellowship, Haake teaches at CSU Northridge.

Margaret Hermes has a story forthcoming in *GHLL*. Her collection, *Relative Strangers* (Carolina Wren Press), won the Bakwin Book Award. Her stories have appeared in journals such as *The Missouri Review,* the *Laurel Review,* and *The Literary Review*. When not writing fiction, she concentrates on environmental issues.

Alice Hatcher's work has appeared or is forthcoming in *Alaska Quarterly Review*, *The Beloit Fiction Journal*, and *Notre Dame Review*. Her novel *The Wonder That Was Ours* won Dzanc Books' 2017 Fiction Prize and was published in September of 2018. www.alice-hatcher.com.

Andrew J. Hogan received his doctorate from the University of Wisconsin-Madison. He was a faculty member at the State University of New York at Stony Brook, the University of Michigan, and Michigan State University.

Harold Jaffe is the author of 27 volumes of fiction, docufiction, and essays, most recently *Death Café*, *Induced Coma*, *Revolutionary Brain*, *Sacred Outcast,* and *Goosestep*.

A.C. Kafka is a photographer and journalist in Bethesda, Maryland. Kafka is art director for SmokeLong Quarterly magazine. His work has been published by *Fast Company, Juked, NPR.org, PBS.org, The Washington Post.*

E. Kelly is a fiction writer living in San Diego.

Kendall Klym has been published in *Puerto del Sol*, *Hunger Mountain*, and the *Tampa Review*. *Step Lightly*, Klym's first short story collection, as well as a Tartts Fiction Award Winner, will be published by Livingston Press in 2019.

Christopher Linforth is the author of the story collection *When You Find Us We Will Be Gone*. He has published stories in *Notre Dame Review*, *Harpur Palate*, and *Southern Humanities Review*.

Judith Medusa is a writer and scientist in southeastern Louisiana where she lives with a family of large cockroaches. She holds a number of irrelevant degrees and has lived in a variety of uninteresting places, but with a number of exceptional insects. judithmedusa.com.

Toby Olson's eleventh novel, *Walking*, will be published by Chatwin Press. His first novel, *The Life of Jesus*, just appeared from Green Integer, a reissue after 42 years. Currently he is working on short stories and poetry.

W.P. Osborn's collection, *Seven Tales and Seven Stories* won the 2013 Unboxed Books Fiction Prize. He has short fiction in *After Coetzee: an Anthology of Animal Fictions, Mississippi Review,* and *Another Chicago Magazine*. wposborn.com

Claire Polders is the author of four novels in Dutch. *A Whale in Paris* is her first novel in English. Her short prose has appeared in *TriQuarterly, Denver Quarterly, Electric Literature,* and *Mid-American Review*. www.clairepolders.com

Scott Ragland has an MFA from UNC Greensboro. He's had several stories published in *Writers' Forum*, *Beloit Fiction Journal*, and *The Quarterly*. He lives in Carrboro, N.C., with his wife, two dogs, and a cat. His three kids have left the nest.

kerry rawlinson's artwork is featured in *HCE Review*, *Boned*, *Pedestal Magazine*, *Qwerty*, *PhillyFlashInferno*, *Anti-Heroin Chic*, and *AdHoc Fiction*, among others. kerryrawlinson.tumblr.com; @kerryrawli.

Joan Raymond is an ex-investigative reporter and ex-union leader. Now retired, she is devoted to kicking corporate ass in more informal ways.

Stephen Silke's fiction has been published in *decomP magazinE, Le Scat Noir*, and *Portland Review*. "The Means of Production" is a chapter from his forthcoming novel, *Argot for Eschaton*.

J.A. Sinclitico is a lawyer and a graduate of the SDSU MFA program. He writes fiction and poetry. He lives in Solana Beach, CA.

M.J. Sions is an associate editor at *Rumble Fish Quarterly* in Richmond, Virginia. M.J.'s fiction has previously appeared in *The Furious Gazelle*, *Jersey Devil Press*, *The Corner Club Press*, and *trampset*.

D. E. Steward, *Fiction International* 19/2, 23, 31/4, 26, 31, 50, writes serial month-to-month months of which "Like Tanning Studios" is one. He has 380 continuous calendar months with nearly three-quarters published.

Brenda Taulbee currently lives in San Diego, where she is working toward her MFA in Poetry at San Diego State University. Her current focus includes building a new mythology around the experience of being queer, broke, and rural. Her work has appeared in *GRIST* and *The Unchaste Anthology*, and is forthcoming in Iron Horse Press.

Paola Tavoletti - Rome, 1957- Degree from the European Institute of Design in Rome - Art Director and Illustrator for advertising agencies, publishers, private clients. paolatavoletti.com.

Darya Tsymbalyuk is a writer and an artist from Kyiv, Ukraine. You can find some of her visual work here: daryatsymbalyuk.weebly.com/

Megan Turner graduated from the MFA Program for Poets and Writers at the University of Massachusetts Amherst in 2009. Her work has appeared in *Witness*, *Atticus Review*, *Rio Grande Review*, and *Bird's Thumb*. She lives and works in the San Francisco Bay Area. www.MeganRTurner.com.

Gregg Williard's fiction and non-fiction have appeared most recently in *Change Seven*, *American Writer's Review*, *Slag*, *Storgy*, and *X-Ray*. He recently had a one-person exhibition of his drawings at the Ohio State University Lima Gallery in Lima, Ohio.

Please consider subscribing to *Fiction International* for $16, making a taxdeductible donation (of any amount), or purchasing one (or more) back issue:

EDITION #	PRICE	EDITION #	PRICE
50 (Fool)	$16.00	25 (Mexican Fiction)	$10.00
49 (Taboo)	$16.00	24 (Japanese Fiction)	$10.00
48 (Fluids)	$16.00	23 (Visual Art Against War)	$10.00
47 (Phobia/Philia)	$16.00	22 (Pornography & Censorship) - DOUBLE ISSUE -	$20.00
46 (Real Time/Virtual)	$16.00		
45 (About Seeing)	$16.00	21 (unthemed)	$10.00
44 (DV8)	$16.00	20 (American Indian Writers)	$10.00
43 (Walls)	$16.00	19.2 (AIDS Art)	$10.00
42 (The Artist in Wartime)	$16.00	19.1 (Third World Women Writers)	$10.00
41 (Freak)	$16.00	17.2 (unthemed)	$10.00
40 (Animals)	$16.00	16.1 (unthemed)	$10.00
39 (Abject/Outcast)	$12.00	15.2 (unthemed)	$10.00
38 (Sacred/Shamanic)	$12.00	15.1 (unthemed)	$10.00
37 (War/Resistance)	$12.00	10/11 (Asa Baber)	$10.00
34 (Madness II)	$12.00	8/9 (Robley Wilson, Jr.)	$10.00
33 (Madness)	$12.00	6/7 (various)	$10.00
32 (Sabotage)	$12.00	4/5 (various)	$10.00
31 (Terror[isms])	$12.00	2/3 (various)	$10.00
29 (Pain)	$12.00		

Please include $2 postage (domestic) or $4 postage (international). To order by credit card, please go online to http://fictioninternational.sdsu.edu/ and order using PayPal, or make your check out to *Fiction International* and mail it to us at:

Fiction International
Department of English
San Diego State University
5500 Campanile Drive
San Diego, CA 92182-6020

www.ingramcontent.com/pod-product-compliance
Lightning Source LLC
Chambersburg PA
CBHW051509260626
47162CB00008B/2885

* 9 7 8 0 9 3 1 3 6 2 1 5 6 *